Bad Loyalty

A Trudy Wilson Mystery

Russ Crossley

53RD STREET PUBLISHING

Acknowledgments

Thank you must go to my first reader, Rita Schulz, for her invaluable insights into this story and these characters. Without her willingness to slog through the first draft this book wouldn't be as good as it turned out to be. Thanks, Rita.

And I must thank my editor, Colleen Kuehne, who has so often saved this writer from embarrassing gaffs. Thanks, Colleen, you are the best.

The Trudy Wilson Mystery Series
Shear Murder

Bad Loyalty

Buzzcut (to be released in 2015)

Dedication

This one is for, Simon. Miss you, buddy.

Trudy didn't think Bruce could hurt anyone, never mind commit cold-blooded murder…until she received the call.

"I've been arrested—for murder."

Shrill cries of the seagulls in the sky above the plaza startled Trudy back to reality. The seagulls hung around the plaza looking for scraps. Suddenly they all screamed loudly, then flew into the fog-enshrouded sky outside the hair shop's picture window, leaving a flurry of white and gray feathers behind. The mustard-yellow, banana-shaped receiver in her hand felt suddenly cold and heavy.

Fear gripped her like a vice. Fear for her friend. Fear she thought she'd put behind her returned to invade her world.

She immediately recognized the voice—Bruce Carstair's deep voice, edged with sadness—yet his words were clipped and tense, not at all like the last time she'd seen him, six months ago.

He'd been happy then. Happier than he'd been in a long time, having seemingly put the murder of his sister behind him. Or at least he'd finally managed to come to grips with Sharon's untimely, unfair death.

In her mind's eye, she pictured the tanned, swarthy biker with radiant blue eyes the color of a hazy sky, the long, dark hair that draped off his broad shoulders, and the easy smile. Bruce Carstairs, who'd helped her to rekindle her life and give it meaning when all seemed lost. Bruce, who'd dragged her from her own despair, had become a true friend.

Though he was much younger than she, she felt sometimes he understood her better than her own husband of twenty years.

They first met almost a year ago, here in Fairview, Oregon, when Sharon Carstairs, Bruce's sister and Trudy's employee, was murdered.

Trudy had been accused of the murder. Now it seemed she would have to bail Bruce out of trouble. She was more than certain the big guy was incapable of murdering anyone.

Introduction

This novel is a sequel to the first novel about hairdresser, Trudy Wilson and her friend, Bruce Carstairs.

The series had its gestation many years ago at a writing workshop taught by Dean Wesley Smith and Kristine Katherine Rusch.

A few years before my wife and I had been a franchisee for a major hair shop chain so I knew well the troubles of the young women in the hair service industry like those in this story. Sadly, many of these women come from broken homes, and many have failed personal relationships. Some have substance addiction problems, which are their Band-Aid solutions for their personal problems.

The idea of this series is to focus on one woman, Trudy who, like many heroes, quickly discovers she can do more than she thinks she can. As in many classic hero journey stories she accepts the challenge reluctantly, but is soon drawn into an adventure. An adventure where she must overcome seemingly impossible odds to save her friend.

I hope you go back after reading this sequel and pick up the first novel to discover how the Trudy, Bruce friendship became so deep and loyal.

So join Trudy on this adventure, and check out the excerpt at the end.

At some point I will write another Trudy and Bruce adventure so if you enjoy this novel contact me on face book or twitter and let me know what you thought.

I hope you enjoy the ride.

January 2012

Bad Loyalty

A Trudy Wilson Mystery

by

Russ Crossley

Published by 53rd Street Publishing
1st edition Copyright © 2012 Russ Crossley
2nd edition Copyright © 2015 Russ Crossley

Trade paperback ISBN: 978-1927621387
E-book ISBN: 9781466142688
Cover image © Saporob | Dreamstime.com
Cover design by R. Edgewood
Cover and interior layout copyright 2014
by 53rd Street Publishing
Published by:
53rd Street Publishing
Gibsons B.C. Canada
www.53rdsteetpublishing.com

CHAPTER ONE

"I'VE BEEN ARRESTED—FOR MURDER."

Shrill cries of the seagulls in the sky above the plaza startled Trudy back to reality. The seagulls hung around the plaza looking for scraps. Suddenly they all screamed loudly, then flew into the fog-enshrouded sky outside the hair shop's picture window, leaving a flurry of white and gray feathers behind. The mustard-yellow, banana-shaped receiver in her hand felt suddenly cold and heavy.

Fear gripped her like a vice. Fear for her friend. Fear she thought she'd put behind her returned to invade her world.

She immediately recognized the voice—Bruce Carstair's deep voice, edged with sadness—yet his words were clipped and tense, not at all like the last time she'd seen him, six months ago.

He'd been happy then. Happier than he'd been in a long time, having seemingly put the murder of his sister behind him.

Or at least he'd finally managed to come to grips with Sharon's untimely, unfair death.

In her mind's eye, she pictured the tanned, swarthy biker with radiant blue eyes the color of a hazy sky, the long, dark hair that draped off his broad shoulders, and the easy smile. Bruce Carstairs, who'd helped her to rekindle her life and give it meaning when all seemed lost. Bruce, who'd dragged her from her own despair, had become a true friend.

Though he was much younger than she, she felt sometimes he understood her better than her own husband of twenty years.

They first met almost a year ago, here in Fairview, Oregon, when Sharon Carstairs, Bruce's sister and Trudy's employee, was murdered. Trudy had been accused of the murder. Now it seemed she would have to bail Bruce out of trouble. She was more than certain the big guy was incapable of murdering anyone.

"Where are you?"

"Vancouver."

"Washington?"

"The other one."

She thought for a moment. No, couldn't be. What could he be doing there? "Canada?"

"Yeah." At least he didn't talk your ear off. "Trudy, please come here. Please help me. You're the only one I trust." He sounded desperate.

"But, Bruce I…" Rocky would be pissed. She stopped herself. What did she care if that self-centered son of a bitch husband didn't like it? He only cared about how much money she brought in. The job he'd promised he'd get finally came through, but it had lasted all of two weeks. Until Mr. James found him with that fifth of whiskey stuffed in his back pocket.

"Trudy, please. I know you have that new gal. What was her name—"

"May," Trudy said, finishing his thought for him.

"Yeah. May." He paused. "Trudy. I'm in a real jam."

"What about the bike shop guys? Ya know them."

Bruce worked as a bookkeeper for a motorcycle shop owned by Hell's Angels in Seattle. Not that he was involved in their lifestyle, though to look at him you might think so. He lived the part sometimes, enjoying the parties and the women who liked their men on the dangerous side. Fringe benefits, he called them.

"I can't talk about anything else on this line. Just please come and get me outta here."

Trudy thought he meant the phone line was bugged. It probably was. The world had become a paranoid place since 9/11.

"Okay," she said with a heavy sigh. "I'll be there sometime late tomorrow night. I've got a few things to take care of here first."

His voice brightened. "Thanks a million. I knew you wouldn't let me down."

Trudy set the receiver in the cradle and gazed into the distance across the parking lot. The fog was rising to reveal a sky filled with reds, yellows, and oranges as the sun was about to disappear. The ball of fire hung low on the horizon, making the few clouds erupt with color. She sighed.

May was in the back, working on a perm for Cecile Aimes. May was a godsend for the business. After the unfortunate mess with the sheriff and the murders, Trudy had become something of a minor celebrity on the coast. When she'd placed an ad in the local paper to find a replacement for Sharon, May was the first to apply.

The dyed-blonde hairdresser had worked at the most prestigious hair shop in Fairview. The town hierarchy was on her extensive client list.

T

his client, Cecile Aimes, was a minor—except in her own mind—celebrity herself. She had been the chef on a nationally syndicated cooking show for twenty years before returning to Fairview. Nice lady, but a little standoffish when Trudy was around. May said it was because she didn't want her adoring fans to mob her. Until she'd walked into the shop the first time, Trudy had never heard of the TV cook.

May Carpenter was a woman with infinite patience, which made her popular with the local ladies. The business had improved to the point where Trudy and May worked six days a week, and there was a part-time apprentice for Fridays and Saturdays. Trudy still closed on Sundays. Not because of a particular religious bent, but because, like God, she need a day of rest to recharge her batteries.

"Something wrong?" asked May, walking toward her, wiping her hands on a towel. The towel reeked of perm solution. She wore black nylon slacks and a purple, short-sleeve shirt. She wasn't fat by any stretch of the imagination, and for a woman nearing forty, she still had a good figure. At least her husband of twenty-two years, Jack, an independent building contractor, seemed to think so. May joked that his job made him Carpenter the carpenter.

"Yeah. I'm gonna have ta go to Vancouver," said Trudy. May's brow wrinkled and her eyes were quizzical, so Trudy explained. "Sorry, May, but I have ta go to Canada. Bruce is in trouble. He needs my help."

May and Jack had met Bruce six months ago when Bruce visited the coast. It had been summer then and that week had been very special. They were very fond of the large man, and the four of them were now fast friends. May would understand.

"How long you gonna be gone?"

Trudy looked away, afraid to look into May's pale gray eyes. "I don't know, exactly. I guess as long as it takes."

Trudy glanced up when she heard May smirk.

May's eyes danced in the low light from the overhead fluorescent tubes. She had a wry grin across her pale-peach-coated lips. "Yeah, I understand. You go. I'll take care of things here. I know what to do."

On many a night, Trudy and May sat in Trudy's kitchen sipping wine and telling war stories. Life stories, really. They'd discussed the Fairview murders, and Trudy and Bruce's involvement in solving them.

The new town sheriff was a woman named Flo Henderson. She had left the crime-ridden streets of New York for the friendlier life afforded small tourist towns.

When she'd found out about the Fairview murders, she'd paid Trudy a visit. She'd assured her she had no intentions of letting such a thing happen in future. She was still a client of the shop. May's, of course, but what the hey, a buck was a buck.

Since attending the shop on a regular basis, Flo had become friends with both the hairdressers. She'd been suspicious of Bruce until Trudy let her in on the details about how he'd risked his life to save her.

Trudy was sure the sheriff had checked Bruce out with the new, fancy computer system she'd purchased to update the capabilities of her new police force.

The money they'd recovered from the previous sheriff's skimming activities had more than paid for the equipment upgrade. Too bad about his deputy, now serving time in the state pen. He hadn't been all bad.

"Trudy," May began, her eyes filled with tears, "I know how important that man is to you. So you go and I'll make sure the home fire stays bright."

Trudy nodded and headed for the wooden coat tree at the rear of the shop. It was in the small office at the back behind the flat-gray painted door. Along the way, she passed Cecile, who had her nose buried in one of the supermarket tabloids she read while she was here.

Keeping up on the news of your friends? Trudy thought.

Cecile glanced up from the black cushioned hair-cutting chair as Trudy passed, nodded, and offered a thin smile. Trudy offered a closed-mouth smile, though if you looked in her brown eyes, they were pretty much free of expression. You might even say bland.

She pushed the door inward until it bumped against the coat tree. She stepped inside. There, next to the metal shelving with the shop supplies, was the worn wooden coat tree.

Her faux leather jacket hung on one of the hooks. She pulled it off and slipped in one arm, then the other. She shrugged her shoulders and the jacket fell into place. She left it unzipped. She turned and stopped to glance at the desk.

The bills from yesterday were still there, laid out where she'd left them. She'd been trying to balance the receipts when Bruce's call interrupted her. She couldn't get the totals to match, no matter what she did. She shrugged and walked onto the cutting floor, closing the door behind her.

She must've looked worried, because May stood with her hands folded over her chest, a look of concern on her face. Her deep frown revealed her care for her friend and boss.

"What?" asked Trudy upon seeing May's face.

"How you gonna get there?" asked May.

"By car, of course. I can't fly." Trudy flapped her arms, as if they were wings. "I'm not a fuckin' bird." She grinned at her own joke.

"C'mon, you know what I mean."

Trudy dropped her arms to her sides and the smile on her face disappeared. "It'll make it."

May shook her head. "I don't think so. That piece of shit barely gets you to work every day as it is."

Trudy grimaced. "Well then, if I don't take the POS, what will I use?"

May uncrossed her arms and moved to stand behind Cecelia, who sat staring straight ahead, pretending to read her paper. She was, of course, listening to every word. Small towns live and die by gossip.

Since Trudy was a bigger celebrity since the murders than Cecile was, she knew Cecile'd ride that coattail if she had juicy stuff to share with the gals at her cribbage club at the casino.

"Take Rocky's pickup."

Trudy cast her pale eyes toward the floor and caught herself before she shuffled her feet like some child at her mom's knee. "I know I should, but…"

"But nuthin', lady. You go tell him you're taking it and he can have the POS while you're away." May's tone sounded firm.

Not as firm as Trudy felt.

Rocky was a far better man in her eyes than she knew he truly was, since that day on the beach when he'd saved her life. Trudy nodded, but inside she wasn't so sure. She knew what Bruce would say. He shared May's feelings about her alcoholic husband.

"Yeah, I will." She kept her eyes on the gray tiled floor as she hurried outside into the parking lot.

Mall employees were to park their cars in the back of the mall so the spaces closest to the outlet stores were left for the convenience of the visiting shoppers, or sharks, as May jokingly dubbed them.

When the lease had been up for renewal, May had talked Trudy out of moving to another location away from the outlet mall. She'd been glad for it when the strip mall she'd been considering burned down along with every shop in it.

Trudy regretted that Mr. Swinson's butcher shop had burned to the ground, though the smell of perfectly cooked meat seemed to linger in the air for days afterward. She couldn't help but smile to herself. It was as if the whole town smelled like one big barbecue fest. Poor Mr. Swinson.

The air smelled like rain today. Then again, didn't it always? She walked past the shoe outlet and the kitchen appliance store without a glance. The covered walkway would protect her from any rain that might develop, at least until she made it to the rear parking lot.

CHAPTER TWO

She stepped off the curb where there was an access lane that led to the staff parking area and walked into the lot through the gap between the low-rise buildings.

The sun was trying in vain to break through the gray clouds as they roiled across the sky overhead; scattered rays of sunlight stream across the horizon like rays of gold.

Trudy wasn't able to see the beach from here with the low hills between her and the ocean, but the stiff breeze that hit her in the back as she walked toward the red Chevette meant the ocean would be angry today. The waves would be beauties. She shuddered at the casual thought.

Too many people died due to that ocean, far too many. The image of Sharon's blonde hair, fresh-washed face, and sparkling blue-green eyes flashed across her mind and she felt infinite sadness fall over her. She shook the feeling off, and after pulling out her key ring, the one with the GM logo, she unlocked the car door.

Bad Loyalty

She sat behind the steering wheel and started the engine.
It started immediately and she breathed a sigh of relief.
She knew where to find her wayward husband at this time of day.

CHAPTER THREE

SHE TURNED OFF HIGHWAY 101 onto the black pavement of the parking lot outside the Whaler Bar and Grill. She glanced at her thin-banded Timex. It was a cheap Korean knockoff, but it kept decent track of time.

The heavy, twin wooden doors that made up the entrance to the local's booze shack stood before her. Over the doors was a carved wooden sign with a rough facsimile of a blue whale, a smile on its face and a spout of water shooting from what the artist, if you could call him that, thought a whale's blowhole might look like. Trudy smirked, then thought, what am I? An art critic...

With her small, black, faux leather purse slipped over one thin shoulder, she walked up to the double doors. She reached for one of the handles and it suddenly flew toward her. She stepped back and a man wearing a baseball cap with the logo of a local fishing supply store barged through the doors with his head down.

He must've noticed her because he stopped to study her. His face was covered in gray stubble, and a shock of gray curls stuck out from the sides of his cap.

He wore a blue-and-red lumberjack shirt, black rubber boots, and heavy, dark green work pants. He had a lit cigarette dangling from dry lips. He was swaying badly and reeked of stale booze and cigarettes.

"Huh... sorry..." he muttered as he passed her.

Yuck.

She held the door open with one hand and stuck her head into the smoky bar. The place was quite dark.

It took her eyes a few seconds to adjust to the dimly lit room. Finally she made out the chairs and tables strewn randomly throughout the place and the polished wood bar with a large mirror behind it at the far end of the room. She stepped inside and immediately felt the need for a shower. The place stunk something awful, a pungent mix of mold and piss, mingled with stale liquor and cigarettes.

Must be poor air circulation, she thought. She wrapped her arms around her body and slowly walked toward the bar. As she got closer, she could see the red-haired bartender smiling at her. His white shirt unbuttoned at the collar, no tie, and he was clean-shaven. An older man sat at one of the stools facing the mirror. Trudy could see the man's grizzled features in the mirror's reflection as she approached them.

"Why, hello there, missus. What can I be doin' for ya?" the bartender smiled warmly, his green eyes sparkling in the low light.

Ever since she had lost the weight, men showed considerably more interest in hearing what she had to say. The increased attention made her feel strange.

"Uh...hi...I'm looking for my husband."

"Oh," said the bartender. His eyes dropped to the bar and the smile disappeared from his face.

He picked up a white cloth and began to idly concentrate on polishing the shiny wood surface of the already highly polished bar. It looked to Trudy like the finest teak. "And who might your hubby be?" he asked.

"Rocky Wilson," she said, amused at his reaction to her being here to find a wayward husband. No doubt when the wives showed up, sparks tended to fly. Well, she certainly wasn't here for that. She needed his truck, nothing more.

The red-headed bartender pointed toward a particularly dark corner of the room. "He's in the corner."

The old man didn't look up from his glass of beer.

Trudy turned to look into the corner where the bartender pointed and saw that the light hanging over the half-moon table in front of the black leather horseshoe-shaped booth was out.

She shielded her eyes with her right hand. Her purse slipped a little, so she adjusted it, then, with her hand covering her eyes, she walked toward the booth. She made out the outline of a man-like shape crouched in the booth hunched over a glass of flat beer.

When she stood in front of the table, a pair of bloodshot eyes stared up at her. She sat down across from him.

"Rocky. I need your truck."

Her husband stared at her, saying nothing. He fumbled in his right pants pocket and pulled out a set of GM car keys. He threw them across the table. They clattered to a stop in front of her. She smiled thinly. That had been easy. Maybe too easy.

"Is something wrong?" she asked, attempting to keep her tone light.

Rocky said, "Everything." His speech was slurred from the drinks he had consumed so far today. No doubt quite a few, as usual.

He was coming home very late most nights, having consumed copious quantities of alcohol. He had begun to smell of the stuff all day, every day. She wanted desperately to know what was bothering him, but he didn't want to talk. He just said everything every time she asked him what was wrong. She didn't know how much longer she could put up with his silence.

Without her, though, she didn't know what would happen to him. He wasn't mean to her or beat her or anything like that, he just drank too much. She sighed and without saying anything more, she dropped the keys for the POS on the table in front of him.

"I'm gonna be outta town for a few days. May's looking after the shop. Do you want me ta call you later?"

He nodded his head and then cast his gaze back into the depths of his glass. He took a sip of the warm beer as she stood, looking down at the pathetic figure he'd become.

She walked away without looking back.

Once outside, she let the tears flow down her reddened cheeks. What the hell am I gonna do?

The truck was parked at the far end of the little lot. She walked over to it and opened the door. She sat behind the black steering wheel for a long time, wiping away the tears with her fingers until at last they stopped.

She shook her head to clear her thoughts and then turned the key in the ignition. The truck's engine roared to life. It was far more powerful than her POS and she liked to drive it. It really gripped the road.

She backed the truck up, and after making a left turn, headed north along the coast highway toward the house she and Rocky occasionally shared.

She needed to pack and make an important call before she left town.

CHAPTER FOUR

THE BLUE AND WHITE SPLIT-LEVEL HOUSE where they had made their home when they moved to Oregon from Seattle came into view between the stands of tall fir trees that lined the road. From the front window, like many homes in this area, you could see the ocean.

Yup, it was a high-surf day. No doubt the tidal warnings would be in full swing.

She walked up the natural stone pathway she'd built herself, then up the red cement staircase. She unlocked the door and it swung open noiselessly.

She would have liked being greeted by a favorite dog or cat, like when she was a child growing up, but with Rocky away a lot and her crazy hours at the shop, she didn't want an animal to suffer from neglect.

She closed the door and flipped on the light switch. The little decorative window next to the door didn't throw a lot of light into the foyer.

She had taken off the old, worn forest-green wallpaper and painted the walls a light peach color, but while that helped a little, the area was still the darkest in the house. The brown, short-shag carpet that Rocky insisted on keeping didn't help.

She stopped to pick up the mail. There was an electric bill and two advertising flyers. It's never good news, she thought, glancing at the white envelope with the plastic window. Her name was there, not Rocky's. She'd have to put a check in the mail tonight so it would be paid while she was away. Couldn't have the poor guy without lights while she was away. Not that he'd notice anyway.

She slipped off her navy-blue windbreaker, put it away in the hall closet, then went up the stairs to the upper part of the house. The front, floor-length drapes were closed so she walked over and pulled them open to reveal the distant view of the ocean. She stood for a few seconds and gazed at the waves attacking the shoreline. It was a dangerously beautiful sight.

Like Sharon had been, she thought. She immediately regretted the thought. Why couldn't she get that woman out of her head?

She walked into the kitchen, pulled the banana-shaped yellow phone from its wall-mounted cradle, and used the clear plastic buttons to dial the sheriff's office.

After two rings, the new receptionist, Ella Simpson, answered. "Fairview sheriff's office." Ella always sounded so cheerful. She was just a happy person.

"Ella, it's Trudy Wilson calling. I'd like to speak with Flo."

"Trudy, how nice," she sounded genuinely pleased. "Sorry, sheriff's outta the office right now. You want me ta raise her on the radio?"

Trudy laughed. The woman's sunny disposition was truly infectious.

"Naw, Ella don't bother her. I would like to speak with her, though, as soon as she gets in. It's kinda important."

"You bet."

"Thanks a bunch. Bye."

Trudy hung up, confident that Ella would be immediately on the radio, relaying her message. Ella was not one to sit around and wait. The woman's energy and enthusiasm were attributes that made her a valuable commodity to the community.

Trudy leaned back and glanced at her thin Timex. The black arms had moved two minutes when the phone rang. She smiled to herself and picked up the receiver after the second ring.

"Thanks for calling me back so quickly, Flo," she said. She heard the husky chuckle at the other end.

"Ella said you wanted something important?" Right to business. That's what made her a pro. No chit chat.

"Bruce's been arrested in Vancouver."

"Which one?" asked Flo.

Trudy grinned. Only true west coasters would think to ask this question. The lady had done her homework. Though she didn't ask what he'd been arrested for.

"Canada."

"Do you know which department has him? They have a few there."

"Huh…I don't know. He didn't tell me."

"Huh, huh…well, once you know, call me back and I'll make a few calls for you."

"Thanks, Flo." Trudy sighed.

"Oh, and by the way, what's he charged with?"

Now came the tough part. Trudy hesitated. Friend or not, Flo was still a sworn officer of the law, and murder was a serious crime.

"Murder."

"No fuckin' way," came the quick reply. She sounded pissed. Trudy pictured the sheriff, sitting in her cruiser, her pure white face reddening and her blonde curls waving side to side as she shook her head in disgust.

Boy, she thought, I really gotta get the hairdresser shit outta my system. I'm always thinking about everybody's hair.

"I know. It's total bullshit."

"Okay, once you find out what's happening, call me right away. I'll give a buddy of mine from the RCMP a quick call and let him know you're on your way. His name's Rod Baker. Good guy. Good cop." She paused. "How're you getting there?"

Trudy laughed. "Thanks, Flo. I'm taking Rocky's truck. My ol' POS would never have made it that far. I'm lucky if it gets me across town."

It was Flo's turn to laugh. "Okay. I'll call you back as soon as I hear anything more. And, Trudy…"

"Yeah?"

"Don't worry. I'm sure Bruce'll be cleared."

"Yeah." Trudy hung up the phone and stared at it for a long time without moving. The battery-operated clock that hung off the wallpapered kitchen wall over her head ticked loudly in her ears. She heard the motor in the refrigerator come on. She noticed that the room smelled of onions.

A trail of tears began to flow down her pale cheeks from her swollen, red-rimmed eyes.

CHAPTER FIVE

FLO PULLED THE WHITE CRUISER with the gold-and-black sheriff's logo on both doors away from the curb after finishing her call with Trudy. In bold, black lettering on the rear trunk lid was the word SHERIFF.

She wasn't surprised that Bruce was in trouble with the law. She'd done some background checking on him and discovered the connections he held in that motorcycle business outside Seattle. He wasn't directly connected with any of the owner's activities, but he wasn't squeaky clean, either.

A few disorderly conduct arrests at local bars, and one assault case in the past four years. No convictions, but it meant he wasn't an angel.

Flo steered the cruiser onto the highway and headed south back to her office. As soon as she arrived, she planned to make a few calls to people she knew from the law enforcement community in Vancouver. She was certain they'd be able to shed some light on this mess.

As she pulled the car into the parking stall, she saw that her deputy Jason March was out on patrol—his cruiser was missing from its parking slot. Good. He wasn't the best deputy she'd ever hired, but he seemed to be getting the message.

She'd hesitated in hiring him, with his low scores at the state police academy, but on a small-town budget, she needed to stretch every dollar. Especially with the recent equipment upgrades.

She stepped from the car and walked into the office with her report folder under one arm. She'd instituted patrol reports, much to Jason's chagrin.

"Sheriff," said Ella. The coffee-colored woman's row of brilliant white teeth seemed to brighten the dingy room.

The station house was old and run-down. The many layers of ancient paint were all that seemed to hold the place together. Her petition to the town council to provide the sheriff's department with better quarters had thus far fallen on deaf ears. She was being ignored and it bothered her.

"Hi, Ella," said Flo, a thin smile across her lips. She knew she was frowning. Ella would understand. She always did.

Ella spun around in her black office chair to face forward as the phone on her desk rang. Flo hurried past her to her private office. The glass, wood-framed door rattled loudly as she slammed it behind her. She normally kept the door open as part of her open-door policy. Something she'd promised in her election campaign.

She moved behind her large oak desk and sat in the high-backed, gray tweed office chair. With her feet, she pushed the chair backward on its steel rollers in order to reach her two-drawer credenza.

She pulled her keys from her pants pocket and quickly located the key that opened the gray steel cabinet. She slipped the shiny silver key into the lock and turned it.

Leaving the key in place, she pulled the top drawer open and there, on top of her "closed" files, was her old business card holder.

She hoped they remembered her. She had met a number of RCMP and Vancouver City cops at the Organized Crime Conference in Portland a year ago. One of them might be able to help her.

She flipped through the cards until she found the one she was looking for. Corporal Rod Baker, RCMP, Vancouver Drug Section.

She swiveled her chair to face the desk and placed the white card on her desk blotter. She lifted the receiver and dialed Rod's direct line. His line rang three times until it kicked to a voice mail recording.

Damn, she thought, he isn't there and I hate these fucking things. Why can't they have secretaries or something, like the good ol' days? She smirked. What the hell am I thinking? Then again, having a cute male butt running around out there instead of Ella might be fun.

His message finished, indicating that he wasn't in the office today but would be tomorrow.

She left her name and phone number, saying it was important she speak with him, then hung up.

She rested her arms on the desk and thought she might try Phil Singh. He was a Vancouver PD homicide guy she knew. If Bruce were in the VPD lockup, then Phil would definitely know about it.

She flipped through the cards again until she found Phil's. This time the line rang once, and before a second ring, he answered.

"Detective Singh," said a soft voice that reminded her of silk bed sheets. He sounded kinda bored.

"Hi, Phil, it's Flo Henderson from Fairview, Oregon."

There was a pause, then a snort of laughter. "Flo. How nice to hear your voice. You've made this broken-down old flatfoot's day. How the hell are ya, eh?"

Flo smiled. "Phil, you son of a gun. I'm great. Made sheriff here in Fairview. Nice job. Ya know, after what happened with the former sheriff and all."

Phil's voice turned grim. "Yeah, I heard about that mess. That guy was a real son of a bitch, eh?"

"Yup. But listen, that's not why I called. Do you remember how a local guy and woman worked together to solve that case?"

"Yeah, sure; they helped a state cop named Sanchez, didn't they?"

Flo nodded. "Yup. Well, it seems the guy, a Bruce Carstairs, seems to have gotten himself in a little trouble with you up there north of the 49th."

"Okay. Give me a minute and I'll check in the computer."

Flo heard the click of keys being pushed as Phil keyed in Bruce's name. "You got a DOB?"

Flo had no idea what Bruce's date of birth was. "Nope, sorry. I'd say he was about thirty-two or thirty-three."

"Okay. Here it is…" Phil paused. He must've been reading the file information on PIRS.

The Police Information Retrieval System linked all Canadian police forces' files in one central data depository. Great idea, which police departments in the states envied.

"Oh, shit. Yup, looks like your boy's in a heap of trouble. In fact, he's up to his armpits in shit," said Phil. For a veteran cop who'd seen just about every vice human beings were capable of, even he sounded amazed.

"What is it?" asked Flo. She tried and failed to keep the anxiety from her voice.

"He's been arrested for murder—he's accused of killing the daughter-in-law of the prime minister of Canada."

CHAPTER SIX

BRUCE SAT IN THE STEEL-GRAY PAINTED CELL, staring at the polished aluminum toilet and sink resting against one wall. The bed, bolted to the wall, was comfortable against his butt. His long, black hair hung about his broad shoulders like a waterfall of pure night. His pale skin glowed from the light of the overhead boxed fluorescent lights. Even those were encased in heavy wire mesh.

He glanced at the magazine lying next to him on the bunk. Movies stars. Assholes, he thought. Now he'd be the celebrity of the moment. He thought back to what might have gone wrong.

His mind wandered taking him back to the events that led to him being in this cell.

***

He recalled Cherie. She was some hot chick. He pictured her in her tight blue jeans and red cotton tank top. Her heavy breasts stood perfectly erect, even without a bra. Her long blonde hair, neatly permed into flowing curls, ran down her back like a train of shimmering gold. Her tanned skin also reminded him of that gold-painted broad in that spy flick from the '60s.

His old roomie, Howard, loved those cheesy movies and had watched them endlessly after they came out on video.

Cherie had definitely been a hottie. Too bad she hadn't mentioned her husband before he'd slept with her.

And too bad she was dead. He'd really liked her. She'd been fun. He felt grief overcome him, but he knew the cops were watching him on their closed-circuit monitors, so he held back the tears.

It was like reliving the horror of his sister's death. It was a fuckin' nightmare. He hoped Trudy would be here soon. He needed a friend right now—any friend.

He was tired. The party had taken a lot out of him. The night that began at the Ranch Hand Bar and Grill and then moved to Spike's place near the beach had been a long one. He sighed heavily.

Spike Logan was a local wannabe of the Angels who'd never gotten his patch; he was an associate, just like Bruce was. Sure, being an associate had its rewards. Booze, dope, and broads may be fun, but they also made life complicated.

Bruce knew that for sure, now.

He had never really wanted to be a full-fledged member of the Angels anyway. It wasn't his thing. Looking like one and being one were very different things. He was a damn good bookkeeper and he needed to live life on his own terms.

The extended party last night had been a doozy. Booze flowing and more-than-willing women plentiful. Music blaring. All the mix for a good-time-was-had-by-all ending. Not this time, though.

When he woke up this morning, he couldn't remember much. His head throbbed due to a seriously wicked hangover. Next to him lay Cherie. He never knew her last name until after he was arrested. He shook her, but she didn't move. He realized when he touched her that she was abnormally cold.

He checked her wrist for a pulse and found nothing. She looked like she was asleep, but he knew she was dead.

He stumbled into the living room wearing only his boxers. Spike lay on the couch, facedown and naked. Bruce shook him and the tough guy with his bleary, blood-shot eyes stared up at him, an angry expression on his face.

"What the fuck?" he asked, his word slurring.

"Cherie's dead," said Bruce. He grasped one side of his head and used his free arm to steady himself by gripping the arm of the brown tweed couch. Glancing to the picture window, he saw that the sun was beginning to climb into the eastern sky. The glowing ball of orange fire was becoming brighter by the second. In another half hour, this room would be filled with the rays of the new day.

"Who?" asked Spike, his face changing to one of concern. From his expression, it was plain he didn't need this shit in his house. Rental or not, it spelled trouble for a guy in his position.

"Cherie," said Bruce more forcefully. "Ya know, the broad I picked up at the bar last night."

Spike looked puzzled for a moment, then his memory cells must've kicked in because he became pale and suddenly sat up as if the alcohol in his system had dissipated. "I remember now," he said his voice solemn. "I think you'd better leave."

"What? There's a dead girl in my bed…"

"Right the fuck now!" Spike's eyes were narrow and his voice gave the room a sudden chill. Bruce shivered involuntarily.

Clearly, he had to leave. He turned and made a beeline for the bedroom. He stole a final glance at Cheri's still, naked figure, lying spread-eagled on the bed. Her ample breasts stood like twin peaks from her chest. Her long, blonde hair fanned out from her head. Her eyes were closed and she looked peaceful as he quickly dressed in his white sport socks, blue jeans, and black tee shirt.

He slipped on his Daytons, then stomped each foot down until the boots were securely in place. Lastly, he slipped on his black leather jacket and hurried from the room.

Spike sat on the couch, watching Bruce walk across the room toward the front door. He had slipped on a pair of black jeans and sat with bare feet and a bare upper body. He was smoking a cigarette.

"Sorry," said Bruce, casting an eye at Spike, who nodded. His inky eyes were focused on the worn, forest-green, oval throw rug that lay on the scuffed and marred hardwood in front of the couch.

Bruce pulled the front door open then he hurried down the cracked cement walkway and the two stone steps to the driveway where his rebuilt bike sat, leaning on its steel stand. The gas tank was painted royal purple and the yellow lettering painted across it read "Sharon's Ride" in honor of his late sister. His late sis had loved the feeling of her long hair trailing in the wind as she rode on the back of his motorcycle.

He straddled the bike and kicked the stand in place with his right foot. He turned the key in the ignition and stepped hard on the starter pedal. The engine roared to life. He revved it a couple of times and then gave it some gas and eased out the clutch. The bike leapt forward and he steered onto the black-paved road. The road was too small to have painted lines.

The dilapidated bungalow sat at the end of a dead-end cul-de-sac near the edge of a park.

He smirked. Not much of a park—more like a wild forest. Perfect for wild parties. No neighbors, no complaints.

He heard the waves at the beach and smelled the mix of salt water and green forest around him as he sped down the quiet street. The house wasn't far from the beach.

He rounded a corner shielded by a stand of maple trees, their leaves pale green. The leaves moved about as if in some fall dance; a light wind had sprung up. The warmth of the sun felt good on his face.

As he neared the corner, he saw two cars parked across the road, their noses creating a V shape. The cars had light bars on the roof, which were flashing. Cops.

He slowed the bike as he neared the roadblock until he saw there were cops with guns drawn, crouching behind open car doors, aiming straight at him. He stopped in front of the cars.

"Get off the bike and put your hands above your head." The sound was amplified by a speaker on the roof of one of the police cars.

He knew, if he didn't comply with the order, they would shoot him, no doubt at all.

He stopped the bike, turned off the engine, and kicked the stand in place. Carefully, with his hands visible, he stepped off the bike and stood beside it with his hands over his head. I feel kinda stupid, he thought.

"Lock your fingers behind your head, then lay facedown on the ground," came the next order.

Again he complied, albeit a bit awkwardly, given his size. He lay still as he heard booted footsteps approach.

"One hand behind your back," said a deep male voice.

He did so and felt the cold steel of a handcuff being slipped over his wrist and then secured with a ratcheting sound.

"Now the other."

Again, he did so, and again he felt the handcuff being locked in place. Now he wouldn't be able to move. He felt two sets of strong hands grab his arms and lift him up.

He saw there was a shit-load of cops. Had to be at least twenty. They holstered their automatic pistols. All were young, both the men and the women, and all had grim expressions on their faces.

"Hey, guys," he said, trying his best to sound as innocent as possible. "What's up?"

They didn't say a word as they pushed him toward the open door of one of the cars, and while holding his head so it wouldn't bump against the doorframe, placed him inside. The door slammed behind him. He sat in the car, staring at the cops milling about. A man and a woman cop climbed into the front seat of the cruiser. The man spoke into a microphone, apparently to dispatch. A tow truck would take his bike away.

The woman turned and looked at him. "Do you know why you're being arrested?" she asked. He shook his head. He felt a sinking feeling deep in his stomach. He knew why, but he just couldn't believe it. Spike had fingered him.

"Is your name Bruce Carstairs?" she asked. Her eyes were hard and free of emotion.

He nodded.

"Well, Mr. Carstairs, you are under arrest for suspicion of the murder of Cherie Lavois…" she proceeded to read him his rights, which he barely heard as his mind raced, trying to remember what happened the previous evening after he arrived at the house. He couldn't remember anything past coming through the front door after Spike handed him the bottle of beer…

"Do you understand your rights as I have read them to you, Mister Carstairs?"

He blinked. "Yeah, sure," he said dully. The car had begun to move. The flashers were off and they quickly left the roadblock behind.

They weaved their way through the windblown trees until they came to the junction with the two-lane highway. The traffic was light, the car quickly made it into the traffic, and they headed north.

Bruce eased back in the seat, the cool, hard steel of the cuffs digging into the soft flesh of his wrists.

What the hell was he gonna do? "Fuck," he muttered under his breath.

He saw the two cops in the front seat cast sideways glances at each other and smirk at his predicament.

He felt despair run through his being. He didn't remember anything else. It was like there was a void in his mind. A hole where his memories disappeared. Something like this had never happened to him before, no matter how much booze he drank or how much grass he smoked.

Trudy. He needed Trudy. There was no clock on the wall or window and they'd taken his watch. Pretty hard to kill yourself with a Seiko, but he'd heard of stranger things.

He still didn't know who Cherie was, but the cops seemed to be worked up about something. His legal-aid lawyer would be in tomorrow morning. Maybe he'd find out then.

***

No matter how many times he ran over the events surrounding his arrest in his mind he still couldn't determine who had framed him for Cherie's murder.

"'Yeah," muttered Bruce, his voice echoing off the brick walls surrounding him as he leaned back against his cell wall. "Fuck."

He hoped Trudy would get here soon. He'd made the right decision to call her for help. She was the only person he trusted.

CHAPTER SEVEN

TRUDY NEARLY DROPPED THE TELEPHONE RECEIVER. She felt it slipping from her grasp but managed to retain control of herself.

"What the hell....?" she asked under her breath. "That can't be right." Her mind reeled with crazy thoughts. How would Bruce know anyone like that?

"Flo, something has to be wrong. Bruce would never fucking kill anyone, much less the daughter-in-law of the prime minister of Canada. That's bullshit..."

Flo Henderson, her voice cool and calm, interrupted her friend's tirade. "Listen to me, Trudy. All I know is what my contact tells me. I haven't been able to reach my guy at the RCMP yet, and until I do, I won't have any more information."

"Sorry. It's just that I know this guy. He wouldn't kill anyone, especially after what happened..." her voice trailed off.

She could almost hear the gentle nod of Flo's head as she attempted to comfort her. "Yeah, I know." There was a pause. "So, you gonna go up there, or what?"

"You bet your ass I am." Trudy surprised herself with the determination in her voice. "I've already packed my stuff and put it in the truck. I was just waiting for your call."

"Okay, but be careful. I'll be waiting for your call when you get there."

Trudy felt her eyes fill with tears. They tasted salty as they flowed down her face to her lips. "Thanks, Flo, for your help. It means a lot to me."

"You're welcome," Flo said cheerfully.

Trudy hung the receiver back in the cradle. She wiped away the tears with the back of her right hand and then glanced toward the carpeted steps that led to the three bedrooms on the upper level. Rocky was no doubt still sleeping off yesterday's libations before starting on today's round. She never knew how he made it home every day, but then again, she didn't want to know, either.

Sunlight streamed into the living room as she crossed the room to the top of the staircase, which led to the foyer and the front door. She hurried down the stairs without looking back.

Her white Nikes made no noise on the carpeted staircase.

Upon reaching the landing at the bottom, she pulled one of the natural-stained wood-slatted closet doors open and extracted her faux leather jacket. She'd bought it last spring at the discount outlet store in the mall. Eighty percent savings was a good deal in her book.

Its dull, black, simulated leather shone in the light streaming through the fogged glass of the narrow window next to the solid pine front door.

She closed the closet and opened the front door. The air was filled with the freshness of the sea air and the blooming roses and daisies that lined the sides of the driveway.

She smiled and immediately a flash of guilt for feeling so good crossed her mind. She had no right to feel good, but she couldn't help herself. It was a beautiful day for a drive. The sun was warm and the air was fresh, though the wind, which was light this time of day, took some edge off the warm rays of ol' sol. She loved late fall days like this on the coast; it reminded her of home in Seattle. She closed the door behind her and made sure it was locked. She tried to turn the brushed-brass doorknob, twice.

She dismissed her thoughts of Rocky. Regrets. Who needed them?

She moved to the driver's door of the blue pickup and swung the door open. It had been oiled recently so it made little noise—just a small, swishing sound. I wish he took as good care of me as he did this hunk of metal, she though bitterly.

The engine started as soon as she turned the key, the V8 rumbling at a low purr. She put it in gear and backed out.

She had to make one stop and then would hit the road. It was an eight-hour drive to Vancouver and she felt tired already. She rolled down the driver's side window so she could take in the smells of the sea and rain forest. She reveled in the coast. It permeated her being and made her feel alive. The atmosphere of the place was the one thing that held her here.

She wound through the forest that lined the road to the highway, well below the posted speed limit. She loved the green of trees and the smells: the flowers in spring, the rain in winter, the salt air.

She almost closed her eyes but resisted the urge, preferring to keep her eyes on the road ahead.

A sudden honk from behind made her cast her eyes in the rearview mirror. A brown station wagon had pulled up close behind her. She glanced at the speedometer and realized she was only going twenty miles per hour.

She shrugged her shoulders, then cast an apologetic gesture at the driver behind her. Not that he would see it, but it didn't hurt to at least feign an apology.

She stepped on the gas and was soon at the highway. She turned north and easily found a space large enough to get onto the road.

She followed the highway to the outlet center, where she entered the visitor parking area. She'd only be a few minutes, so she'd park in front of the shop and say her good-byes to May.

She pulled up in front and turned off the engine. The shop lights were dark—it was still early. She could make out that the office door at the rear was partially open and the light was on, meaning May was in the back preparing for the day ahead.

She stepped out of the truck and slammed the door. As the parking lot was mostly empty, it echoed off the brick walls of the shops that lined the giant, ugly strip mall.

Trudy saw a blonde head appear from behind the closed door, with a frown on her face. It was May. Her frown turned to a slight smile as she saw who it was.

She rushed to the door and unlocked it. She was wearing those wooden sandals that had become so popular. Trudy could hear them slapping the tiled floor even through the heavy glass.

She had on a pink-and-white flowered short-sleeved dress shirt and a pair of brand-new blue jeans that looked like they'd been painted on. The male customers will really like this outfit, May, she thought to herself.

May stepped back as Trudy entered, then, once she was inside with the door closed, she reset the deadbolt.

Together they walked in silence to the back room.

"I need you to sign something," said May once they were seated at the two chairs, one in front of the office desk, the other to the side.

Lying flat on the brown, laminated surface of the heavily cigarette-scarred desk were two white cards with the logo from her bank in the upper left corner. She gazed at them and immediately recognized them. They were account signature cards.

"What are these for?" asked Trudy, already actually knowing what they were.

"While you're away, I'll need access to the accounts to pay bills and such," said May, her tone all business.

"Yeah, I guess so…" Trudy paused to open the desk drawer and pull out a blue ballpoint pen. "Can't Rocky look after this shit?"

May gave her a withering look.

Trudy nodded. "Yeah, I know. Don't say any more."

She reached for the cards and pulled them toward her. She read them over carefully. She certainly hadn't understood all the legalese when she'd signed them the first time, and this was no different; but all the same, she liked to make the pretense she knew what they meant.

She held the pen over where the x's were on the two cards and signed her name, in full, the legal way.

When she was done, May smiled warmly, took the cards, and placed them in her purse. Really, a cloth bag that hung off one hook of the wooden coat tree.

"Come on, let's get a coffee at the Snack Shack before you have to go," said May.

Trudy suddenly felt the oddest sense of foreboding come over her. This seemed too familiar. Hadn't she gone for coffee with Sharon just before she disappeared? She immediately shook it off and smiled at her friend.

"Yes, let's. And I'll tell you what—I'll pay."

***

Thirty minutes later, Trudy was back on the highway headed north. She quickly arrived at the junction, which led to Portland and all points north.

She began to think about Bruce, sitting in his cell in Vancouver. She couldn't believe he'd ever be involved in a cold-blooded murder, though Flo told her that the cops seemed pretty sure he'd done it. She needed more information. She decided to call Flo once she got to Portland and stopped for gas.

She stepped harder on the gas pedal and felt the surge of power as the extra horsepower that she definitely had never experienced in her POS came to bear. The truck quickly caught up with the massive house on wheels in front of her. She moved her foot to the brake and slowed down before she mated with the massive vehicle.

Oops, she thought, *this is going to take some getting used to.*

CHAPTER EIGHT

Flo picked up her phone on the first ring after Ella mouthed to her it was the call she'd been waiting for.

"Rod?"

"Yeah. Hi, Flo." Rod Baker's voice sounded world-weary. Flo knew from bitter experience that the war on drugs was unwinnable. The weekly law enforcement bulletins always seemed to be the bearer of bad news for cops on the drug beat.

"How're you?" she asked. Even though she tried to control it, she knew her voice sounded clipped. Damn, she thought. This guy's a friend, and I need friends right now.

"Trouble?" asked Baker, obviously picking up the inflection in her voice.

He'd understand, she knew he would. Good cops helped good cops—that was the unwritten rule, and they were both good cops who cared about what they did for a living.

"I need your help," she stated flatly. The small talk could wait. She stole a glance at her watch. Trudy would be near Portland and would no doubt be calling to see if she'd found anything more about Bruce's situation.

When Rod didn't say anything, she took it as her cue that he was waiting for her to continue. So she did. "A friend of mine is in deep trouble up there and I need to find out what's happened. I spoke with Phil Singh—do you know him?—VDP homicide. Anyway, he said I better check with the Mounties because my friend is in the lockup in someplace called…" she paused to look at her note pad. "White Rock."

"Well, that certainly sounds like trouble," said Rod slowly.

"Yeah—right. Could you check it out and let me know what's goin' on?"

"Would that guy's name be Bruce Carstairs?" asked Rod.

Flo eased back to sink into the cushion of her high-backed ergonomic office chair. Oh, shit, she thought. I have a bad feeling about this.

"As a matter of fact, yeah, it is. Why?" she asked cautiously.

"Well, your boy made the morning papers up here. Offing some ordinary scumbag is no big deal. Might get ya a small article at the back of the sports section. Ya know, after the funny papers. But this guy? The daughter-in-law of the PM—now that's first-rate stuff. Sex—Drugs—and Rock and Roll? Wild parties? Really juicy stuff, if you go in for that sort of thing." Rod sounded almost amused. Almost. He was a serious cop. His sense of humor was limited at the best of times.

She pictured him the last time she saw him. In his rumpled golf shirt, faded blue jeans. His sunglasses sitting atop his balding head.

He was a little overweight, but not too bad. A couple of well-fed love handles hung over his belt. He chewed gum. The fruit stuff, sugarless. For his diet, he said.

In actuality, he'd quit smoking some two months before the conference and found that chewing gum calmed his nerves, especially when he couldn't get Canadian smokes in Portland.

He didn't sound like he was chewing gum right now.

"Has Bruce been charged?" asked Flo.

"Yup. He's going to a prelim in a couple of hours. What can I do for ya?" Rod, always to the point.

"I just need to have the address where he's being held."

"Why?" asked Rod, sounding quizzical.

"Cavalry's on the way," said Flo.

She wrote down the address on a yellow post it note as he recited it to her. "You comin' up here?" he asked.

"Nope. See ya, Rod." She paused. "Oh, and Rod?"

"Yeah?"

"Thanks, I really appreciate this. Any time—"

He chuckled cutting her off. "No worries, Flo, us cops gotta stick together."

She heard the click at the other end then hung up the phone by replacing the black receiver in the cradle with a resounding slap. She leaned forward on her elbows, her hands grasped together, her fingers intertwined. She stared at the rain that had begun to fall like pellets of angry bees, striking the large picture window that looked out over the highway.

"Now it's up to you, Trudy, "she whispered gazing at the scrawled address.

***

Trudy left the dark clouds and Portland far behind on the multi-lane I-5 highway. She decided to keep on going until she need gas, then she'd phone Flo.

Fear of finding out the truth kept her going. She glanced at the truck's gas gauge; it read half full. Good thing she'd filled the tank at the station halfway to Portland, otherwise she might have had to stop by now.

She slammed one hand on the steering wheel, making the large truck sway slightly. A car beside her honked at her. She glanced at the driver, gave him the one-fingered salute, then stepped hard on the gas pedal.

The big V8 engine quickly put distance between her and the other driver. She sighed and eased back on the pedal. What the hell was she doing? Bruce was in trouble and she was fingering other drivers on the road like some white trash.

She decided she better get it over with. The gas gauge had moved a little off the middle mark, so she gazed at the signs ahead on the side of the highway and saw that there was a grouping of gas stations at the next turnoff. After glancing in the large side mirror that protruded from the right side of the truck and in the rearview mirror, she maneuvered into the slow lane.

There was a sudden sharp blare of a car horn behind her, which made her steer back into the middle lane. She glanced over her right shoulder and saw the smaller car from before, right behind her. It had been in the blind spot.

She shook her head and slowed down to let the car get past her.

The driver, a middle-aged man with dark hair waved his fist at her as she sped past. She shrugged her shoulders and grinned apologetically as he hurried past her.

He honked his horn to punctuate his displeasure.

She made if off the highway without further incident and found a Chevron station with three pump islands for gas and one set up for diesel. Each pump had space for two cars, so six could gas up simultaneously.

She pulled up to one of the islands and stopped next to the front pump. She turned off the engine, swung open the door, and stepped out. Just then the little car with the dark-haired man appeared behind her, pulling up to the rear gas pump.

She rolled her eyes and sighed. Damn my luck, she thought.

She kept her eyes averted as the man got out of his car and walked around to the pump.

He glanced at her, an angry expression in his eyes. "You should pay better attention to your driving." He said it calmly, but with sufficient menace so she'd get the message. "A woman traveling alone can get into all sorts of trouble, if you get my meaning?"

Trudy didn't say anything. She kept her eyes focused on the gas pump, watching the numbers change as she filled the tank. The man finished first. Made sense. Small car.

He moved around his car after replacing the pump handle. Trudy stole a glance at him. On his belt, he wore a black leather knife case. He had on white runners. He had a sleeveless, white tee shirt with tattered edges where the arms would normally be attached to the shirt.

"I'll be watching you, bitch."

Trudy began to tremble as she watched the man get in his car and start the engine. He tossed her a menacing glare as he sped away.

A man came running toward her wearing a uniform of light blue shirt, navy pants, and black runners. He was waving his arms and shouting. "Hey, that guy didn't pay!"

This wasn't her day. That was for damn sure.

The guy was closer now and she could see by his nametag that his name was Bruce B. Another Bruce, she mused.

"That guy used a stolen credit card," said the man, his face flushed from the sudden exertion. She could see by the bulbous stomach hanging over his belt that he wasn't used too much physical exertion. The button just above his belt strained to keep the shirt together; stretch lines ran like a ring of waves where a pebble had splashed in a still pond.

"Do you know him?" The man's green eyes looked hopeful until she shook her head. "But you was talking to him."

She shook her head again and this time added a small shrug of her narrow shoulders.

"I'm gonna call the cops," the man said. He turned away and walked toward the office. He didn't move as fast as before. More like he was sauntering than walking.

The trigger of the gas pump handle suddenly clicking in her hand startled Trudy. The tank was full. She glanced at the numbers and saw the total was nearly fifty dollars. Good thing she'd gone to the bank before leaving. The truck was a real gas hog. Good thing Rocky only drove to the bar and back most days. She sighed. But at least the thing's reliable.

She closed the little door that covered the refill nozzle after replacing the plastic gas cap and turned to walk toward the station's little store.

Out of the corner of her left eye, she caught some movement and stopped.

A little car sped through the spot where she was about to step. She caught a flash of the face behind the wheel, grinning at her. It was the asshole, punctuating his point.

The little car's engine whined and disappeared around a corner at high speed and out of sight once more.

She broke into a near run and hurried inside the station's store. Her hands trembled. She braced herself against a counter set up as a coffee bar overlooking the gas station's lot.

"You okay, miss?" It was the attendant. His now white face gazed at her with genuine concern in his eyes.

"Yeah," she said, feeling her knees buckle slightly. The man moved to her side and held one of her arms, holding her up.

"Marcie, call the cops—and an ambulance—right now!"

Trudy didn't know who Marcie was, but she hoped she was fast. That son of a bitch could be coming back right now. He might have a gun. He did have a knife.

Her knees finally gave out as the thoughts of the grinning man flashed through her mind. She hit the side of the tan-colored counter and used it as a support to slowly sink to the floor. The attendant held her arm and made sure she made the trip with the minimum of force. He let go once she'd completed her journey.

She sat on the floor, her knees pulled up to her chest, hugging them, her face buried in her black slacks. She couldn't control the trembling or the feeling of overwhelming fear that gripped her.

"Marcie, hurry!" His voice sounded like it was in a dream, but this was definitely no dream—more like a nightmare.

Finally, after what seemed like an eternity, she heard the warble of a siren approaching. Low at first, then getting louder with each passing second.

She heard the squeal of brakes as the siren's echo died.

The door to the store burst open and two cops, one woman and one man, burst in with their pistols drawn. They wore forest-green uniforms with gold badges over their left breasts.

They both wore rimmed, dark sunglasses, so Trudy couldn't see their eyes, and they wore no hats.

The woman had dirty-blonde hair pulled into a bun and a slim build. The man was about six feet tall, with a military style flattop, broad shoulders, and arms like a bodybuilder.

Great, Trudy thought, Arnold Schwarzenegger is rescuing me. She giggled to herself when she stretched out Arnold's name, like some of those late night comedians did on TV.

The woman saw her sitting on the floor and quickly moved to crouch down next to her, holstering her pistol. She removed her sunglasses while her partner stood in a shooting stance, his gun's barrel scanning the station for possible targets.

Trudy saw serious brown eyes staring into hers. "You okay, ma'am?" her voice was pretty normal and surprisingly calm.

Trudy nodded.

"Okay. Sit tight while we make sure the perp is gone," said the woman. She indicated to her partner to search the rest of the store.

The woman stood, drawing her service automatic from the holster again as she followed her partner. Trudy lost sight of them.

She heard slow footsteps, and finally two figures appeared before her with their hands locked over their heads. The attendant didn't look too impressed and the woman, black with short, tight curls, looked genuinely frightened. Her eyes were wide as saucers. She kept stealing furtive glances behind her.

"Keep moving," said a stern male voice.

The attendant and the woman, who must be Marcie, stood in front of her like some convenience store police lineup. Trudy shook off the thought that this was ridiculous.

"Those people aren't the guy who threatened me," Trudy said.

"Where is he?" asked the woman cop to the two prisoners.

"I told you," said the attendant, his eyes flashing with annoyance. "He didn't pay. He drove off. I saw him try to run down this lady—with his car," he nodded toward Trudy.

"Okay," said the male cop, obviously satisfied with the response. "Put your hands down and go about your business. We need to talk to the lady."

The attendant and his female partner dropped their hands to their sides like they were dead weights. "Boy, you try to help people and this is the fuckin' thanks you get..." Bruce the attendant muttered as they disappeared from Trudy's sight.

The two cops, their sidearm's holstered, crouched down next to Trudy. "You wanna go outside and get some air?" asked the woman, attempting to sound compassionate. Difficult after the extreme adrenalin rush only moments before. It took a lot of practice for cops to make the switch to low gear. Sometimes it took years of being in dangerous situations. Unfortunately, the life of a cop often played havoc with personal relationships.

Trudy nodded. She took in a gulp of air, realizing it had been several minutes since she'd breathed normally. No wonder she felt light-headed.

The lady cop—the gold-plated tag over her right shirt pocket said her name was Sheppard—smiled thinly to reassure her, held out a hand, and helped Trudy to stand. The guy—his nametag identified him as Devlin—hooked his thumbs over his gun belt.

The portable radio hanging off his right hip crackled. He removed it from his belt and mumbled something she couldn't hear into it and then placed it back in its holder. His sunglasses hung by one arm off his left shirt pocket. He removed them and slipped them over his eyes with one smooth, practiced motion.

Yeah, this guy thinks his shit don't stink.

Supporting her with one arm, Sheppard helped Trudy outside into the sunlight. The warmth felt good against her face. The air was rife with the smell of gasoline.

The police car was parked in front of the station door with its flashing light bar lit up. Sheppard stood beside Trudy as Devlin moved to the car. He slipped in the passenger door and turned off the lights. He stepped back out and closed the door behind him.

He leaned back against the hood of the car, crossed his arms over his wide chest, and studied the two women.

"Why don't you tell me what happened?" asked Sheppard, a slight smile crossing her red lips. She unbuttoned a leather pouch on her belt and extracted her notebook. She casually flipped it to a blank page.

Do they train all cops to do it that way? It reminded Trudy of the first time she'd met Delores Sanchez. She wondered how the detective's recovery was coming. Last time she'd talked to her, Sanchez had said the force was giving her a desk job until she'd fully recovered from her injuries.

"I cut some guy off by accident when I was leaving the highway and he followed me and threatened me. Like the attendant said, he almost ran me over in the station parking lot."

Sheppard nodded, and like good cops everywhere, recorded Trudy's every word. She nodded to urge Trudy to continue. "You get a look at the guy?"

"I don't know," said Trudy. She meant it—the whole thing seemed unreal, like it hadn't happened at all.

Sheppard looked into her eyes. "What's your name?" she asked.

"Trudy—Trudy Wilson."

"Okay, Trudy, so where you headed?"

"Canada."

"Big place, Canada." Sheppard smiled warmly, her brown eyes sparkling.

Trudy smiled thinly. "Yeah. Vancouver. To visit a friend."

Sheppard nodded. "Is there anyone we can call?"

Trudy knew immediately that Sheppard suspected something was wrong with her story. There wasn't, but Sheppard didn't know that. Middle-aged woman, driving a truck with Oregon plates, headed for Canada by herself. Not exactly normal.

"Yeah. Flo Henderson. She's the sheriff of Fairview. She's a friend of mine."

"Okay. You go sit in your truck. We'll check this out and make a few calls." Sheppard raised one hand to grasp Trudy's left arm in an attempt to reassure her. "It'll be okay, right?"

Trudy nodded and walked away toward her car. She glanced back over her shoulder and saw Devlin head inside the gas station store. No doubt to interview the attendant and the girl.

Sheppard stepped through the driver's door of the police car. Trudy saw her pick up the mike attached to a radio on the cruiser's dashboard before she turned away.

Once at the truck, Trudy opened the driver's door and sat behind the steering wheel, leaving the door open. She needed air. She closed her eyes and leaned her head against the seat back.

Bruce. I need you. You would know what to do.

The woman cop's approaching booted footsteps interrupted her thoughts. Trudy opened her eyes, nodding her head forward.

The woman stood, her hands at her sides, her face expressionless. "We have a description of the car and the guy from the attendant. No license plate number, but it's a Washington plate, so we think he may be a local." She smirked, a sardonic grin crossing her face. "We have a few yahoos round here. We'll catch 'em."

Trudy smiled weakly. "Yeah. Can I go now? I have a long drive."

"Sure." The cop wheeled around and started back toward the police car. She stopped and turned her head back toward Trudy just as she closed the driver's door. Fortunately she'd left the window rolled down.

"Oh, I almost forgot. Flo Henderson said to tell you she needs you to call her ASAP. She says it's important."

Trudy nodded and then rolled up the window. Before starting the truck's engine, she glanced at the passenger door and saw that the lock button was down. She did likewise with the driver's button. She sighed, then started the engine. It roared to life.

She put it in gear and pulled away from the pump stand. She made it back onto the highway and started north. She felt suddenly overcome with fatigue and decided to look for the next motel sign and stop for the night. She'd call Flo as soon as she got settled in. Something important, the lady cop—Sheppard—said. She didn't like the sound of that.

What else could go wrong today?

CHAPTER NINE

Bruce stared at the building that housed the courtrooms across from the police station. A large parking lot filled with cars, vans, and trucks separated the buildings. The buildings were no more than three stories and reminded Bruce more of a collage campus than a government complex. The city hall, police station, and courthouse were in a cul-de-sac on a side road. Once in the loop, drivers had to keep going round the loop to the next building's parking lot.

The RCMP station held a lot of cars, and there were a few of their white patrol cars, as well as civilian vehicles of all shapes and sizes.

Bruce was escorted, with his hands cuffed in front of him this time, across the parking lot by a squad of RCMP officers, each carrying a secured automatic on their hip. Bruce thought they must've recruited from the local football team because they were the biggest cops he'd ever seen. Each one was built like Arnie: massive arms and chests that seemed to strain the buttons of their light tan uniform shirts.

When they neared the steps leading into the courthouse complex, Bruce saw why they were needed. There was a gauntlet of reporters to get through. TV cameras, photographers, and newsies with note pads clamoring over each other to get near their quarry. Bruce Carstairs, the killer of little Cherie Lavois, wife of the son of the Prime Minister, Pierre Lavois. This was big news.

Bruce kept his eyes focused on the ground, averting his gaze from the crush of the reporters. When they saw him coming, they shouted questions at him. Bruce ignored their calls and jeers.

The cops made a wedge shape. They must've done this before, thought Bruce bleakly. They quickly and quietly moved through the group like they were slicing through a pizza.

Two cops held the smoked-glass doors open and the little troupe made it inside. There was a locked side door, where a large man in a different shade of brown shirt and brown pants stood, holding it open. He wasn't a cop. The Mounties wore black trousers with a yellow stripe down the side. The man with dirty blond hair in the brown uniform had shoulder flashes that said he was a deputy sheriff for the province. The sheriff's here performed a very different duty than in the United States. They were officers of the court who acted as guards and who provided prisoner escort as well as managing the pre-trial jails. They weren't responsible for policing. The RCMP and city police forces were the law enforcement officers in British Columbia.

This sheriff wore a scowl on his face, and like many of the male cops Bruce'd met here, had a regulation brush cut.

Once the group was inside, a dark haired deputy sheriff closed and dead bolted the door, leaving behind shouting reporters, who pushed against the door until the sheriff gave them a withering look, his dark eyes piercing.

The reporters must've seen this man before because they backed off immediately. They looked none too happy at not being able to speak to the prisoner.

One of the cops handed the sheriff a folded white paper. He nodded and the cops then went out the door they'd come in and Bruce and the sheriff were alone.

"Have a seat," said the man. He nodded toward a wood bench with a row of wooden spindles to support your back. The bench had an elegant curve to it and looked quite old. The wood appeared to be solid oak. It was stained a dark brown, with a shiny lacquer coat over the top of that, which made it gleam in the florescent light.

Bruce smiled thinly though the sheriff continued to be free of any human expression. His eyes were dead as if his soul was missing. And given what he'd no doubt seen in his job, Bruce was certain any humanity the man had had when he started this job had long ago disappeared.

Bruce moved to the bench and sat down.

The sheriff stood beside a closed, solid wood door, his muscled arms crossed over his wide chest. He occasionally glanced at his watch. He didn't even look in Bruce's direction.

After what seemed like hours, and was in fact only a few minutes, the door opened and another uniformed provincial sheriff appeared. He was a brown-haired man who wore his hair short, but not the brush cut favored by the others. He was an equally large man. He spoke in a low tone to the first man, who nodded. They turned and together they approached Bruce where he sat on the wooden bench.

"Stand up," said the new arrival, his blue eyes hard and his strong, clean-shaven jaw set.

A pro, thought Bruce.

"I'm gonna removed the cuffs. Don't try anything or Rusty here will shoot you." He nodded toward his partner, whose expression remained a void. "Understand?"

"Yeah," said Bruce. He understood "shot while trying to escape" perfectly well.

They entered the courtroom, which was jammed with reporters sitting in the rows of plain, wooden, brown benches behind a short wall of polished, stained, wooden spindles. A gate in the middle admitted those allowed into the area of the judge's bench and the witness box. To the left, in front of the empty judge's bench that rose above every other seat in the large room, was a woman bent over what Bruce knew was the recording device used by the court reporter to record everything said in this room.

Two plain, wood tables sat facing the judge's bench. No one sat at them yet, and off to the right against the wall was the prisoner's box. Someone had erected a wall of glass that he supposed was bulletproof. Bruce stared at the glass as the two guards flanking him led him to the box where they offered the seat. He sat down and the two sheriffs stood, one on either side, their hands clasped in front of them in a casual manner. Their eyes scanned the audience of reporters, looking for any threat.

Bruce was always amazed how sheriffs here, unlike their counterparts in the States, didn't carry sidearm's.

A gray-haired sheriff came through another door to the left of the judge's bench. He stood with his arms at his sides. "All rise," he said in a deep, booming voice.

A woman appeared in an almost floor-length black robe, with a file folder tucked under one arm. She wore gold-rimmed reading glasses perched at the end of a square nose and dark eyes, and sat in the high-backed chair.

She swiveled to face the courtroom. She nodded to the sheriff who'd led her in, and he moved to the right of the judge's bench, where he assumed an identical pose to the uniforms guarding Bruce.

The judge placed the file folder on the desk in front of her, dropped her head of blonde curls, the ends slightly silver, and read. Her eyes quickly scanned the top page. She hefted a large, wooden gavel and tapped lightly on the desk to quiet the murmur that had permeated the room. The reporters had buzzed throughout the time that Bruce had appeared.

"Mr. Carstairs." The blond-haired sheriff beside Bruce motioned for him to stand. He got to his feet and faced the judge. She removed her reading glasses and looked him over.

"How do you plead, Mr. Carstairs?" she asked, her voice deep and throaty and her eyes cool.

"Not guilty, your honor," said Bruce, his voice firm with conviction. He wasn't going to let them intimidate him. He knew he hadn't killed that girl.

"Are you represented by council?"

"No, your honor."

"Then council will be appointed for you, Mr. Carstairs. I so order." The judge brought the gavel down again on the bench with a resounding bang.

She made a move to stand and the gray-haired sheriff dropped his hands and moved closer to the bench.

"All rise," said the sheriff.

The entire courtroom rose as one and the judge, her long, black robe billowing behind her, hurried down the two steps and through the door.

The situation seemed so unreal to Bruce. This couldn't be happening.

The two muscular sheriffs guided him from the courtroom into the prisoner transfer room. The blond sheriff re-attached the handcuffs and nodded to the dark-haired sheriff, who disappeared through the door, closing it behind him with a thump.

"Your escort will be here soon," said the sheriff, his voice humorless.

Bruce sat on the hard wooden bench with his hands cuffed together in front of him. A feeling of despair engulfed him again. The bright sunshine that was streaming through the high windows over the front doors to the courthouse belied the dark clouds that had appeared in his life.

Where the hell was Trudy?

CHAPTER TEN

IAN WELLMAN STOPPED AT THE POLISHED TEAK DOOR and took in a deep breath. He straightened his red striped power tie at the collar of his pure-white cotton shirt fresh from the dry cleaners. He could feel the sweat in his armpits and hoped the salty excretion wouldn't stain the dark suit jacket.

The finest silk worms had spun the material for this suit and he'd paid a princely sum for it.

His right hand trembled slightly as his left turned the brass doorknob. The PM was in a foul mood these days. A fact that Ian couldn't fault the man for.

He took the plunge and pushed the door inward, stepping into the prime minister of Canada's parliamentary office.

Pierre Lavois sat behind an ornately carved, solid oak desk, his eyes focused on the documents in front of him. To his right sat a computer screen. One of the new thin screens. His red striped tie hung loosely about his neck and he wore no jacket.

His light blue shirt had razor-sharp edges running up the sides. His thin gray hair was neatly combed and reading glasses sat perched on his narrow nose. He was a thin man with gray eyes, who liked his ruddy face clean-shaven.

Lavois glanced up from the document he'd been reading as Wellman entered the room. He frowned.

Wellman, catching the prime minister's expression, felt a gulp starting and quickly suppressed the feeling. A much practiced and gifted civil servant, he prided himself on his outward control. This time it didn't fail him.

"What's the latest?" asked Lavois, his impatience evident in his voice. He eased back in the black leather chair and removed his glasses, holding them with one hand by the folded-together arms. His was a very expensive and very comfortable chair. It was the same one he'd sat in as a cabinet minister until two years ago, in another wing of the parliament buildings.

His promotion to head of the party and the PM office had been controversial and hotly contested, but he had managed to quell most of his political enemies with ripe and juicy gifts.

"I have the latest from the CSIS station in Vancouver." The Canadian Security and Intelligence Service wasn't supposed to become embroiled in internal criminal matters, but the chief of the Vancouver office was an old friend of Lavois' from his days at Carlton University.

Wellman handed Lavois the document, a plain white piece of fax paper, without comment.

Lavois took it from him and placed his reading glasses back atop their perch on the tip of his nose and read the three sentences of typed script.

He placed the document on his desk blotter and again removed his glasses. "Get me my son, right away."

"Yes, Prime Minister," said Wellman, thankful to be dismissed so quickly. The PM had been hard on him lately. He didn't seem to like Wellman. Wellman knew his days were numbered anyway, having been selected for the job by Lavois' predecessor. At least he knew which son to call. Lavois did have three.

He retreated from the office, closing the door softly behind him.

Lavois steepled his fingers, his eyes fixed on the dark-stained, polished teak panels that made up his office wall. On one wall hung a portrait of Sir John A. MacDonald, the first prime minister in 1867. Lavois glanced at it and sighed heavily. Things were very different in those times. Different problems—different solutions.

The black telephone on the left side of his desk rang twice before he picked it up. It was Willie, his favorite of his six children.

"Father?" asked Willie Lavois, the strain evident in his voice.

No doubt he hadn't slept much since the news of his wife's death. The marriage was a bad one, though Willie was reluctant, like most young men, to admit his mistake. Ever since the wedding, a little over a year ago, relations between the newlyweds had been going steadily downhill. Now this happened. It was a public relations nightmare and a personal crisis for his family. Pierre had never even met his daughter-in-law's family.

Cherie was—or had been, he corrected himself—an impulsive girl given to late night parties with the most unsavory of characters. William Lyon Lavois had married her in a civil ceremony in Vancouver, believing she'd grow out of her party-girl phase.

He'd informed his parents a couple of days afterward. The Lavois family were strict Catholics who did not handle the news well at all.

They'd sent him to university in Canada's third largest city to study engineering, not to party and marry some 'bimbo,' as his mother referred to Cherie. This event had forged a wedge between mother and son, which Pierre feared would lead to permanent dysfunction.

After the quickie marriage, Willie told his father that he was in love, as if that made any difference to the family business, which was politics.

Pierre continued to speak with his son only because Willie was his personal favorite. Now that this had happened, Pierre Lavois knew he would come to the rescue again.

"Yes, my son," they spoke mostly English to each other, though both were fully bilingual, having grown up in Ottawa.

"What news?" asked Willie.

"Not good, I'm afraid. My sources tell me the biker who was picked up by the RCMP is pleading not guilty. This means a lot of publicity."

He heard his son's voice choke as he was speaking. "I'm sorry."

"You should've thought of that before you ran off with this girl." Pierre rolled his eyes. The boy had a way of attracting trouble. At least he'd been low profile since he'd started studying at UBC. The University of British Columbia had one of the best engineering schools in the country. Pierre had thought a gift horse had dropped in his lap when Willie said he wanted to major in engineering. Three thousand miles from the capital was the perfect way of minimizing any damage Willie managed to inflict on Pierre's political campaigns. First for party leader, then the top dog, headaches and all.

Maybe every cloud did have a gray lining; it certainly wasn't lined with silver.

"Father…" began Willie, his voice edged with anger. He was hurting and Pierre wasn't helping the situation by digging up old grievances.

"Yes, you're right," said Pierre with a small sigh. "Sorry, son."

"You gonna help me or not?" asked Willie, his voice choked with a mixture of anger and sorrow.

"I'll do what I can," said Pierre. He kept his voice level to appear aloof from his son's emotional upheaval. Inside he was conflicted with revulsion and love for his favorite son. He felt his child's pain emanating from the receiver.

"Where can I reach you?" asked Pierre. Willie was often not in his dorm these days, preferring to spend time in the student lounge, also know as "The Pit". It was a bar with lots of music and cold beer to keep the campus lively for those students who made their home on the campus grounds.

Willie had managed to get himself barred temporarily on more than one occasion, but right now sympathy seemed to be running his way, so he spent a lot of time, and a lot of his allowance money, at The Pit.

"I'll call you tomorrow," said Willie tersely. "I want the son of a bitch in jail, forever." Willie hung up, leaving a dial tone behind, humming in Pierre's ear.

He carefully set the phone's black receiver back in the cradle and gazed at it, his head resting on his chest. He hated to do it, but he needed to get directly involved. The problem was that he also needed to maintain distance from the investigation and the prosecution of this biker.

The least little thing that suggested he was involved would be picked up by the press and make his life hell during question period in the House of Commons. His political enemies would be looking for any chink in his armor to exploit for their own personal gain. Brownie points in politics were the notch in the belt these people live by, including him. He wouldn't be sitting here if he didn't follow that credo. Being the new kid in the big chair meant he needed to keep as low a profile as possible right now. But he wasn't about to sacrifice his family.

Using his intercom button, he buzzed for Wellman. The weasely little man quickly appeared, looking proper and neat, as usual. The guy must be a fag, thought Pierre. Regardless, Wellman irritated the hell out of him. At the next opportunity, he'd fire the guy's ass out the door.

"Wellman, get me the RCMP Commissioner. Tell him I need him over here as soon as possible."

Wellman's eyes flitted but the silly smile he always wore remained intact. "Yes, Prime Minister. Do you wish to me to schedule an appointment?" Under his right arm pressed against his side was a black appointment book that he lifted and flipped open to the day's activities. He flipped it forward until he found an empty space. "I see you have a spot available next Tuesday at ten…"

"Wellman," interrupted Pierre with a steadfast glare, "everything this week is canceled. I want to see the commissioner in the next hour, or tell LaFrance he's out of a job. Got it?"

"Yes, sir. Immediately." Welman slapped the appointment book with one hand, the silly grin still on his pale face. He had a lot of work to do to rearrange the PM's unexpected schedule change.

Wellman closed the door behind him, wondering how long this mess with the PM's son was going to affect the neatly organized world of Ian Wellman. He hoped it wasn't going to be very long until they returned to the normal course of the office, but as it would turn out, he couldn't be more wrong.

CHAPTER ELEVEN

Trudy saw a sign that said there were three hotels at the next turnoff, with a couple of restaurants. This made it the perfect place to pull off for the night. She'd also call Flo and get an update.

She had promised her friend she'd call her from Portland, but she had tried to make it to the border before stopping. The incident at the gas station had shaken her badly, so her eyelids felt like lead after the adrenaline letdown. She knew she'd have to stop before she killed herself.

She made the off ramp turn and drove down the ramp to the stop sign. She could see the three hotel signs down the road to her right, so she turned and started toward them.

The first one said they charged thirty-nine dollars a night. Yup that would be the one. No doubt the others were equally reasonable, but this one was a national chain of low-priced hotels, which would suit her just fine. She hoped there was room on her credit card.

She'd tried to get Rocky to give up his card, but he said it was his insurance policy "just in case," and she'd agreed it made sense.

A drunk with a credit card. It was only a matter of time and she knew it. She only hoped it wasn't now. A fifteen-hundred-dollar limit could be eaten away fairly quickly in the wrong hands.

She pulled into the parking lot just as the sun began to disappear behind the low hills on the horizon to the west of the highway. She wished she could see the ocean like at home. She loved the sea. The sounds and smells meant she was home. Even in Seattle, she and Rocky hadn't lived far from the ocean.

She stopped the truck's engine and glanced at the gas gauge. She was down to a quarter of a tank. She'd have to re-fill in the morning. She'd passed a gas station near the off ramp, so she'd stop there.

She stepped out onto the black tarmac of the parking area. There were neat yellow lines painted on the blacktop to delineate the parking spaces. There were few cars in the lot right now.

The low-rise building was only two stories, with the rooms connected by an outside covered walkway. The office, with a glowing red "open" sign, was on the main level. She walked toward it, gazing at the pale-blue-and-white building that comprised the hotel, or more properly called a motel. Funny what the advertising companies called a hotel these days.

It looked okay, but it certainly wasn't the Waldorf.

She entered the office, accompanied by the tinkle of a bell that hung over the door to let the office person know she was there.

A woman who appeared to be no more than thirty came from the back. She wore a lime-green tee shirt and white jeans. Her copper-red hair hung down to her shoulders, or would've if she didn't have it pulled back over her ears. It wasn't styled, so Trudy suspected it hung down over her eyes at the most inconvenient times.

The woman smiled warmly when she saw Trudy standing in front of the brown wooden service counter.

Trudy returned the woman's bright smile.

In one pink-finger nailed hand, the woman held half a bran muffin.

"Sorry to interrupt," said Trudy, nodding toward the muffin.

The woman laughed brightly. It felt good to hear laughter again. It seemed to Trudy as if she hadn't heard anyone laugh for years.

"Oh, no. I should've let this back there," said the woman, indicating the pale gold curtain at the rear of the reception area. She placed the remainder on the desk and wiped her hands to remove any crumbs. "Bozwell will take care of that," she said.

"Your husband?" asked Trudy.

The woman laughed again, the corners of her eyes crinkled slightly. "Oh, my, no. It's my cat. He loves bran muffins, does ol' Boz."

Trudy couldn't help but smile at that one. A cat who loves muffins?

"What can I do for you?" asked the woman, returning to business. She placed her hands on the desktop with the white register book open. Not many places used a book anymore. Most used a computer or index cards or some other system of maintaining customer records.

"I need a room for the night," said Trudy. She thought it obvious until she considered she might look like a salesman trying to sell the owner something.

"Hmm…" the woman gazed at her, her expression changing to a frown as if she were deep in thought. Her pale forehead wrinkled and her green eyes shifted to the open register.

"Is there a problem?" asked Trudy, wondering what the problem could be. The parking lot was mostly empty, for God's sake.

"No. Not really," said the woman. She flipped over a page in the book as if she was unsure of her answer.

"Uh...it's just that we have a tour group coming in later and we might be full." With one pink-tipped finger, she ran down a line of the book until she stopped and nodded. One side of her hair fell forward and with one hand, born of a reflex, she pushed the wayward hair back behind her ear.

"Okay." She grinned and glanced up at Trudy, the lightness returning to her eyes and her voice. "We do have one room on the top floor. It's at the end nearest the highway, so you might get a bit a noise, but the bed is soft and the coffeemaker works."

Trudy nodded and reached into her black, faux leather handbag that hung off her left arm. She pulled out her brown leather wallet and extracted her credit card from the pocket that held her cards.

The woman smiled briefly, then slipped the card through the machine that would send Trudy's vitals to the bank and make sure she was good for the price of a room. It came back okay. She nodded and picked up the register in one hand and placed it atop the counter.

She turned it toward Trudy and asked her to fill in the blank line with the details of her address and other contact information. Trudy completed the spaces and turned the book back to her host.

The woman reached under the counter out of Trudy's sight and pulled a shiny brass key with a little cardboard tag with black numbers: 233. She also took an imprint of the credit card.

"In case there are any additional charges," explained the woman.

Trudy nodded, placed her credit card back in its proper place in her wallet, slipped her wallet into her purse, and left the office.

She stopped at the truck long enough to get her black leatherette bag that contained her clothes and toilet items. She made sure the truck was secured, then headed up the wooden stairs to the second floor.

The sun had disappeared and the streetlights that dotted the edges of the paved parking lot crackled to life, flickering on one by one, creating long shadows over the dark payment.

The stairs creaked underfoot as Trudy reached the top step and turned left. She followed the numbered doors until, sure enough, she came to the last room, number 233.

She slipped the key into the lock and turned it. The lock clicked lightly and she pushed the door inward with the flat of one hand. There was a bank of light switches by the door. She flicked the nearest one and the lamp next to the bed lit up.

The low, red shag carpet and garish flower-covered duvet looked clean enough, but sorely in need of replacement. Not the best place to stay, but it looked clean. There was a wooden table bracketed by two worn chairs that needed a new coat of stain to keep them bright. The red cushions, which were supposed to match the rug, sagged in the middle but again looked clean.

At the foot of the bed against the wall was an older model television, bolted to the low, two-drawer dresser. A remote was attached with Velcro to the top of the TV. Attached to the remote was a stretch-cord band so the user wouldn't be able to easily walk off with it. Not that she thought a stretch-cord band was much of a deterrent until she looked closer and saw that the cord had a steel wire running down the middle of it. Looking at the age of the equipment, Trudy wondered why anyone would bother anyway. She shrugged.

There were short curtains on the window that faced the parking lot that closed in the middle. The light from the street coming through the window made the room glow with an eerie light.

She walked over and pulled the curtains shut until there was only a slit of light visible in the middle.

Fortunately, the curtains were lined so they would block the bright streetlights. At least she'd manage to get some sleep.

Next she threw her bag and her purse on the bed and walked to the telephone on the cheap, pressed wood nightstand that sat next to the queen-size bed. She plopped down on the bed next to the telephone and her bottom made the bed sag. She bounced on the bed, causing the ancient springs to shriek in protest. The room smelled musty and reminded her a little of mothballs. She wrinkled her nose.

Great, she thought, every time I move, the thing will probably wake me up. She blinked her eyes and there was an audible click of eyes that were drying out because she was so tired. The strain and the long day had taken a lot out of her.

She saw that the beige, push-button phone sat on a plastic mount. At the front of the mount was a slider with a plastic tab sticking out. She pulled the tab and, like a drawer, it opened until she could see the list of instructions for dialing long distance, local, and person-to-person calls.

She reached across the garish red coverlet and retrieved her purse. She opened it and the latch clicked. She pulled out her little telephone book of important numbers. Flo would probably be home by now unless there was some major crisis. She studied the instructions for person-to-person and dialed nine zero.

"Operator. How may I help you?" the man's voice sounded bored.

"I'd like to make a person-to-person call from Trudy Wilson to Florence Henderson." Trudy gave him the number and decided the guy didn't deserve a polite 'please' at the end. He hadn't earned it. She earned it every day in her job, damn it. Even when those nasty old bitches gave her a hard time. Yup, she'd earned it, all right.

There was a gentle click and a phone began to ring at the other end.

After three rings, the guy interrupted, but Trudy could hear the line still ringing in the background. "Sorry, lady, I don't think there's anyone home."

"Just a couple of more times," she said curtly.

The guy heaved a bored sigh, but didn't say anything else. The phone rang twice more, then someone picked up.

"Hello." It was Flo's voice, no doubt about it. Trudy felt a shiver of excitement. It was good to hear a friendly voice.

"I've a person-to-person call for Florence Henderson from Trudy Wilson," said the bored voice of the male operator.

"Yes, I'm Flo Henderson."

"Go ahead."

There wasn't a click or any such sound to indicate he was gone, but Flo spoke first. "Trudy?"

"Yeah, Flo it's me." Trudy could barely contain her enthusiasm at speaking with her friend.

"Trudy," Flo breathed a sigh, evidence of her relief at hearing Trudy's voice. "I was so worried about you. I received a call from the Washington State Police saying you'd been attacked. What happened?"

"Nothing. I'm fine, just got a little sidetracked. I'm just north of Seattle. Not too far from the border. I just couldn't keep going."

"I spoke with my contacts and Bruce is in deep shit, up to his neck."

Trudy felt her inner resolve disappear and her shoulders slump. "Tell me," she said.

"I'm told the evidence is pretty good, and they have a witness."

Trudy sighed heavily.

"That isn't a conviction," Flo reminded her.

"Yeah. I know. But, fuck."

"Listen, you see this guy I know in Vancouver. His name's Phil Singh. He's a homicide dick with the Vancouver PD. Good guy."

Trudy reached for her purse and pulled out a pen. Flo gave her the phone number and address, which she wrote in her telephone book.

"Okay, Flo. I'll call you when I get to Vancouver."

"Good," said Flo. "Take care of yourself. It's not over yet."

"Bye," said Trudy, with a thin smile playing across her lips as she hung up the phone.

There was the sound of footsteps outside her window, then a man's voice calling her name. She felt a stab of fear run through her slight frame. She stiffened and held her breath, hoping whoever it was would go away. She hoped it wasn't the same guy from the gas station.

She saw the doorknob begin to slowly turn. Someone was coming into the room. She didn't recall if she'd locked the door. The chain hung loosely beside the wooden doorframe, swinging freely.

What the fuck should I do?

CHAPTER TWELVE

Rocky's red-rimmed eyes stared at his first mug of amber liquid for the day as he sat on the padded black barstool.

 Sam stood leaning against the row of steel fridges that lined the wall underneath the large mirror that also ran the length of the wall behind him. His arms were crossed over his chest as he chewed loudly on a piece of well-used gum. He cracked and popped the seriously flavorless piece of white rubber in his mouth as he studied his one customer.

The Whaler Bar and Grill was a hotbed of activity after five o'clock, when most decent folks finished their daily work. Not this guy, though. Nope, Rocky Wilson was as good as an old pocket watch his father used to own. Everyday at opening he'd be in here to get his morning pick-me-up before going off to do whatever it was drunks did during the day. Sam stole a glance at his watch. Rocky'd be back at five, as usual, to delve into his fuzzy world of too much booze and too many smokes. Just like every day.

Sam caught himself. *Damn, I have to get the hell out of here and get a real job.* Sons of bitches like Rocky were really getting to him. He knew a career change was in his future. He nodded and smiled thinly when Rocky glanced up at him, a silly, lopsided grin across his ruddy, puffy face.

"Another?" asked Sam.

Rocky shook his head, tipped his glass back, and drained the remaining beer in one swallow. He stepped off the stool that stood far enough from the floor that you had to rest your feet on the crossbars between the legs while sitting. It wasn't the most comfortable position, but it worked well enough.

He wobbled slightly, then steadied himself by placing one unwashed hand on the bar.

"Where you off to today, Rock?" asked the bartender.

"Gonna see a man about a job."

"Uh, huh." He didn't really give a shit, but if this bum thought that someone would hire him, who was he to judge otherwise. Maybe it was a garbage man. Didn't exactly need to be all spit and polish for a job like that.

"But first, I gotta see May. Gotta keep an eye on the business while Trudy's away," Rocky muttered to himself as if he were reminding himself to take a piss. He turned away and headed for the large oak doors that exited to the parking lot.

Watching him leave, Sam shook his head.

***

Once through the doors, Rocky winced at the sunlight that streamed down from the clear, blue-sky overhead.

He held one hand up and gazed about until he spotted the red Chevette, sitting not too far from the entrance.

He ambled over to the driver's door and opened it—he didn't bother to lock the doors, hoping someone would steal the damn thing—then he sat in the driver's seat. He fumbled with the keys until he found the ignition key. The square one with the General Motors logo on it. He slipped the key into the slot on the steering column and turned it. Nothing happened. Nothing. No sound of any kind. The piece of shit was dead.

Rocky sat back in the high-backed, stained, light beige-and-white checked seat and stared at the little car's dashboard. "Fuck," he said out loud, his voice echoing in the quiet confines of the car. What the hell was he supposed to do now?

***

May held a perm roller ready to do the next strands of Emily's hair. Emily was the young sales girl at Pop's Shoes here in the outlet mall. Next to her was a black tray on wheels, filled with different colors of perm rollers. Emily liked the white for the looser curls. May envied her long, almost virgin hair. She smiled to herself. Based on what Emily told her since starting here as a customer a few months back, she was certainly no virgin.

"So what's new with Rob?" asked May, trying to keep the conversation going by talking about Emily's latest beau. She was growing tired of hearing Emily complain about the fucking manager of the shoe store, who was always trying to hit on her. His toupee never seemed to be on straight. Not that you were supposed to notice. Slightly gray at the temples and black on top, like some off-shade hat, was a little obvious.

Emily's face reflected in the mirror in front of the station where she sat in the black cutting chair, squished like she'd bit into a particularity bitter lemon. Her face was buried in a Hollywood gossip rag. The kind the old ladies liked to read when they were back here.

You're getting your time, kid, thought May.

"I gather he's history," said May, with a false smile and a smirk on her lips.

Emily nodded as she glanced up. A grin broke out on her young, smooth-skinned face. It was the type of skin most women May's age envied to the point of obsession.

Emily buried her eyes back in the magazine, preferring to remain silent.

May went back to working on the girl's perm, making sure there were sufficient rows of rollers to create the desired effect.

She sighed inwardly. It would be nice if Trudy were here. There were a lot of heads to do. She glanced over her left shoulder at the two gray hairs waiting in the lobby for their roller sets. She could get one going after she finished Emily's perm set up, but the other would have to wait a little longer.

Eventually she'd have all three going at once. But no doubt one of the old bags would complain to her and she'd smile and nod like she always did and pull out her best empathic face. It seemed to placate the old ladies.

She needed different looks in her arsenal for different people. Men needed sly smiles; those seemed to work best for the male ego. Old men, they were the toughest. They wore their skins like battle armor. That's why they favored old male barbers, not stylists. That, too, would change over time, as more of the younger men who had grown up with stylists became the norm.

She knew she needed to get to the bank later and make the deposit. There would be a delivery from the beauty supply company later today and she needed to write the check. So much to do. She sighed audibly.

"Something wrong?" asked Emily, not glancing up from a picture of Tom Cruise.

"No, of course not," said May, pasting a thin smile across her lips. Wasted, really, because Emily didn't even glance up. At least the cow could make an attempt to show she cared.

It wouldn't be long now and she'd have the funds to blow this town and leave these sniveling, pampered bitches behind her.

May picked up another roller and began to roll a few strands of hair around the white plastic. She almost had them all in so she could start applying the solution.

The phone on the front desk began to ring.

"Excuse me," said May. Emily murmured something unintelligible as May walked away toward the front of the shop. She wiped her hands on her black apron that covered her black slacks and beige top.

The old ladies sitting at the front nodded and she cast them a white, toothy smile as she picked up the receiver.

"The Hair Club, how may I help you?" asked May brightly.

"May, it's me, Rocky."

May spun away from the old ladies so they wouldn't see the scowl that came across her face. What the hell did that creep want? If he were trying to hit on her again it would be the last time. Her husband said he'd kill the son of a bitch next time.

"Yeah," she said, her voice low so as not to advertise her annoyance.

"The car broke down and I need some money from the shop's business account to fix it."

May rolled her eyes. "I don't think I can do that. Trudy would have to give the okay."

His voice became angry. "I don't need her fucking permission. That money is a much mine as it is hers…"

"That's not what I mean," interrupted May, "the money in there is enough to cover expenses and that's about it. If I give you some, then we might not make rent, or I won't get paid. I don't work for free, ya know."

The edge came off Rocky's voice now; he sounded like a sulky kid who'd been told he has to go to bed. "Yeah. I know. But the car's at Hank's Auto and Pete tells me it'll take five hundred bucks to get it back on the road."

May sighed. Sometimes she couldn't help but feel sorry for the guy. "Okay. Okay. Drop by the shop tomorrow at noon. I'll figure a way to cut our expenses somehow for this month and loan you the money. But mind you," she cautioned, " If Trudy calls me and says no go between now and then, the deals off. Understand?"

"Yeah, I understand." He hung up.

May turned to face the windows overlooking the parking lot. It was one of those days.

The old ladies smiled warmly at her and she forced a thin smile to her lips in kind. "Won't be long now, ladies," she said. They nodded.

She spun 'round and headed for the perm, sitting at the back. She'd have to step up her timetable. *Damn, this was getting complicated, fast.* It all seemed so easy when you have it on paper.

CHAPTER THIRTEEN

TRUDY WALKED SLOWLY ACROSS THE ROOM until she was near the door. The knob turned slowly as if the world was suddenly on a different time. She could feel her heart beating inside her chest as if it would burst through, like in that science fiction movie from so long ago.

With trembling fingers, she grabbed the sliding door chain and slid it into the slot on the first try. She felt the fear ease slightly. The door suddenly swung open and stopped as the chain was stretched to its limit.

"Ms. Wilson?" asked the man's voice.

"Yes," she said, her voice low.

"Sorry to bother you, ma'am, but my wife said you would need some fresh towels up here."

"Why did you use my first name earlier?"

There was a pause. "Sorry. It's a bad habit of mine. I hope I didn't frighten you?" he sounded genuinely concerned.

"Well, you sure as fuck did," said Trudy. Removing the chain from the slider, she opened the door partway, enough to see who was outside.

A man with dark hair, a trace of gray at the temples—he kept it cut short—stood holding two neatly folded white cotton towels.

His blue eyes were concerned. He had a slim build and was obviously a little older than his wife. He had a dark mustache, with a few gray strands running through it. He wore a short-sleeved, checkered blue-and-red dress shirt, untucked over a pair of faded blue jeans.

"Really, Ms. Wilson, I'm truly sorry," he said.

"Its Mrs. Wilson, and you damn well should be." Trudy was angry at being frightened by the man. He looked remorseful, so she let her shoulders relax.

"Forget it," she said, taking the towels he offered her in outstretched hands.

"If there's anything else you need, Mrs. Wilson, please call the front desk, anytime, day or night, and me or Liz will be happy to be of service." The man offered his hand. He smiled thinly. "My name's Armand Felgar. My wife and I own the place."

Trudy took the offered hand in hers and shook it. His grip was one of those she hated. Loose and soggy.

"Okay, thanks," she said. She closed the door and made sure it was locked and the chain in place. Felgar's footsteps retreated into the distance.

There was a roar of a bus engine below her window. The tour group must've arrived. She walked to the bathroom, with its white tiled floor and plain white fixtures. The white plastic shower curtain hanging beside the white porcelain tub gleamed in the light. She gazed at herself in the mirror.

She dropped the towels on top of the closed toilet seat.

The dark circles under her eyes were coming through the makeup she'd applied to her pale skin this morning when she'd started off on this little road trip. Her curly, mouse brown hair, with gray streaks shot through, sat like a lump of used, blackened, steel wool atop her head. It needed a wash, but she was too tired to think about a shower right now. That could wait until morning. She gazed at her clear-coated nails and saw that the edges were chipped and worn. Her slim fingers, which had once been on the chubby side, looked like old lady hands.

Maybe she was in over her head. She'd been lucky the last time.

A lot of people had been hurt last time, some of them fatally. But Bruce needed her and she felt she had to find a way to help him. She hung her head in her hands and began a low series of sobs.

After several minutes, her eyes dried. She couldn't cry anymore.

She walked back into the room and flopped back onto the bed. Yeah, it was soft; Liz had been right. She closed her eyes and felt her mind drift. It wasn't very long before she was snoring softly. It would be several hours before she woke.

***

Trudy woke to a sound like water rushing by in sheets. It was the sound of traffic on the freeway, not too far away. She opened her eyes in a darkened room. She was still dressed. Glancing at the red digital alarm clock next to the bed, she saw it read 7:30. Was it in the morning or the evening?

She squinted and made out the little "a.m." indicator to the left of the numbers. It was lit.

Oh boy, she thought, *I've slept all night in my clothes.*

She pushed herself from the flowered coverlet and yawned. She stretched her arms over her head and blinked repeatedly to clear the sleep from her eyes.

She stood and shuffled to the bathroom. She finished her morning constitutional and then padded back to the bed, where she'd thrown her overnight bag. She realized she definitely felt refreshed after a decent night's sleep.

She dropped her clothes next to the bed, reached into her bag, and pulled out her toothbrush, toothpaste, and shampoo. Her bag smelled like oranges, and so did she when she was finished. She smiled to herself.

She padded on bare felt back to the bathroom and closed the door behind her. She locked it. Ever since the murders in Fairview, she'd taken up the habit of locking every lockable door behind her.

She brushed her teeth and then started the shower. She stepped in and began to wash under the stinging spray of warm water. She used the small hotel bar to soap up a face cloth and then ran it over her body. Next she soaped her hair with a quarter-sized dollop of the overly perfumed hotel shampoo. The white liquid foamed up as she applied it to her hair.

With both hands, she ran her fingers through her hair and washed the tangled curls. She closed her eyes and pushed her face into the warm spray.

It felt good to have the warm water cascading down her ample breasts and curves to run down the drain of the white bathtub.

She rinsed her body and then her hair, careful to make sure all of the soap was gone from her hair. Soap buildup in hair was not a good thing. "Always rinse thoroughly" was something they ingrained into you at beauty school.

She turned off the water and stepped onto the bathmat she'd placed near the edge of the tub. It wasn't much of a mat—really more like a small, white, frayed towel, only a little thicker.

She pulled one white towel off the rack near the toilet, where she'd hung the two side by side. She dried herself all over and then, after wrapping the towel around her body, unlocked the bathroom door. She stepped into the room and froze when she spied a figure sitting on one of the chairs next to the little table under the window that looked out over the parking lot and to the highway beyond.

It was a man. His skin was dark from the sun and he wore a wry grin across his dirty, stubble-covered face that made her heart freeze.

She recognized him as the guy who'd nearly run her down at the gas station. She swallowed hard and her heart began to beat rapidly in her chest. *He must have followed me.* She stole a glance at the room's door and saw the chain hanging broken cleanly in half. *He must have broken in while I was in the shower.*

I'm going to die.

CHAPTER FOURTEEN

Sergeant Mike "Hammer" Harris hung up the black telephone with such force everyone in the squad room thought he'd broken it. They quickly glanced back at whatever they'd been working on when they caught the look in Mike's brown eyes. He was mad as hell.

The big man, who stood six-feet-four and weighed two hundred twenty pounds, stood up from his desk, his blue-and-gray striped tie swinging as he pressed both of his meaty hands against the surface of his oak desk. He didn't have but a few ounces of fat on his muscled frame. He worked out nearly every day to keep his body trim and lean. His granite-like jaw, clean-shaven face, and brush cut gave him the appearance of a hardened drill sergeant about to run the recruits though the drills.

His desk was an old one. He refused to let the boss buy him one of the new computer workstations that were so favored by officers in the RCMP's SCU.

Mike had been promoted to a detective position with the Serious Crimes Unit fifteen years ago and he'd seen his share of grisly murders and serious crime. What he'd seen would be enough to fill most Hollywood producer's nightmares for years to come.

This case—this murder of the prime minister's daughter-in-law—was turning out to be a nightmare. His contact in The Canadian Security Intelligence Service had just told him that CSIS had been snooping around asking questions about his suspect.

He didn't like it one bit. It smelled of political interference, and that pissed him off more than anything else. Right now, he was gonna have it out with the boss. Inspector Barbara Kelso was gonna get the "Hammer" treatment.

Mike had earned the nickname when, at his job interview for the SCU, he very nearly blew his chance at getting the job by telling the review panel that he wouldn't 'put the hammer down' on a fellow officer if he found his brother officer had committed a crime. The nickname, like most, started out as a mild ribbing by his fellow officers and ended up sticking. Not that he'd admit it, but he kind of liked the image it portrayed of him as a tough guy.

He stormed across the room to the inspector's office. Six pairs of wary eyes followed his progress. They knew better than to make eye contact when he was like this.

Once there, he threw open the door. The glass in the wood-framed door rattled as it hit hard against the rubber doorstop.

Inspector Barbara Kelso was sitting behind a light gray, laminate workstation, staring at her computer screen, reading an e-mail. A woman nearing forty, she cut a trim figure in her navy suit and white shirt open at the collar. Her hair was short but neatly cut into a straight style. There wasn't a trace of gray yet, and she wore no glasses.

A master's degree in Criminal Psychology from the University of Toronto had leapfrogged her into her present job as boss of the SCU, a position she'd held for the past three years.

There were those skeptics who thought she'd been promoted because she was a woman until they'd met her will of iron and her keen mind.

She glanced, stone-faced, at Mike as he made his grand entrance into her office. He stood before her desk, the steam almost visibly rising from his ears. His white face was flushed crimson.

He crossed his arms over his wide chest and tapped one foot as he waited for Barbara to finish.

She read over the e-mail and then started to key a reply.

"Barbara…" he began until she held up one hand, signaling him to stop. He locked his rugged jaw and gritted his teeth. With the same hand, she motioned for him to sit on one of the steel-framed, padded chairs in front of her desk.

He watched her key in the message she'd started and hit the "send" button. She then swiveled her high-backed leather chair to face him, her hard blue eyes fixed on his. "I know," she said, her voice calm.

"You know? How? I just got the call from my contact at CSIS," he said, feeling his anger dissipate a little to be replaced by amazement. How did she do it? She was always one step ahead of everyone else.

"That e-mail message was from one my contacts." She smiled humorlessly. "You're not the only one with friends in low places, you know."

Mike shrugged. A slow grin crossed his face and his shoulders relaxed. He liked the boss. She was the best boss he'd worked for in his twenty-two years in the Mounties. She was honest to a fault, tough, yet loyal to her troops.

The latter made the SCU one of the most sought-after units to be in these days, even though the work was tough on a person and their personal life usually turned to shit because of the nature of the cases they were assigned. Many of the men and women who worked here were divorced, some more than once.

Murders, rapes, and unbelievable cruelty were the staples of this job. It was hard to leave it at the office when you went home at night, or in the wee hours, as the case may be. Mike had seen more than one cop lose himself in an ocean of booze. And some damn good ones, too.

Mike was one the few survivors, possibly because he thrived on catching the bad guys. His arrest record was the best in the unit.

"What the fuck are those spy pukes doin' messin' with my case?" asked Mike.

Barbara eased back in her chair and her clear, expressionless eyes were fixed on his anger-filled face as she spoke. "Mike, I don't know yet, but you can be damned sure I'm gonna find out, even if I have to go to the top."

Mike knew she meant the Commissioner of the Royal Canadian Mounted Police at the national headquarters in Ottawa, who reported directly to the prime minister of Canada. He knew also that what she said she would do always got done. The members of the SCU had learned that right off the bat when she'd come into the unit and cleaned out the older cops that were dirty up to their collective elbows. A real bloodbath. Messy, but he totally respected her for it and she seemed to respect him.

Yup, she was what they would've called one tough broad in the old days. These days they called her the boss.

The corners of her eyes crinkled and she leaned forward to rest her elbows on her desk's gleaming top.

He glanced at the wooden "in" basket that sat near the front of the polished oak desk. There were a few loose papers in it, while the "out" box had a small stack. One thing about being the boss was the ever-increasing round of reports, documents, and forms that needed to be looked at each day. Never mind the lists of incoming and outgoing e-mails. Whatever dumb-ass said, "the electronic super highway would be paperless" had never been a cop.

"So, what ya got for me on the case so far? The sup's been up my ass on this one." She even talked like one of the guys.

Mike shrugged and dropped his meaty hands to the armrests on the chair. He felt wedged into the damn thing. It wasn't designed for a guy his size. He shifted his weight in a vain attempt to get comfortable.

"Not very much. We're still waitin' for the autopsy. The coroner says he should have his report in to me by tomorrow. It looked to me like she was strangled, though there're no finger marks on the neck."

Barbara nodded grimly.

"We've closed the Angel's party house down and have the forensic guys going over it with their usual fine-tooth comb. The head of the team says they may have some pretty good physical stuff for me." He shrugged again and continued. "All I really have that's solid right now is the witness, and I don't think much of him."

Barbara nodded at this one. No, from what she'd read in his jacket, Spike Logan was not the most reliable character to have to hang your case on. A biker wannabe. A low-level associate of the Hell's Angels fingered Bruce Carstairs as the killer.

Logan's track record with the law wasn't great. Nine minor arrests. Low-level drug pusher, part-time, small-time hood. Probably an enforcer for the collections wing of the Angels.

They had him in a holding cell on a minor possession charge. The house had been dirty. Not much, but enough to hold the guy. Maybe Mike could apply a little pressure and see if he could crack the guy's nuts for him.

"You gonna have a talk with this Logan guy?" asked Barbara.

"Yeah, but I wanta wait for some more physical stuff first. We got twenty-four before he's out on the street again. I expect he might run to ground, or his buddies might take him out for even talking to us. You know they don't like any signs of weakness in a potential club member. This may be the only opportunity to talk to the piece of shit."

Barbara smiled and shook her head. "Now, Mike, you know you're not supposed to call suspects names."

Mike grinned. "Why not? It's fun."

"You get the hell back to work," said Barbara, shooing him out of her office with a wave of her right hand.

He grinned and walked back into the squad room, closing the boss's office door behind him. The glass rattled as it closed. He walked across the room, a sardonic grin across his rugged face until he stopped in mid-stride. His eyes narrowed as he moved behind his desk and stared at the mess of papers across its worn, scarred surface. The boss agreed with him, but what the hell was she gonna actually do about it?

Oh, well, he thought. *I can always finish off the Thompson* double-homicide report for the crown counsel. It was due tomorrow and the trial was in thirty days. He smiled at that. Another successful prosecution about to be added to his belt. That made ten this year, and the year was still young.

He bent over the keyboard of the computer that sat on his desk and began awkwardly typing in the information into the templated form. Young Joey, the new kid with the degree in computer… sumthin'—he had no idea about this shit—had helped him with that one. The dumb kid even suggested he get a newer model computer.

He rolled his eyes at that. Yeah, right, like he'd get newer model. What world did that kid belong to?

Carefully Mike typed in the next few words, stopping twice to fix a couple of spelling errors. One of these days he had to figure out how that spell checker, as Joey called it, worked.

***

Barbara Kelso watched Mike cross the room and sighed inwardly. The guy was a dinosaur in many ways, but he was a damn good cop. His record spoke for itself.

She picked up the phone and pushed the gray numbered buttons until the phone at the other end of the line began to ring.

A man's voice came on the line. "Hi, Babs." Her phone number must've appeared on his caller ID. This was the only person, other than her late husband, who had ever called her Babs.

"Hi, John. Can I come up and have chat?"

Superintendent John O'Reilly prided himself in always being available to his troops, as he called them. He was the Commanding Officer of the Unsolved Homicide Unit of E Division, which included Vancouver and its surrounding municipalities. He was also Barbara Kelso's immediate superior.

Normally she didn't like to bother him this early in an investigation, but this was far from a normal case and required special attention.

The local and even the national press was all over this one like flies to a corpse.

"Can't it wait until the branch commander's meeting tomorrow morning?"

"No, John, we have to speak right now. It's important."

John O'Reilly was a very astute cop, with thirty years on the force. He knew the sense of urgency in someone's voice when he heard it. "Okay. Just thought I'd ask. Sure, come on up. I've got a few minutes. See you soon."

Barbara hung up the telephone and stood behind her desk. She picked up her black notebook. It was composed of white, lined paper between two lengths of pressed cardboard, a four-by-five safety net where she kept her daily conversation notes and reminders.

She moved around the desk and smoothed her knee-length skirt. She straightened her shoulders and felt the well-tailored suit fall into place, just as it was supposed to. Nothing like quality clothing, she thought to herself.

She walked through the door, leaving it open behind her.

The officers working on their case files glanced at her as she strode past. She kept her eyes straight ahead and avoided eye contact. She needed to concentrate on the job ahead.

This was gonna be a tough one, she could feel it. Those CSIS pukes need some hammering, she thought as she walked past Mike's desk. He didn't look up from his computer screen. The tip of his pink tongue was curled in concentration as he typed his report.

She left the room and stood in the lobby area. It was basically a stopping place for the elevators to discharge passengers.

There were no plants or nice furniture or expensive prints on the walls, like in some corporate offices.

There was a well-used bulletin board with a few "work safe" posters and a sign-up sheet for the office softball team.

She moved to an elevator and pressed the "up" arrow.

She didn't have to wait long. There was a ding and the amber light behind the elevator button quickly went out.

The ancient metal doors opened. The car was empty. Good, Barbara thought, I don't have to make small talk. I must think this thing through, before I lose my cool in front of John. It was hard enough being in a man's world without being able to play by their rules.

Women who lost their temper were hard-ass bitches, while men were just being men. Tough as nails. God, how she hate the double standards. But at least she'd made a good career for herself. A far better one than had been possible only a generation before.

The elevator car stopped on the fifteenth floor and doors slid silently open. She kept her eyes on the executive level's plush maroon rug and nodded at the security guard as she passed his station desk, with the red-and-white Canadian flag to the right. The guard, a white-haired woman of about fifty whom she only knew as Margaret, glanced up from the newspaper she was reading and nodded in that bored way all security guards had.

There was a plain, brown, wooden door at the end of the corridor, with only the room number beside it to indicate it wasn't a closet.

Old Margaret wouldn't be able to stop a rampaging midget, so not having a name on the door would add additional time for the occupants inside if some crazed terrorist circus clowns attacked the floor.

This was the joke amongst the SCU officers at O'Shea's, their favorite bar in the Gastown section of the city where there were a number Irish themed bars and restaurants.

Like cops everywhere, they had their own bar.

There was a numbered keypad next to the door. Barbara keyed in the proper sequence and the lock mechanism clicked. She pushed the door inward with her right shoulder as she turned the doorknob.

The inner office was a small reception area with a plain gray workstation, where the Superintendent's administrative assistant—not secretary—Gary Owen sat behind his computer terminal, typing.

He looked up as the door opened and smiled warmly as he saw Barbara enter. His straight white teeth shone in the fluorescent light of the room.

Behind his desk were two flag stands, one with a Canadian flag and the other with the colorful British Columbia flag. On the wall to his right hung a picture of Her Majesty the Queen in a formal evening gown, smiling benevolently at her subjects. After all, she was the Royal in the Mounted Police, wasn't she?

"Hello, Inspector Kelso," said Gary, nodding at her. "You may go right in. The superintendent's expecting you."

Barbara nodded silently and walked through the door to Gary's left and into the inner office. Near the window, with a view of planes taking off at the airport not very far away, a man of fifty years, his dark hair peppered with gray, sat in his tall, black leather chair, waiting for her. He wore a sky-blue dress shirt with a matching tie. He was trim and fit for a man his age, and his dark eyes were hard and serious.

His ruddy face smiled tightly as he rose from his chair, extending his right hand in welcome. She took his hand in hers and shook it.

Simultaneously, as if they'd rehearsed it many times, they sat opposite each other and John leaned back, his elbows resting on the arms of his chair. His fine Italian suit pants didn't make any sound as he regained his seat.

"Can I get your something, Barbara? Coffee?"

Barbara shook her head. "No, thanks, John. No, I've come up here because one of my guys is choked about some developments on his case."

"Hammer?" asked John, the smile having been replaced by a serious frown. What was odd was he'd never used Mike's nickname. In fact, she didn't even know he knew Mike's handle.

She nodded. "Yeah. It seems CSIS has been interfering with this case, and you and I know that those bastards are not supposed to get involved in domestic matters. For God's sake, John, they're supposed to be hunting spies, not murderers."

John raised one hand to silence her. He sensed her frustration.

"So what do you want me to do about it?"

This surprised her. John had always backed the troops, no matter what. Barbara sensed something different in his tone. Somebody'd gotten to him, as unbelievable as that was.

She decided she'd better back off for now. She shrugged. "You know, sir. Make the usual calls and such and get those guys off our backs so we can get this case wrapped up."

She saw a glint in the corner of one eye as John O'Reilly leaned forward across his desk on his elbows, his fingers interlaced. He spoke softly.

"Why don't you and Hammer meet me at O'Shea's. Say about six?"

She nodded dumbly. This was almost too much. The super had never gone for a drink with the "boys" since she'd been at the SCU. And as far as she knew, he'd never done it before she'd gotten here.

"Uh…yes, sir. Of course."

She stood and walked out of his office.

She glanced back and saw that the superintendent had swiveled his chair to face the window. She closed the door softly behind her and headed for the door to the corridor but stopped and faced Gary. He had his head of blond hair down, focusing on the incoming pile of mail.

"Uh…excuse me, Gary. Can I ask you something?"

He glanced up from a white envelope he was opening and nodded, a puzzled expression on his face. She rarely called him by his first name.

"Yes, ma'am."

She moved to stand over him, her arms at her sides. She nodded toward the super's door. "Is he okay?"

"Yes, ma'am. Why?" The eyebrows were both arched on his young, pale face and his mouth hung open. If you looked up the word "confused" in the dictionary, you'd probably see his face.

She waved her right hand. "Nothing. I was just wondering, that's all."

Once out in the corridor, she immediately pushed the down button, not glancing up in Margaret's direction. She stood and watched the orange number above the elevator doors change as she thought about what had just transpired.

Suddenly it dawned on her. A bug. There was a bug in the super's office. The question was, were there also bugs in her office too. Her face paled as the elevator door slid open and she stepped inside for the ride to the fourth floor, where her office was.

Anger rose inside her. The bastards were bugging their own kind. This was getting messy real fast.

CHAPTER FIFTEEN

Trudy felt the blood rush from her brain. She was trapped in a motel room with a madman. He sat there with his unshaven, dark, stubble-covered features split in a grin she could only describe as evil. His dark eyes glowed as if he was seeing presents under a Christmas tree.

"What do you want?" asked Trudy. Her voice cracked as she wrapped the towel tighter around her. Rivulets of shower water trickled down her neck from her wet hair, making her shiver.

The man held a small object in his right hand. He pushed a silver button on it with his right thumb, and a steel blade sprang from the object with a deafening sound of metal on metal. It sounded to her like thunder in the quiet room.

He didn't say anything, but his dark eyes narrowed and he started to move forward in the chair, his sights fixed on her. She glanced at the door to the room and thought she might try to run. In her heart she knew it was useless. He looked mean and could probably move faster than she could.

She knew she was gonna die.

Suddenly the door to the room burst open and two uniformed arms with automatic pistols stuck through the now open door.

"Don't move a muscle…" said a female voice.

The man's eyes shifted and Trudy saw fear cross his face. He kept the switchblade on the arm of the chair, the blade pointed toward the ceiling. A knife wasn't much good against an armed assailant. Guns could reach out and touch someone, while knives were for close-in combat.

The female cop—it was officer Sheppard—moved into the room and kept the man covered with her gun while her male partner, Devlin, from yesterday, came in behind her with his gun holstered. He knocked the knife out of the man's hand and then hoisted him to his feet. He expertly pressed the guy up against the wall and began to frisk him. He found no weapons, but he did find a wallet in the right rear pocket of the guy's black jeans.

He grunted and with one hand extracted his handcuffs from a leather holder on his belt. He slipped them onto one wrist, reached up and dragged the guy's other hand behind him, and quickly had him wrapped and ready to go.

He pulled him by the shirt collar until he had him standing before Trudy and Sheppard.

Sheppard grinned at her partner and then holstered her weapon. She nodded at Trudy and cast her eyes at Trudy's only covering.

"The bastard got you just out of the shower?" asked Sheppard.

Trudy nodded meekly.

Sheppard glared at the guy. "You son of a bitch. Good thing we were close when the call from the manager came in. He said he spotted a man breaking into Ms. Wilson's room."

"Can I get dressed?" asked Trudy. "I feel kinda funny with all of you in here."

Sheppard nodded to her partner. "Why don't you take the suspect to the car and have a chat with him while I wait outside Ms. Wilson's door until she's dressed?"

Devlin nodded and pushed the would-be killer, who now had his head down and seemed as tamed as a new bronco. Devlin had his right hand firmly gripping the guy's left arm to make sure he didn't run. Of course, with the steel bracelets, he'd be noticed if he tried.

Sheppard followed him out and pulled the door shut behind them. The lock was shot and the door was broken, but it still closed enough to give Trudy privacy.

Trudy began to tremble and tears rolled down her cheeks in a river of emotion. She was alive but felt like she'd just died and been resurrected.

She dressed hurriedly in blue jeans and a mustard-yellow sleeveless top. She put on open-toed faux leather sandals. It wasn't supposed to be exactly a heat wave outside today, but it wouldn't be cold, either. Sixty-two would be the high.

She threw open the door and moved to sit in one of the chairs that surrounded the table under the window. She pulled the curtains open to let the light in as she sat down.

Sheppard stepped into the room. She had her notebook out and a pen in her left hand.

Her face was a mask of concentration as she moved to sit across from Trudy. She sat down and placed her notebook flat on the table.

"You okay?" asked Sheppard. A flash of concern traveled through her eyes.

Trudy nodded even though she didn't actually feel okay. She just wanted to get the hell out of this place.

Her eyes must have reveled otherwise because women everywhere, when they see others going through a crisis, can't help but try to comfort them. Sheppard reached across the table and rested one hand on Trudy's. She smiled weakly, nodded, and then retracted her hand.

Trudy nodded her thanks, her eyes drooping at the corners.

A single tear escaped her right eye and traveled down her pale cheek.

"Is this the guy from the gas station?" asked Sheppard.

Trudy nodded and cast her eyes downward.

"His identification says his name is Simon Renault. He's from Red Deer, Alberta."

Canada? Why the hell would this guy be trying to kill her?

She'd thought at first this was a random event when she'd met the man at the gas station. What the hell was going on? Trudy's mind whirled possibilities.

"He's got some minor stuff on this side of the border, nothing serious. Until now. Though he's not talkin'."

"Is he a biker?" blurted Trudy. She grimaced inside. She should've kept those thoughts to herself.

Sheppard seemed surprised by that question. "I don't know, why?"

"No reason," said Trudy, with a shrug of her narrow shoulders.

Sheppard frowned and glanced down at her notebook. "You know what's odd? The car he's driving has Washington plates."

"Yeah," said Trudy agreeing. "That is kinda funny."

"You're not holding out on me, are you? I mean, the guy did try to kill you."

Trudy shook her head and tried to keep her face as impassive as possible.

Sheppard's eyes narrowed. "Okay, Ms. Wilson. We'll contact you when we need you to testify. I have your home number and address in Fairview."

"Any idea when you might need me?"

Sheppard grinned. "Oh, don't you worry; it'll be quite a while. We're kinda backed up with cases round here."

"Well, if that's all…" said Trudy, rising from the chair and moving to where her small suitcase sat ready to go. She just needed to collect stuff from the bathroom and then she'd get on the road again. She wanted to put a lot of distance between herself and this place after she thanked Mr. Felgar. She regretted being so rude to him yesterday. His quick action calling the police probably saved her life.

Sheppard nodded and walked to the door. She stopped as she opened it and turned her head to look at Trudy, who was busy now in the bathroom, collecting her toiletries and putting them in her black leather satchel.

"Ms. Wilson, I've left my card on the table for you. If you want to talk anytime, please call me."

"Okay, thanks," called Trudy, her voice echoing in the confines of the bathroom. "Tomorrow's another day," she muttered to herself so that Sheppard couldn't hear her.

***

Sheppard shook her head and then left the room, closing the door behind her. She knew Trudy was in far deeper trouble than she was willing to admit.

She also knew there was little if anything she could do about it. Maybe she'd call Trudy's friend the sheriff in Fairview and fill her in.

Maybe the sheriff would be able to talk some sense into the woman. Before she got into some real trouble. Yup, that's what she'd do, she decided as she walked down the open walkway toward the wooden staircase to the parking lot.

The boards creaked underfoot and the breeze, with its scent of pine, washed over her as she hurried to join her partner.

They had a lot of paperwork to do to get this scumbag bedded down. She hadn't mentioned to Trudy the possibility that, if this guy was connected, he'd be out on bail by this afternoon. And Sheppard was certain he was connected, all right.

And probably a biker gang, and those guys could be nasty if you were in their sights.

CHAPTER SIXTEEN

TRUDY ARRIVED AT THE CANADIAN BORDER unsure of what she should do. Maybe if she told the customs border guard that she was here to visit Bruce in jail, they might not allow her in the country. From the couple of times she and Rocky had been to Vancouver, she still had so little knowledge of Canadians and how they thought.

They'd not been searched or questioned much when entering the country, but she felt her stomach do flips as she stopped at the red stop sign just before the booth. There was a car in front of her, and yellow metallic poles lined the lanes with camera boxes atop them. She wondered what they were for. Maybe they liked to get a picture of everyone coming and going?

The car in front of her began to move away from the booth, heading north. She stepped lightly on the gas and the truck moved forward until she was next to the booth. The young man in the blue uniform shirt with the gold badge over his left breast pocket had a black mustache and bored looking, dark eyes that seemed to look inside her as if he were a human x-ray machine.

The butterflies of her nerves deep in the pit of her stomach twitched under his steady gaze.

He handed her a colored card without saying anything. He reversed his right hand and pointed toward the pull-out with white-lined parking spots in front of the one-story building. "Pull over there," he said in a somewhat bland tone.

Trudy nodded, too afraid to say anything.

This was new to her. She thought for a second she might have done something wrong, but then how could she have? She'd just arrived.

She pulled into the stall and turned off the engine. She sat and watched the blue-uniformed customs agents, with their dark cargo pants, polished, ankle-length boots, and sky blue shirts, moving about the office inside the building. There were rows of large windows that lined the building's exterior, making the parking area visible to those inside and vice versa.

Finally a female officer, with her chestnut brown hair pulled back into a ponytail, the end of which trailed down her left shoulder, came out of the building toward her.

She stopped next to the truck. "Are you Trudy Wilson?" she asked, her dark-skinned face a mask of seriousness mixed with boredom.

"Yeah," said Trudy, her voice edged with reservation.

"I need you to follow me," said the woman, stepping back to allow Trudy to open the door, which she did.

Trudy stepped out and closed the door, leaving the driver's window down. She cast a glance at the truck.

"Don't worry, it'll be fine," said the woman, as if she were able to read Trudy's mind.

It was then that Trudy noticed the smell of sour manure in the air. As this area consisted of farms on both sides of the border, it wasn't surprising. It did explain why these agents weren't the happiest people on earth.

She followed the agent into the building. Inside there were a few agents standing around sipping from coffee mugs and talking in hushed tones. They glanced at Trudy as she went by, each averting his or her gaze as they caught her eye. The office was filled with the musty smell common to offices where there was lots of paperwork done. Ink, coffee, and dust filled her nostrils.

The agent held a low-slung gate made from the same material as a counter, which stood about waist high. The material was a laminated, pressed wood the color of straw. Behind the counter were two older metal desks where two agents sat with their booted feet resting atop the desks. They nodded to the woman agent as she and Trudy passed them.

Finally they arrived at the end of the short corridor, where there was an open office door.

The female agent motioned for Trudy to go inside, then spun and headed back to the front office.

Trudy hesitated momentarily and then walked through the door.

Sitting behind a desk wearing a navy sport coat, white shirt, and navy blue tie, was a dark-skinned man talking on a telephone. He was leaning back in the chair and Trudy could see the pistol hanging down from a shoulder holster under his left arm.

He grinned warmly as she moved into the room and swept one dark-skinned hand toward a chair that sat in front of the desk

It was the metal-framed type, with a well-worn green vinyl cushion to protect the user's butt. The chair wasn't particularly comfortable, but it was at least a little better than standing.

Trudy moved the chair back and sat down.

"Okay," said the man, nodding to her. "My guest has arrived. I gotta go."

He hung up the black, hard plastic receiver in the cradle and leaned forward in his chair. "You must be Ms. Wilson." He said it like he'd been expecting her. She certainly didn't know him. His dark eyes glinted with humor. He knew he had the advantage at this point.

He held out his right hand. "I'm Phil Singh."

She started at him dumbly not lifting her hand. She'd been through far too much shit to fall for this.

He smiled and chuckled. "Sorry, it's just that Flo Henderson said to expect you. I've been here for a couple of hours waiting for you to show."

At the mention of Flo's name, it suddenly dawned on her. Yeah, this guy was the friend Flo had asked her to look up.

He was gonna help her. Yeah. With all that had happened to her, she'd nearly forgotten the guy's name.

Trudy felt her face grow hot. She smiled weakly. "Sorry, it's just that I've been through a lot getting here, and your name slipped my mind." She held out her hand, felt the warmth of his handshake as he grasped hers. It was a good one. Not too tight, yet not too loose. She hated those sloppy ones.

He chuckled. "Yeah. That's okay, don't worry about it. Say, what do you mean, all you been through," he asked. The smile faded from his dark complexion and a look of concern grew in his dark eyes.

Trudy sighed and then explained about the guy from the gas station and how he'd slipped into her motel room.

Phil nodded without saying anything as she talked. He was obviously a practiced listener. Good trait for a cop to have in his toolbox. He waited to let her finish before he said anything.

"I think we better arrange some help for you," he said grimly.

She felt fear rise in her throat. She looked at him wide-eyed. "What do you mean?" she asked.

"I think someone's not too happy with you and Bruce. I've talked to a buddy of mine in the Mounties, and he seems to think something's not right in Denmark." Phil caught her look of puzzlement.

He grinned. "Sorry. I made a little joke." He held up a thumb and forefinger to show how tiny his little joke was.

Trudy forced a smile across her face.

He frowned. "No, I think there's far more to this case that meets the eye."

He stood from behind the desk. "You follow me and we'll go my place. I don't live too far from here."

She gazed at him with growing suspicion.

He smiled warmly. "My wife will treat you to some of her home cooking and we have an extra bedroom for you," said Phil. "Honest." He held up his hands as if in surrender.

"I couldn't intrude…" Trudy began to protest.

"Nonsense," he interrupted with a wave of one hand. "Flo helped me out on a couple of cases. It's the least I can do to pay her back. Now come on, let's go." He started for the door and together they walked through the front office past the bored agents in their cocoon of fresh horse manure.

"Thanks, guys" said Phil with a wave of his hand as they walked by. One of the agents, wearing two gold bars attached to shoulder straps on his blue shirt, waved back. He had slick, short-cut, jet-black hair combed neatly to one side. "You're welcome, Phil, anytime."

Phil went out a door opposite hers and she saw him climb behind the wheel of a silver Firebird.

That certainly wasn't a cop car, not unless the Vancouver cops were issued sports cars now.

She went through the door to the parking area and climbed into the truck. After starting the engine and backing out, she pulled away and started to drive up the highway headed north on the two-lane road.

Phil pulled out in front of her and she matched his speed as they headed north. He is certainly the precursor to good things, she thought as they rolled north. At least she hoped it would be. The truck seemed to hum beneath her now that she was nearer to Bruce. Maybe she could even see him today, if Phil could arrange it. If not, then tomorrow was another day.

CHAPTER SEVENTEEN

PHIL TURNED INTO A SIDE STREET OFF THE KING GEORGE HIGHWAY. It wasn't really a highway. It was a road comprised of two wide lanes in either direction. There were traffic lights at most of the intersections like state highways back home.

Trudy followed him into the right turn, her turn lights flashing amber to signal the rushing traffic behind her she was leaving the highway. Drivers here seemed to follow awfully close. This sure is a busy place, she thought as she made the turn.

The street was lined with small, leafy trees on either side. The leaves were a pale green and moved about in the slight breeze. It was a warm day, but not too hot. Neatly painted homes—rust colored, dark blue with white trim, and natural wood stained ones—sat like rows of little cottages running up and down both sides of the quiet street. Kids on bikes and skateboards lined the sidewalks, laughing and playing, unaware of her or her truck.

Trudy smiled to herself. This was what neighborhoods were supposed to be.

Three houses in, Phil pulled into a freshly blacktopped driveway and Trudy followed, coming to a stop beside his car. The driveway was wide enough for more than one vehicle to fit comfortably. She turned off the engine and rolled up the driver's window. She regretted having to do so with the scent of roses and other fragrant flowers filling the air of the neighborhood.

The gardeners must've been out in full force this past spring, given the abundance of flowering plants that lined the driveways of the houses around her.

She stepped onto the driveway and saw that Phil had also got out. He glanced down the street toward a couple of boys riding bicycles.

"Satinder. Kaldeep," he called the names, which caused the two boys to stop and stare back at him. He glanced at Trudy and grinned, then turned again to face the boys. "Come here," he said as he waved to them.

They smiled and remounted the bicycles and started toward him. They stopped at the foot of the driveway. They looked inquiringly at Trudy.

They reminded Trudy of two puppies, confused by their master.

"Boys, I want you to meet, Mrs. Wilson. She's going to be staying with us for a few days."

They nodded and smiled. "Nice to meet you, ma'am," they said in unison and together nodded their heads politely toward her. Their voices were gentle and friendly, a good sign of well-trained children.

Inwardly Trudy sighed. She loved kids—even though she'd never had any of her own—provided they were well behaved. These two, she had a feeling, were gonna be the good kind.

"Nice to meet you, boys," she said.

"Okay, guys, run along until your mother calls you for dinner," said Phil. He positively beamed.

He was obviously very proud of his two sons, and from the quality of the clothing they wore—gray Nike tee shirts, open-toed leather sandals, and matching blue-and-white striped shorts—they appeared well looked after, as well.

But then again, appearance could be deceiving.

She followed Phil up the cement stairs leading from the driveway to the front door of the white stucco split-level house. The door was a solid piece of carved oak and the stucco gleamed in the sunlight. There was a half-moon, yellow-tinted window over the door. Phil pushed on the door, which was unlocked, and it swung inward.

He stepped inside and she followed. In the entryway, which was tiled in black and gray slate tiles, he doffed his shoes and slipped into a pair of open-backed, powder-blue slippers. She'd never been in a house that did that. She slipped her shoes off onto a little maroon-colored mat that sat in the entryway by the door. The light coming through the half-moon window brightened the entry. It looked yellow in the dim light.

"Do you have any slippers?" asked Phil.

Trudy felt her face grow red and shook her head.

He chuckled and opened the closet to reach down and pull out a pair of woman's open-toed, dark red slippers, and dropped them in front of her. "Use those," he said and winked at her with a mischievous gleam in his eye. "We've just put in new kitchen tile upstairs and my wife is on a terror about anyone walking on them with bare feet or shoes."

Trudy smiled thinly and nodded.

"What were you saying about me?' said a woman's voice from overhead at the top of the landing. Trudy couldn't see who was talking.

Phil laughed. "Sorry, Ranjit. I was just explaining the rules to our guest."

"Well, don't make her wait in the lobby, for goodness sakes, Phil. Bring her up here." The woman spoke with underlying warmth that made Trudy feel good inside.

Leading the way, Phil lead her up the two short flights of powder-blue carpeted stairs to the upper level of the house. They reached the living room. Trudy cast her eyes about. She was amazed how much it reminded her of her own home in Fairview, except this was tastefully decorated. A brass-and-glass clock hung over the stone fireplace that lined one wall, opposite the stairs and comfortable, overstuffed furniture. The chairs and the couch were a tan color with specks of blue and red thread running through it.

There were two matching glass-and-brass lamps on two pine end tables. In one corner, near the large front window overlooking the street, sat a television and a stereo unit. A larger wooden stand filled with CD's sat next to the stereo stand.

"Well, what do you think of my little kingdom?" asked Phil.

"You mean mine," said a dark-haired woman with skin the color of mocha. She was wearing a beautiful, pale green dress and shawl with gold trim at the edges. Her hair was cut neatly to her shoulders and she wore a wide smile on her elegant face. She wore a light shade of red lipstick and her dark eyes sparkled upon setting themselves on Phil. He embraced her and kissed her lightly on the right cheek.

She pushed him away and tapped him lightly on the shoulder. "Oh, Phil, it's not like we've been apart for days. You only went to the border and back," she said, scolding him playfully.

He feigned hurt feelings and rubbed his shoulder. "Sweetheart, I'd like you to meet Trudy Wilson."

Trudy smiled weakly and held her black handbag by its strap like some pickpocket would suddenly pop out and run off with it. Her fingers worried the strap.

"Trudy, this is my wife Ranjit, also known as Randy Singh."

Randy wrapped her arms around Trudy and hugged her lightly, then pulled back and gazed at her. Her brown eyes were measured in their assessment of the Oregon woman.

"Phil tells me you've been through a lot," she said, her smile kind and filled with reassurance.

Trudy only nodded.

"Why don't we have some tea first, then you can freshen up. I'll show you to the room where you'll be staying. Okay?"

Trudy nodded again. Her cheeks grew warm. They must think I'm deaf and dumb.

Randy lead they way into the kitchen, where a forest-green teapot sat surrounded by three matching china cups on a pine table covered with a flowered tablecloth. There were four matching chairs with wooden spindles for the person seated to rest their back against.

The walls were papered with cheery yellow flowers, and the appliances—stove, fridge, and built-in dishwasher—were plain white. The cove counters were butcher block style, with a row of pale, yellow, stone containers marked flour, sugar, and coffee lined beside a double, steel sink. The cupboards were plain, dark, brown wood with brass handles.

There was a small window over the sink, with frilly, white curtains on either side. Trudy surmised it looked out over the backyard. A plain, brown door with a window set in it opened onto a sundeck at the rear of the house.

They sat and Randy poured them each a cup of steaming, pale green tea. There were things floating in the cup.

They looked like small bits of plants or leaves. Trudy grimaced at the sight of the foreign matter.

Randy smiled as she watched Trudy study the contents of the white cup. "It's okay. Those are real tea leaves. Indians make their tea without the convenience of tea bags. Just don't swallow the leaves themselves. Leave a bit of the hot water in the cup when you're done."

Trudy nodded and raised the cup to her mouth. It smelled of rose petals and jasmine. It felt soothing and she hadn't even tasted it yet.

She took a tentative sip and the warm tea went down her throat.

It tasted surprisingly good, unlike any tea she'd bought at the supermarket.

Randy grinned at Phil, who smiled warmly. They in turn each took a sip from their cups. "Rather pleasant, don't you think?" asked Phil.

Trudy nodded and sighed. These were good people. It was nice to meet some good people for once. It seemed like years since she'd felt so immediately at home in a strange place.

She felt her head nod and her eyes droop. A heavy sense of fatigue suddenly gripped her.

Trudy glanced at the old, white-faced Timex with the with a thin, faux gold band on her left wrist. It was only four o'clock in the afternoon. She had to get down to see Bruce as soon as possible. She cursed herself for not going there directly from the border.

She tried to stand, but her body felt like it had lead weights attached.

She caught a glimpse of Randy's dark eyes, a slight frown now marring her fragile features in a look of concern.

She planted her hands on either side of the tabletop and tried to push herself to a standing position with limited success. The world was suddenly off kilter.

Phil bolted from his chair and held her up by her right arm. Randy nodded toward the staircase just outside the entrance to the kitchen from the living room.

Trudy couldn't fight off Phil as he helped her up the stairs into a bedroom. It contained a single bed with a bright red comforter thrown over it and a small dresser with a mirror attached to the back. It was as if they'd been expecting her.

Phil helped her to the side of the bed and eased her down. Once she was seated on the soft bed, her head begged for the pillow. She fell down and landed on the soft pillow and felt her eyes drift shut. Her nostrils were still filled with the gentle smell of the tea. She felt her shoes being removed and then heard a soft click as the door to the room was closed.

Her mind drifted to thoughts of Bruce's smiling face as she lost consciousness. Hers would be a dreamless sleep.

***

The room was quiet when her eyes fluttered open. The sound of voices seemingly far away came through the bedroom walls. She sat up and tried to recognize her surroundings. She was in Phil's house— at least she knew that much. She stood and looked at herself in the mirror.

What greeted her was a fright wig of hair stuck at an odd angle, a nest of brown curls all tangled like some medieval forest. She ran her fingers through her hair and straightened her clothes. She noted her overnight bag had been dropped just inside the door.

She stopped for it and set it on the bed. She hadn't removed the covers and they were rumpled by her sleeping form. But not very much.

She'd slept like someone who hadn't had sufficient sleep for a long time. She realized that maybe she hadn't.

Tentatively she opened the door to the hallway. The sounds of a television drifted up the hall, accompanied by the muffled tones of hushed voices. They evidently didn't wish to wake her.

She moved down the hallway until she saw Randy, sitting on the over-stuffed sofa, her head turned toward the television. She was smiling brightly and her eyes sparkled in the artificial light of the lamp on the end table next to her.

She must've caught the movement because she turned her head just as Trudy came into view. The smile disappeared from her face and she immediately rushed to Trudy's side. She raised one hand to stop anyone else who was out of Trudy's line of sight from getting up.

Randy put an arm around Trudy's waist. "Let's get you cleaned up. Phil will take you down to the RCMP lockup after you have a shower and get your face on and eat something."

Trudy nodded weakly, not able to fight off this woman's goodwill any longer.

Together they arrived at the bathroom, and after making sure there were sufficient clean towels, Randy smiled at her and closed the door behind her.

Trudy used the toilet first and then undressed and turned on the silver-colored taps in the pink porcelain bathtub to adjust the water until it was the right temperature. The pale gray tiles on the floor complimented the color of the pink fixtures. Trudy stepped into the tub and pulled the gray plastic shower curtain closed to keep the water from splashing all over the floor.

There was a bar of deodorant soap on the seashell-shaped soap dish set into the design of the wall. Trudy picked it up and began to lather with it.

She soaped her body and the wonderfully fragrant scent of the soap enveloped her senses. She closed her eyes and let the warm water cascade over her naked body. There was a bottle of drugstore shampoo at one end of the tub.

She grimaced. She'd have to talk to Randy about that, for sure. She opened the bottle and used some to create a foamy hat for herself.

She placed the bottle where she'd found it and pressed her hand flat against the wall underneath the showerhead and let the spray hit her squarely on the face. She held her eyes shut tight.

She stood for several minutes.

Suddenly she felt a sob begin deep inside her and well into two rivers of tears that ran down her cheeks to mingle with the warm spray. Her body shuddered as the sobs weakened her. Oh, God, she thought. Not again. Not again….

Eventually she regained control and stepped back to take a few deep breaths to calm her. She rinsed her hair and her body of all remaining traces of soap and then reached down and turned off the taps.

As she stepped from the tub, she noted the bathroom was buried in a moist fog. She had to squint to make anything out in the small room. She reached for the row of switches and turned on the overhead fan. It whirred to life. Not that it would do much to clear the room. She liked her window in the bathroom back home. When open, it minimized the fog from the shower.

She reached for one of the pale peach towels that hung from a shiny aluminum bar on one wall and unfolded it. It was large enough to allow her to dry her body and afterward wrap it around herself for the trip to her room. She needed fresh clothes now that her skin and senses were refreshed.

She moved across the hall, a wispy, lavender-scented fog following, wafting around her. She caught the sound of a child's laugh that echoed off the walls of the narrow hallway as she opened the door to the bedroom. She smiled to herself. The innocence of a child. If only she could be so innocent once again.

Too much had happened. Far too much. Her life had changed when Bruce's sister was murdered. Her being accused had frightened her at first, but eventually they had ferreted out the real killer.

She closed the door and quickly dressed in clean clothes, dropping the dirty ones on the floor next to her bag. She'd ask Randy about washing them later.

Dressed in a loose-fitting, pastel-yellow top, blue jeans, and black, low-heel loafers, she looked at herself in the small mirror that hung off the back of the dark pine dresser and saw a new woman staring back at her. She smiled and realized she felt better than she had in days. That sleep had been very good for her.

Good thing she hadn't gone to see Bruce earlier. Knowing him, he would've worried about her when he saw the dark circles under her eyes. He had enough on his plate as it was.

She brushed her short curls into place and put her black-and-gray-handled brush on the dresser.

She walked back into the hallway and followed the sounds of the television program and more gales of occasional laughter. As she neared the living room, she put on her best game face.

When she appeared, Randy glanced over and a warm smile crossed her face. The woman positively glowed with optimism.

She sprang to her feet and rushed over to throw her arms around Trudy again and give her a warm hug. She stepped back to see a slightly flushed Trudy and placed her hands on the sides of Trudy's arms.

A broad, red smile and sparkling eyes gazing at her, studying her. "Don't you look good?" she asked brightly.

Trudy smiled weakly. "I feel pretty good, too." She scanned the room until she spotted Phil, sitting on the couch, his arms wrapped around his two sons. His eyes were fixed on the two women, watching them. He smiled when she caught his eye.

"Can we go see Bruce now?" asked Trudy. She'd come a long way for her friend and she desperately wanted to see him and talk to him.

Randy was wearing a different dress this time. It was a deep red with gold trim around the edges, only it wasn't a dress, really, something else. She also wore modest gold earrings in her ears below her flowing hair.

"Your dress is beautiful," said Trudy, unable to keep her eyes off the fine embroidery work of the dress. The way it flowed around Randy distracted her from her mission.

Randy smiled. "Come on in the kitchen with me. You need to eat something before you go to that awful place." Randy gave her a knowing look as if she'd seen the local jail herself.

Trudy's stomach did feel empty. She hadn't eaten since the morning and it was now—she glanced at her Timex—it was after nine. She wondered if it was morning or evening. The boys being here and the sound of the television suggested it might be at night.

She nodded and smiled and followed Randy into the kitchen. She sat at the table while Randy opened the oven with one hand, wearing a blue-and-gray oven mitt she'd left on the counter next to the stove. She pulled out a plate filled with food unlike any Trudy had ever seen.

"I'm sorry we ate a few hours ago. This might be a little dry." Randy seemed genuinely apologetic.

She placed the plate in front of Trudy on an orange, green, and white placemat. "It's hot," she cautioned.

Trudy nodded and picked up the fork that sat beside the plate and gazed uneasily at the food. There was what looked like meat in some kind of brown gray, a pile of vegetables that looked like lumpy mash potatoes, and two slices of thin, flat bread.

She took a piece of a vegetable and tentatively placed it in her mouth. Randy had taken a seat across from her and watched carefully as Trudy's face broke into a smile.

Randy grinned and nodded.

This was good. She next took a forkful of the meat with the gravy and tasted it, too. The meat was so tender it melted in her mouth. She finished the meat first, then went to work on the vegetables until they, too, were gone.

She finished her meal by using the bread to sop up the remaining gravy. She felt sated as she gazed at the now empty plate.

"What the heck was that?" Trudy asked, using a white paper napkin that Randy handed her to wipe off her mouth.

Randy shrugged. "Basic stuff really: lamb, yogurt, vegetables, like chickpeas, and a few magic spices. The bread is called Nan. Old family recipes."

"Well, I must tell you, Randy, that's the finest meal I've had in a long time." Trudy grinned and felt a little foolish to be gushing so much, though it was true.

"It wasn't too spicy, was it?" asked Randy, looking momentarily concerned.

Trudy laughed. "Where I come from, this wasn't evenly mildly warm."

Randy gave her a puzzled expression. "Phil said you were from Oregon?"

"I lived in Texas for a number of years. We invented hot food, what with all the transplanted Mexicans living there. I love the stuff, the hotter the better."

"Well, I guess I have nothing to worry about then, do I?" Randy joined her in a laugh.

Phil walked into the kitchen. "Is there a party going on in here and I'm missing it?"

"No, honey. We were just discussing the food," said Randy to her puzzled-looking husband. She rose from her chair and picked up Trudy's plate and fork.

"Now you two get going. Trudy has a man to see." Randy winked at her with a sly smile across her red lips.

Trudy grinned at the dark-skinned woman. She felt like they'd bonded. Randy'd been so nice since she'd invaded her home. It almost felt like she'd known her for years. Or maybe it was that the family environment had lulled her senses.

She turned and walked behind Phil down the stairs. She'd thought to put on the dark red slippers as this appeared to be one of Randy's house rules. She doffed them at the hall closet doors and reached for her Walmart running shoes.

She reminded herself she was far from home and maybe she'd better keep her emotions in check. Trust was something you earned, not just received. She'd learned that lesson the hard way.

Phil quickly donned his white Nikes and a light, navy windbreaker. "Might be a little chilly later," he explained.

Trudy kept a similar yellow jacket in the compartment behind the seat of the pickup just for such eventualities.

Together they walked out the front door to the driveway. Trudy retrieved her jacket after Phil suggested they take his car. He knew the way and there was no use in taking two cars.

She readily agreed. She didn't wish to be driving in a strange place after what had happened before she got here.

They drove in silence. Not even the car's radio was on. She thought it strange until she realized Phil was protecting her from the news broadcasts. No doubt this was a big story, given the notoriety of the victim's husband.

"I think Randy likes you," said Phil, casting her a brief look of his sparkling dark eyes.

"Yeah. Well, you can tell her that I like her, too," said Trudy, and she meant it.

Philo chuckled. "I told her about your troubles." He steered the car into a left turn down a tree-lined street. There were no houses, only a couple of streetlights hanging from wooden telephone poles.

Trudy could see a flash of a lighted area at the end of the rows of tall trees that lined the road. A breeze had sprung up and the treetops sway like dark warriors in the evening air. The window of the car had been rolled down since they left the house and Trudy could smell the various flowers mixed with the scent of pine trees.

The air smelled good and instantly reminded her of the road into her home on the Oregon coast. Odd that smells activated so many old memories.

They came into the clearing at the end of the road and there were a collection of low-rise buildings, none over three stories. A cul-de-sac with a grassy island in the middle was where the parking lots of the various buildings intersected. You could move from building to building by choosing a different exit from the roundabout.

Clever, she mused.

At the last entrance off the loop, Phil turned in. The parking lot had few cars in it.

A couple of white RCMP cars with their roof-mounted lights and their royal crests on the doors.

Painted on the side of the car just in front of the passenger door was an image of a horse in full flight, its mane flowing as if in a breeze.

There were only a few lights visible inside the building. The twin glass doors to the lobby revealed one area that was lit, as Trudy could make out some light coming from behind the smoked glass.

"This is it," said Phil, steering into one of the rows of empty parking stalls in front of the entrance.

Trudy looked up to see a sign that read "Royal Canadian Mounted Police" in large white letters on a black background, and underneath, in smaller letters, "Surrey."

Phil turned off the car's engine. They got out and started walking across the lot toward the courthouse doors.

"Do you think they'll let us in?" asked Trudy, her eyes wide and her stomach churning.

"No worries," said Phil, a wry smile on his face. He reached in his back pocket and flipped open his wallet, which he extracted with practiced ease. His shiny gold badge gleamed in the lights that bathed the parking lot in intersecting pools of yellow. It reminded Trudy of a gigantic quilt composed of pure light.

She grinned at him. Yeah, he had pull all right. She nodded.

They climbed the plain cement steps until they were at an intercom. There was a large white button below the speaker.

Phil pressed it and Trudy thought she could hear a muffled buzz from behind the door.

A man's sleepy voice answered within a few seconds. "Yeah?"

"Hi, it's Phil Singh, Vancouver PD. I'm here to see Mike Harris," Phil said in a conversational tone.

"He expectin' ya?" asked the voice with an edge of boredom. Trudy could imagine that guard duty at a prison at night when all the prisoners were in their cells was pretty dull.

"Yeah," said Phil.

"Okay. Give it a few minutes. I have ta page him to come to the lobby." There was an abrupt surge in static, then the intercom went silent.

Phil smiled thinly at her as they stood in the evening air. She smiled back.

"I heard you helped solve a case down south?" asked Phil. He was trying to make idle conversation to pass the time.

"Yeah," said Trudy nodding. She didn't want to discuss that time in her life. No, that period of her life, which at times seemed to be decades in the past but was only two years ago, was filled with painful memories. She definitely wasn't ready to deal with any of her baggage.

After waiting a few minutes, a large man wearing a dark blue dress shirt with a matching tie hanging loose about his bull-like neck came into view. He wore what looked like cowboy boots, the tops of which disappeared in the stovepipe gray slacks. She knew they were boots because of the sharp, pointed toes with the silver-colored tips.

He strode purposefully toward them, his strong face expressionless and his eyes hard and filled with a resolution that made Trudy feel a slight sense of intimidation. That, coupled with his crew cut, gave him a formidable appearance.

He expression changed to a wide smile when he spotted Phil. He moved to the door and pushed on the bar and the door swung open.

"Hey, Phil. It's good to see ya." he moved aside to let them in and the door closed behind them, locking with a loud click in the silent lobby.

He glanced at Trudy as he spoke. "So, ol' buddy, what you doin' in my neck of the woods?"

Phil cast his eyes at Trudy, then back at his friend. "I'm just helpin' somebody out. Do you know Flo Henderson?"

Mike frowned a little in thought. "Vaguely. Wasn't she that cop in Portland we met at that conference a few years ago?" He smiled slyly. "Wasn't that a doozy?" he slapped Phil on the shoulder with his meaty right hand.

Phil looked genuinely embarrassed. "Yeah," he said without elaborating. "Flo's now the sheriff of a small town in Oregon and she's asked me to help out this lady." He gestured toward Trudy.

"Mike Harris, this is Trudy Wilson."

Trudy nodded and smiled thinly. This was like being in the middle of an ol' boys club. Cops tended to run like pack animals. They liked to keep with their own kind.

Mike smiled and held out his hand in greeting. Trudy took it and could feel the power that ran through this man in his firm handshake. He was obviously very physically strong. He grasped her hand gently, like he thought he might break her arm off, and shook it, then dropped his arm to his side. His other hand rested on the holster that hung off his belt. His automatic pistol was strapped down securely.

"Really? I think I read something about you somewhere. Your name seems familiar." His brown eyes narrowed.

"Before you drive yourself nuts trying to remember, I better just tell you." Phil cast Trudy an apologetic look.

"Do you remember that corrupt cop story out of Fairview, Oregon, a couple of years ago?"

"Yeah." Mike nodded, his expression saying he did recall the story.

"She's the lady that exposed him."

Mike cast her a look of respect. "Okay, lady, that was some piece of work. Good stuff."

He crossed his massive arms over his chest and struck a casual pose.

"Can we go into your office? There's somethin' we need to talk about," said Phil.

Mike nodded. "Yeah sure. Where the hell are my manners?"

He uncrossed his arms and led them to the rear of the lobby. Once behind a false wall of smoked glass, they were in a hallway, which appeared to stretch to forever. Halfway down the long corridor, they turned down another hallway. The air was filled with stale coffee smells, and the overhead lights—composed of boxes of florescent tubes—and the absence of windows gave Trudy the feeling they were entering the bowels of the earth.

They finally stopped at a door with a plate next to it that read, "Room 51." Mike smiled at Phil, casting him a sardonic glance. "We call this room Area Fifty-One."

Phil chuckled and Trudy felt herself cringe at the bad joke. A room of aliens. It seemed to fit. She certainly felt like an alien right now. A stranger in a strange land.

Mike opened the door and ushered them in. Once inside, they could see rows of single desks with desktop computers and telephones. Most were covered in papers and each had two steel, wire baskets with handwritten signs, one that read "in," the other "out." They were alone in the room.

The room had the smell of fresh coffee. Trudy spotted a coffee station against one wall with the coffeemaker and all the fixings, including that powdered cream substitute she used at the shop. She hatred the stuff, but it was cheap and easier to keep than milk or cream.

Mike moved to a desk somewhere in the middle of the pack and stole two chairs from the desks around him for Phil and Trudy.

Once they were seated, Mike laid his arms on the table and eyed them.

"So, what can I do for you?" he asked, getting right down to it. His attention was now focused and the timber of his deep voice was all business.

Phil, for his part, seemed at ease as if he'd been the subject of these types of discussions many times before. He crossed his long legs and folded his hands in his lap.

Trudy felt the butterflies that had been threatening to take flight in her stomach begin to churn. Mike was a large man and his intimidation meter was redlined.

"Trudy is a friend of your suspect, Bruce Carstairs." Phil let the words hang in the still room for several seconds to let them sink in to the collective consciousness of the three.

Mike cast her a knowing glance and nodded. His expression remained unreadable.

Phil continued. "It seems you might have the wrong guy. Or at least that's what Trudy seems to think."

Trudy nodded slowly, keeping her eyes on the large detective.

He frowned and eased back in his chair, which squeaked under the strain. "Is there something specific that makes you think he's innocent?" asked Mike, speaking to Trudy.

"No," she said slowly. "it's just that Bruce helped me with the—" she searched for the right word "—situation, and I know him, and he's not the type of guy who would ever hurt anyone. At least not intentionally."

"Well, that's the crunch, isn't it?" asked Mike, shaking his head.

"We have a witness who says he was high at the time of the murder and says he killed her."

"Bruce doesn't take drugs," said Trudy, surprising herself with the level of forcefulness in her tone.

Mike's eyebrows went up and a grin softened his hard features. "Okay, lady, okay."

Phil grinned.

"Sorry," said Trudy, casting her eyes down. "It's just that Bruce may look like a biker but he doesn't live their lifestyle. He likes to drink beer and..." she hesitated, "...party, as he calls it, with the ladies."

"Do you party with him?" asked Mike.

Trudy cast him an angry look that she knew would peel paint. She'd used it enough times to cow her husband.

Mike only grinned. "Okay, okay, sorry again. I just thought I'd ask." He raised his hands in mock surrender.

"So what can you tell me that I can use?" asked Mike, his expression turning serious again. "Ya know, my inspector has taken a personal interest in this case so whatever you tell me better be good."

"Well," Trudy shrugged, "I don't know the whole situation, so I don't know what I can tell you, really."

Mike eyed Phil, who shrugged. He nodded to the Vancouver detective. "I shouldn't really be telling you anything, but…" the telephone on his desk interrupted them. It made Trudy jump in the quiet room.

Mike raised one finger. He picked up the receiver on the second ring. "Harris," he said into the black phone.

His calm features became a scowl as he listened for several seconds without saying anything. "Okay, thanks," he said finally. "See you tomorrow."

He hung up the phone and the frown that had invaded his features remained fixed like a crease across his forehead.

"It appears my star witness has gone to ground or something worse." He cast Phil a knowing glance.

Phil sighed. When you dealt all day with lowlifes, you realized things invariably happened to them, because they were always pissing someone off. Someone who didn't take kindly to being pissed off.

"What do you mean?" asked Trudy innocently.

"He's probably dead, and it's highly unlikely we'll ever find the body," said Phil.

Trudy's eyes went wide. "Oh," was all she managed to say.

CHAPTER EIGHTEEN

Pierre Lavois gazed at the flames in the fireplace as he sat in the leather wing chair, his long arms on the smooth armrests. The fine leather of the matching couch and chairs that sat before the old stone fireplace seemed to glow in the firelight. The room was dark. The large, floor-to-ceiling windows of the mansion on Sussex Drive were blocked by the thick, burgundy drapes that the staff had drawn to give the prime minister his privacy.

He'd turned out the crystal lamp that sat on the dark, rosewood end table next to his chair soon after he'd sat down to read the daily briefing reports prepared by his political staff.

It was always useful to know what the opposition was up to before you had to face them across the floor of the house during question period.

Parliament can sometimes be a real bitch, thought Pierre. A sigh escaped his lips.

The dancing orange, yellow, and blue flames were now the sole light source in the ancient library.

The room smelled of wood and books. Some of the books were in English, but most were in French. Many of the prime ministers of Canada had French as their mother tongue, including the current occupant of the official residence.

He stared at the flames, wondering what the hell his son would do next.

He hadn't talked to Willie in several days. Wellman said the campus cops kept regular tabs on his favorite child, and they reported he was spending most days at the bar, not in his classes.

He sighed heavily and glanced at the cup of cold tea sitting on the end table beside the chair. He'd d barely had two sips of the tepid, bitter tea before he left it to grow cold. He wanted something stronger right now, but he knew he couldn't. He'd given up alcohol when he'd decided to get serious about politics, back in the '60s.

He'd been headstrong back then. A radical, his parents had called him. Well, what did they expect? His ancestors had been instigators in the French Revolution. He was born to be a separatist.

Over the years, he'd begun to realize that he would have to adopt a centrist attitude toward Canadian politics. He needed those bastards in Ontario, even though most of them were slimy creeps who liked to make money more than they liked sex. They were always looking for favors from the government of the day.

He'd been resistant to most but had, at the urging of his aide Wellman, sometimes given in to appease the party. They could make a new prime minister's life difficult. He'd barely gotten the nomination for head of the party. Support from some of the more shadowy types in the party had cinched his spot. He knew they'd bide their time before hitting him up too much for a few favors.

Who had killed that girl? It seemed unlikely it was the man accused, who was being reported in the national press as the killer. No, he was the scapegoat who'd go to jail for the murder. But who had really killed her?

Deep inside his gut, he feared the worst but dreaded the thought that his son had been involved in the young woman's death. Willie was a stupid, irresponsible fool, but he couldn't kill anyone. He was certain of it.

LaFrance would take care of this matter. LaFrance was the best at his job.

He stood and smoothed his gray slacks and adjusted his thin tweed sweater over his lean frame. He grimaced at the slight twinge in his left knee. Damn thing is never gonna leave me, he thought.

Rowing accidents rarely did. The metal-and-plastic replacement joint seemed to ache more at bedtime than at any other time of day.

He hobbled to the door, trying to flex the joint as he moved until it seemed to lubricate itself sufficiently to ease the pain somewhat.

He opened the library door, and the hall light, though subdued, made him wince until he adjusted the brightness.

His butler Albert Lipman, the cousin of a friend from Toronto, came down the long hallway toward him wearing a light blue shirt open at the neck and a clean white apron over his navy trousers. "Will there be anything else this evening, sir?' he asked, his ruddy complexion fixed in an easy smile.

"No, Albert. Not tonight. See you in the morning."

"Yes, sir." Albert nodded and disappeared through the library door. Albert would ensure the fire was safe and the room prepared for tomorrow's use. He was efficient; that much was clear. One of those small favors, which had been to everyone's mutual benefit.

As he walked slowly down the hallway, he stopped to study the various prime minister's photographs that lined both sides of the hallway.

He wondered if any of them had suffered because of their offspring. He shook his head. Probably not. Probably all had perfect kids.

He finally arrived at the whitewashed oak staircase that led to the upper level of the house. He started up the stairs.

He needed to get a good night's sleep. He'd need to be wide awake for the press conference tomorrow and the long plane trip to Vancouver. He didn't trust those closest to him to straighten out this mess. He needed to find out for himself what was happening with his son and the murder investigation.

His son wouldn't be thrilled with his arrival.

CHAPTER NINETEEN

THE ROOM WAS BARE EXCEPT FOR TWO BLACK, SWIVEL, OFFICE CHAIRS on rolling steel casters. The only other thing in the room was a plain, tan, office table.

Trudy gazed at Bruce. He was unshaven and his dark beard made him look worn and older than his years. His red-rimmed eyes stared lifelessly at her.

This was a lawyer interview room and would be about the only chance for them to be alone.

He looked like a beaten man. Jail wasn't the place for him to be right now. Phil had explained to her that she could put up a bond; it would only be a portion of the one-million-dollar security deposit required. This amounted to about seventy-five thousand Canadian dollars. It would mean she would have to accept a lien on her house in Oregon. Rocky would also have to agree, and that wasn't going to be easy, given the history between him and Bruce's sister.

She first had to know something, and she'd know if told her the truth.

"Did you kill her?" her dark eyes fixed on his tear-swollen pits of lifeless flesh.

"I don't know," he said with a shrug of his stooped shoulders.

He dropped his gaze to the table.

"What?" She was surprised by his answer. Usually someone knew if they'd killed someone.

"I can't explain it…" his voice drifted off. "Fuck." He voice was suddenly louder and filled with a potent mix of anger and frustration. "Someone's framed me, Trudy."

The old Bruce came right through. She felt it flash across the room between them. They would find out who'd done this to him. Someone killed that girl and they were going to find out who. She felt a surge of confidence course through her, making her tremble.

***

The next morning she filed the papers that Rocky faxed to her from Fairview. Phil kept a fax machine at home. The deed to the house and a loan to secure the mortgage was accepted as bail to allow Bruce to be freed from jail.

Rocky hadn't put up much of an argument when she told him what it was for. He seemed almost eager to help. Maybe too eager. She'd have to check into that when she got home.

Phil warned her to expect a gauntlet of press to be outside when they left the building with Bruce. This was a high profile case and one that the fifth estate was making more sensational by the minute. After all, they needed their headlines.

Phil led them to the back entrance reserved for the police and sheriffs coming into the court.

No doubt some of the press people would be staked out there, but he'd have the car ready to take them back to his house.

Trudy wondered why he was willing to help them. After all he was a homicide cop and Bruce was an accused murderer, after all. His explanation had been a little vague. He'd mumbled something about Flo and left it at that. His gaze was averted when he replied, so she assumed she better not talk about it anymore. She made a mental note to ask Flo about it later.

They exited the police station with a "promise to appear" order for ten days time in her purse. No, they weren't about to run, she explained. Guilty people run, she told the bailiff, who accepted her check and the mortgage papers as collateral for the bond. Innocent people stay and face their accusers.

There were two men outside, both of whom were reporters, given the notebooks in their hands and the grim smiles they gave them as they headed for Phil's car. They were both middle-aged men, so had probably been in the business for some time and knew police procedure.

Phil waved them away as they rushed into the already running car.

Trudy and Bruce slouched down in the backseat, not daring to look at the reporters as the car began to pull out. They heard a few muffled words, as if they were under water, as the car began to move.

There was no mistaking the final word of one the men as he shouted "Fuck," at the retreating trio.

They popped their heads up and scanned the road around them, then giggled like children. A sense of relief washed over Trudy.

Bruce's childlike grin faded as he looked into her eyes. "I'm so glad to be out of that fucking place," he said.

"I know," said Trudy. "But you better watch your language around Phil's house. His wife won't like it much and neither will his kids."

"Yes, mom," said Bruce mockingly.

She grabbed his right hand firmly in hers and held it like she'd never let it go. "We have a lot of work to do." She nodded toward Phil, who was now back on the King George Highway heading north. "Phil and his wife, Randy, are gonna let us stay at their place. No one knows we're there, except Flo."

He nodded, his face now serious and his eyes searching.

"You okay?" he asked.

She felt her heart flutter. He knew something was wrong with her. Somehow he always seemed to know when things weren't right with her.

"Rocky?"

She shook her head. "No, not him. Something happened on the trip up here and I don't want to talk about it right now."

He nodded.

They rode in silence until they arrived at Phil's house.

"Some nice digs," said Bruce when they exited the car. Phil thanked him. Bruce spotted Rocky's truck parked on the street.

"Where's the POS mobile? I hope it died its much-needed death."

Trudy grinned at him as they walked toward the door. "Naw. For a mission like this, only the best."

She placed one arm around his waist and he did likewise as they strode side by side up the three cement steps. The door opened and Randy came out to greet them at the top of the stairs.

Her smiled seemed to brighten an otherwise gray, overcast day. Her perfume was heady and smelled like rosewater.

Her dress circled her like a shimmer of gold and silver thread.

"My, that's a beautiful dress," said Trudy.

"Actually, they're called saris, not dresses," said Bruce.

Randy looked at him in wonderment. Phil grinned and nodded.

Bruce shrugged his shoulders. "Underneath this rugged exterior, I'm a closet man-of-the-world."

They all laughed and went inside. Once they were seated in the living room, introductions were made.

Randy had made some tea in anticipation of their arrival. They each took a cup from the mat on the pine coffee table and poured for themselves, then sat back down. The smell of Indian tea dominated the room.

"Darjeeling?" asked Bruce, taking a careful sip of the hot tea.

"Why, yes, and blended with another type from my family's ancestral village in India," said Randy. "My, isn't he full of surprises," she said to Trudy.

Trudy's eyes narrowed. "Yes, isn't he?" She caught Bruce's eye and her eyebrows went up. How the hell did he know this stuff?

Bruce chuckled warmly. "I used to date an Indian girl." He waved one hand in the air as if he were swatting flies. "It was a long time ago."

Phil decided it was time to change the subject. "So what are your plans?"

Bruce hesitated, so Trudy stepped in to answer for him. "I don't know exactly. We'll probably go talk to some of Bruce's friends and see if they know anything."

"I can't condone interfering with a police investigation," said Phil, his eyes gazed at them knowingly.

"Oh, of course not," said Trudy as innocently as possible. "We wouldn't dream of it. Would we Bruce?"

He shook his head. "We know better," he said.

"That's not what I hear." Phil smiled.

Trudy caught the look in his eye. He couldn't officially let them go off and investigate the case while it was still active, but after their conversation with Mike, it seemed he might be willing to look the other way. Boy, thought Trudy, he must really be in deep with Flo.

CHAPTER TWENTY

AFTER ABOUT AN HOUR OF GETTING-TO-KNOW-YOU TALK, which was a pleasant diversion, Trudy and Bruce excused themselves. They wanted to visit some friends.

Randy had made them cheese-and-tomato sandwiches to take with them and insisted they take them. She also gave them two bottled waters, saying they might be gone a while and might need a pick-me-up.

Trudy thanked her and gave her a quick hug. Bruce shook Phil's hand and they headed for Trudy's truck. She insisted on driving.

"Where's your bike?" asked Trudy when they were alone in the truck.

"Impounded for the duration," said Bruce matter-of-factly.

"Oh."

Trudy started the truck and they headed out to the main road. Bruce told her to head south toward White Rock. He said they weren't going to the scene of the crime, which was still cordoned off by the cops.

"Too dangerous," he said, without further explanation. She did as he instructed, knowing full well he knew these people far better than she.

"I know a guy who might be able to help us," he said.

Trudy only nodded and followed the curve of the four-lane road as it merged into two lanes in either direction. This had to be the strangest road she'd ever seen.

Within twenty minutes, they were driving down a steep road to the bottom where it finally became level once again. The beach was on her right now. The small surf—nothing like Oregon, too much island between them and the wilds of the Pacific—came into the sandy gray beach.

With her window rolled down, she could smell the ocean breeze heading inland and took in a deep breath of the salty air. She reveled in the sea air. Overhead, in the cloudy sky, seagulls called to each other.

She concentrated as she steered the truck down the winding, two-lane road that seemed suddenly narrow after being on the highway.

To the right was a steep cliff with lined with large houses that had tremendous ocean views. These houses were very expensive.

Finally the road became straight again as they neared a parking lot next to the beach. Given the cloudy day, the lot had very few cars in it, though Trudy could see men and women walking along a paved path next to a green strip of grass that grew above the tide line. Some had dogs on leashes.

She pulled into the parking lot and chose an empty spot as directed by Bruce. He reached into a pocket of the black leather vest he wore over his plain blue work shirt and pulled out a couple of quarters.

He indicated the meter in front of the truck with a slight nod. "Put these in the meter and wait here for me," he said, his expression serious.

She knew not to question his directions, though she was curious.

She watched him cross the street and climb the wooden stairs of a two-story blue and white house across from the parking lot.

She watched him knock on the door, and the door swung open to admit him. He disappeared inside.

She hadn't bothered to roll up her window because the air didn't smell like rain, as it would have in Oregon. She rested her arms flat on the doorframe and rested her chin on her arms to watch the people as they walked down the pathway.

There were gray-haired retired types, some of them couples and some holding hands. Love anew, she thought.

And there were young men and women jogging and power-walking, all somehow avoiding collisions as they passed each other.

"Get out," said a gruff male voice from behind her. It was said in a hoarse whisper, just loud enough so only she could hear it. She felt her heart almost skip a beat and fear ran through her. She felt a sudden urge to pee.

"Okay," she said, and slowly, with her hands visible, opened the truck's door. It squeaked in protest. It wasn't loud, but her senses were suddenly heightened. She resisted the urge to look behind her, but then her head began to slowly turn in the direction the voice had come from.

"Don't," said the voice, with sufficient force behind it to make her freeze where she stood.

No, I better not, she thought. She moved slowly and closed the door of the truck, then dropped her hands to her sides.

"Let's go across the street," said the voice. "You first. And don't look back."

Trudy nodded.

She walked slowly to the side of the road, being careful to keep her eyes forward. She glanced to either side as best she could and saw that in her limited field of vision there were no cars. She started across.

"Faster, said the voice, which seemed close behind her. So close, in fact, that she thought she could feel hot breath on her neck.

She also smelled garlic in the air around her and stale cigarette smoke. She resisted the urge to wrinkle her nose at the awful combination.

She climbed the wooden stairs, just as she'd seen Bruce do, until she stood before the whitewashed door. There was a strip of aluminum that ran the perimeter of the door. Odd, she thought. I've never seen anything like that before. Could it be weather stripping?

The door swung open and she was unceremoniously shoved from behind and stumbled through, almost landing on her face. She caught herself by grabbing a smooth counter with her right hand.

The room was dim, with dark, light-killing shades pulled over the windows. She didn't know what the hell was going on, but it couldn't be good.

"Hey, Trud," said a familiar voice. Bruce's familiar bulk came out of the shadows to grasp her shoulder. "You okay?"

"Yeah, for fuck's sake." She felt anger from the pit of her stomach. This was all too much.

"Tell the broad to watch her fuckin' mouth," said the same male voice from before.

Trudy saw red. She hated be calling a broad. What did this bastard think he could get away with?

A light came on suddenly, blinding her momentarily. She blinked away the fuzzy colors of red, blue, and green as her vision adjusted to the sudden intrusion.

A tall, thin man with a noticeable, ragged scar that ran down his left cheek grimaced as he gazed at her with hard, dark eyes. Her fear returned.

"Sorry, Trud. My cousin is careful, maybe overly so." He cast the man a brief flash of annoyance.

The guy, who had the thumbs of both hands hooked over the pockets of his stained jeans, stood casually watching her as if he was a lion studying its prey before the kill.

"Your cousin?"

"Yeah. Gary Peters." Bruce nodded at the guy.

"Can't be too careful," said Gary, his brown eyes studying her. "You two got a lotta heat up your ass."

Trudy nodded, her eyes wide. "Why? Is that a problem?"

Gary gave her a stern look. "In my business, yeah—lady." He spat the words at her, his face twisted and his scar now a shade of white. She sensed the rising tension in the room.

His maroon dress shirt, with the long sleeves rolled up his sinewy arms, was open at the collar, two of the buttons undone to reveal a hairless chest. The shirt was stained with something she couldn't readily identify, much like his black jeans.

The smell in the place reminded her of a paint factory she'd been in for a field trip in junior high school. He'd been working on something, probably rather messy, when Bruce had come to his door. She knew she didn't want to know what that something had been. Too much information could be a bad thing and she knew it.

"Um...never mind. Sorry," she said, lowering her eyes to the dusty tiled floor.

141

The floor hadn't been swept in a while and dust and dirt were everywhere. There were cobwebs in the corners and hanging off the window blinds. She wondered how anyone could live in a place like this.

"Yeah," said Gary, his voice dripping with sarcasm. "It's okay, Sam. You get back to work."

A man had been standing in the shadows. He moved into the dim sunlight that managed to come between the slats of the plastic blinds. Trudy snuck a peek when she felt the air in the room move as he went by them. She only caught the briefest glimpse of a short man with large arms and the flash of a knife blade in his right hand.

She wondered if this was the voice that had told her to cross the street. Gary's didn't sound the same, but she wasn't certain.

"So," said Gary, turning his attention to his cousin. "What the hell can I do for you, Bruce?"

"I think you know," said Bruce, his voice hard and his look one which meant he wasn't to be fucked with. She'd seen it before.

Gary shrugged. "Yeah."

He forced his dirty hands into the pockets of his jeans. It was then Trudy noticed he wasn't wearing any shoes. His feet were so dirty they looked like black shoes instead of feet. No wonder the guy smelled of sweat and grime and his short hair looked greasy.

He grinned, but it wasn't one of those humorous ones. His eyes said otherwise. "Listen, I don't know nuthin' about any of that, cousin."

Bruce stepped closer to his dirt-covered relative and glared at him. His muscular arms were against his sides and his fists were clenched like two meaty hammers about to do some serious damage.

"I think you do," he said slowly, with sufficient menace to make Gary's eyes grow wide.

"Uh...listen, you know if I tell you anything..." Gary's voice trailed off as his body stiffened. He looked surprised by something.

Trudy cast a quick glance about the room but saw nothing. When she looked back at Gary, she saw his face grow slack and he suddenly pitched forward.

Bruce caught the smaller man by his shoulders. This was when Trudy saw the knife handle sticking from the middle of Gary's back, the blade buried in a bloody wound. Its large handle was made of wood and the length of the blade was imbedded to the hilt.

Bruce laid his cousin on the dirty floor and rolled him on his side. If he removed the knife, Gary would bleed to death within seconds. He leaned down and spoke to his dying cousin.

"Gary," he said, his voice a hoarse whisper. "Can you hear me?"

Gary's glazed eyes looked up into Bruce's and he croaked something. Trudy couldn't make out what he was saying. Bruce bent his ear close to the man's mouth.

"Say that again, I can't hear you," said Bruce, his voice desperate.

Bruce waved his arm at Trudy to indicate she'd better get on the floor. Whoever had thrown the knife was probably still outside. There was a neat hole in the window, which a beam of light came through that hadn't been there before.

She followed Bruce's direction and crouched down below the level of the windowsill.

Gary whispered something in Bruce's ear, his body trembling as his heart struggled to keep him alive, but it was no use. He shook violently and from between trembling lips he drew his last breath. It rattled and bubbled from his tortured lungs. He coughed and spat blood, a thick trail of red running from his open mouth down his cheek. He was literally a drowning man.

She glanced at Bruce as his eyes came up to meet hers. From outside came the sound of a car's powerful engine roaring to life, followed immediately by the squealing of tires as it sped away, screaming as if it were a wild animal.

Bruce laid his cousin flat on the floor and used his fingers to close his cousin's eyelids as the dead eyes of Gary Peters lost their light. He was dead. His mouth hung open in a silent scream.

"What did he say?" asked Trudy, her voice quiet.

"One word," said Bruce his voice angry. "Frame."

He rose to his feet and moved to the door to the outside. "We better get the hell out of here. If Sam comes back and finds us with Gary's body, he's gonna think we did it and we're fucked. And if the cops find us, we're fucked. Either way, we're fucked." He shrugged and she thought about it for a couple of seconds.

This was happening too fast and he was right.

They threw open the door to the wooden staircase, then ran up the side of the sad-looking, blue-and-white house that needed a coat of paint and thumped as their feet barely touched the steps on the way down. They ran across the street and Trudy threw open the door to the truck. Bruce picked her up and bodily tossed her inside.

She flew across the seat like a diver from the springboard and landed in a sprawl on the passenger side of the bench seat.

She felt him shove her legs aside as he climbed in.

"The keys," he said, his breath short from the exertion of the run down the stairs. His large, booted feet had used two stairs at a time rather than her use of each step.

Her purse was in her left hand in an iron grip. She tossed the bag at him. He rummaged inside and pulled out her keys with trembling fingers. He threw the purse to the floor on her side of the truck and quickly started the engine.

He put the truck into reverse, and with the squeal of tires, he backed out. She held onto the seat with both hands, afraid to sneak a peek over the dashboard.

The truck swayed as he hit the brake hard and shifted to drive. The truck tires squealed again as they sped off.

She heard a disembodied shout. It was an angry voice. Man's voice. She couldn't make out what he was saying, but the tone suggested he wasn't a happy camper. Bruce stepped harder on the gas pedal and she felt the truck fishtail as they entered the main road. She felt it sway side to side as he drove to get them away from the house as quickly as possible.

Suddenly the rear window over her head shattered and glass rained down on them.

She covered her head to protect herself from the sharp glass. When she looked up, there was a red streak running down Bruce's forehead and down the right side of his face. He looked anxious but unafraid.

The truck finally slowed, which meant they were out of range.

"Are you okay?" she asked, her voice revealing her fear.

Bruce only nodded, his pale face grim and his eyes determined. He cast her a quick glanced and smirked. "They weren't about to end this run."

She smiled thinly and her stomach protested as they made a sharp turn. They were on a slight uphill rise now and she used one elbow to push herself upright into a sitting position.

They were on the road leading away from the beach. The same tree-lined road they'd been on before. Up ahead, on the left, was a pub. She knew this by the sign that hung over the front window. It read, THE PELICAN PUB AND BREWERY. Bruce slowed as he saw a sign in the window.

His surprised look and the slight smile as the corners of his mouth turned up told her they were about to make an unscheduled stop.

"Great. I know someone we can talk to about what the fuck is going on around here. Someone who'll help us," he said.

"That's what you said the last time," said Trudy, crossing her arms over her chest. This situation was getting worse and worse.

CHAPTER TWENTY-ONE

THEY WALKED THROUGH THE FRONT DOOR OF THE PUB. The door was unlocked, even though it was still an hour away from opening time.

The bartender—he must be, because he wore a starched white apron tied across the front of his expensive-looking tan chinos—was sweeping the floor in front of the brass and wood bar that ran along one wall of the room. Cherry-red padded stools sat like empty tin soldiers in front of the bar. Behind the long, dark, teak bar was the traditional wall of mirrors reflecting the dirty-blond-haired man's puzzled expression as he watched them enter.

He squinted, as the light behind them must've made their faces unrecognizable. He no doubt could discern the disproportionate size of the two people walking toward him.

Bruce's Daytons made a muffled, thumping sound as he moved across the scarred wooden floorboards.

"We're closed," said the man, his face taking on that annoyed look of someone busy what they were trying to do.

"We're looking for Tommy," said Bruce, a slight smile on his lips as his dark eyes scanned the bar for other people. There were none. Too early for the lunchtime crowd.

They guy leaned on his broom and frowned. "You and a couple of other guys."

"What do you mean?" Bruce's eyes were suddenly alert and his hands at his sides fisted for any threat that might suddenly appear.

Being shot at made him cautious, while it made Trudy's stomach flutter. She looked over her shoulder but only saw the cars outside driving slowly past the front of the bar, with the blue-green ocean beyond. No threats, at least, none she could see. Trudy saw Bruce's shoulders tense.

The bartender shrugged, leaned his broom against one of the wooden captain's chairs around a matching round table nearest him, and began to remove the apron.

He shrugged his narrow shoulders again as his fingers easily undid the white string of the apron that he then tossed over the same chair with a practiced maneuver. "I don't know. Except they were better dressed than you two. Kinda smelled like cops to me, but real badass ones."

Bruce looked quizzically at him, his lips pursed. "Tommy in some kinda trouble?"

"You guys cops?" asked the bartender.

"Nope, we're friends of Tommy's, and if he's in trouble, then we're the cavalry."

The bartender's lips curled at the corners. "Okay. He's upstairs in a spare room I sometimes let the singers use when they have nowhere else to stay." He nodded toward a half open door behind the bar.

"Thanks," said Bruce.

Bruce, followed closely by Trudy, started across the room toward the door.

"And let him know I told those cops nothin', OK?" added the bartender.

Bruce nodded as his heavy boots plodded across the wooden floor. The place smelled clean, as if the smoke that had probably been hanging in the air from last night's activities had dissipated completely.

Trudy followed meekly behind the big man as they left through a plain brown door and found a staircase with a wooden railing running down the length of the right-hand wall, which led to the upper part of the two-story building.

"Follow my lead," Bruce said, his voice a whisper.

Trudy felt a sudden rush of fear. Why was he whispering? A fleeting thought flashed through her mind that maybe they'd torn off more than they could deal with. She steeled herself and decided that she would see this thing through.

She stopped to remove her shoes to lessen the noise of them climbing the stairs. Bruce glanced at her when he sensed she wasn't right behind him. He held up his hands and mouthed, "What are you doin'?"

She pointed to his boots.

He nodded when he realized what she was getting at and grinned, his cheeks taking on a slightly reddish cast. He raised one finger to the side of his head to acknowledge her smart idea.

He then quickly removed his boots and held them by the tops in his left hand.

He would need to have his right punching arm free if they encountered any threats.

They moved carefully up the stairs until they reached the top to find a corridor off which were three closed doors—two on side, one on the other. One of which must be the room where Tommy was. It suddenly dawned on Trudy that the Tommy they were looking for must be Tommy Roper.

She hadn't bothered to read the sign in the window that had drawn Bruce to the place, but she suspected the traveling singer had finally made his way out of that dive in Newport, Oregon, and made his way to Canada.

They tried the first door but it was locked, so they moved to the second. It, too, was locked; this left door number three.

They stood on opposite sides of the door, flat against the wall of the corridor. The smell of cigarette smoke permeated the air in the corridor. It smelled fresh, so someone had come this way recently.

Bruce tried the brass doorknob, and sure enough, it turned. They heard the click as it disengaged, and Bruce pushed inward with the palm of one hand.

"Don't fuckin' move or I'll fuckin' shoot," said a man's shaky voice behind them.

The rooms must be connected, thought Trudy.

"I think he's got the drop on us, Tex," Trudy whispered to a wide-eyed Bruce.

His eyes contained no fear, only annoyance at having been outmaneuvered. Her mouth was suddenly dry. Funny, the things you thought about when you were about to die.

***

Pierre Lavois eased back into the wing chair in his opulent suite of the Vancouver Hotel. The local party was paying the tab, not his PM account, as it did when he was on government business. No, this was a personal matter that involved his son, William Lyon Lavois, who sat across from him in his faded blue jeans, white Nikes, and blue work shirt.

Pierre sighed inwardly. The long brown curls that ran down to his son's shoulders, coupled with his clothes, were reminders of his own heady days as a young idealist in college.

The uniforms of today's youth were reminiscent of those times, though they cost ten, if not twenty, times more.

Right now, his son's brown eyes were cast at the fine Oriental rug that covered the marble floor beneath them. The only sound was the ticking of the antique clock above the marble fireplace.

Pierre was having a difficult time adjusting to the luxurious surroundings that came with the lifestyle of the prime minister's office. It made the son of a workingman blush sometimes at what he perceived as waste.

"So?" asked Pierre. His hands rested in the lap of his Bill Blass navy-blue pants. He wore an open-necked maroon dress shirt with the sleeves rolled up. It made him feel more relaxed when speaking with Willie. Likewise, his RCMP bodyguards had been dismissed from the room to wait reluctantly in the hallway outside the suite.

"So what?" asked Willie, his tone one of defiance, which he knew pushed Pierre's buttons.

However, being a practiced politician had made Pierre good at concealing his true feelings. "Now let's not start off on the wrong foot, Willie. I'm here to help, not to criticize you."

"You and mother never approved of Cherie," said Willie, his voice angry. He looked up at his father, sitting calmly, watching him. His eyes smoldered with resentment.

Pierre nodded. "Yes, you're right. I don't deny this girl was not good for you; that much is true. But when one of our own is in a crisis situation, we come to their aid. That's what families do, don't you think?"

Willie's shoulders, which had visibly tensed, relaxed and his hazel eyes softened. He nodded. "Yeah, I guess so."

Pierre smiled. "Now that we have that out of the way, I'm told that this matter is getting out of control and it might be time to rein in some of the problems that still exist."

Willie looked quizzically at his father. "What do you mean?"

"I'm told another body has surfaced at the home of a relative of this Bruce Carstairs. My sources tell me he's a suspect in that murder, as well. At least, he's being sought for questioning."

Willie looked momentarily elated at this news, then his eyes narrowed as he contemplated his father. "How do you know all this? There's been nothing on the news."

Pierre smiled but added nothing.

***

"Tommy, its me. Bruce Carstairs." His hands were raised above his head and both he and Trudy were frozen as if they were made of solid ice, though Trudy thought she might melt at any moment.

There was a moment of silence during which Trudy swore she could hear her heart beating inside her chest. A trickle of sweat ran down the side of her head and down her cheek.

"B?" asked the voice, trembling with emotion. "Is it really you?"

"Yeah, buddy, its me," said Bruce, his voice soft. He dropped his hands and turned to face the voice. Trudy clamped her eyes shut, waiting for the sound of a gun going off. It would be very loud in this narrow hallway.

Instead, she heard the sound of heartrending sobs. She opened one eye and stole a quick glance toward the sounds and saw that Bruce had a smaller man in his arms and he was hugging him.

Trudy immediately recognized the slight build and fuzzy curls of Tommy Roper. The musician appeared thinner since the last time she'd seen him, if that were possible.

Why a goddamned folk musician would threaten them with a gun was the real question. But right now he looked in no shape to answer any questions. He was sobbing like a baby.

"Let's get him in the room over here." Trudy pointed to the door Bruce had opened.

He nodded and guided his friend down the hallway, with one massive arm around the singer's shoulders to hold him up. Tommy's blue eyes were red-rimmed and he hadn't shaved for a while. His face had a nest of scraggy stubble. The cocky little bastard she'd met in Newport had evaporated, replaced by a bum.

Trudy led the way as they entered. She touched the wall beside the door and quickly discovered a bank of three switches. She pushed them all upward with the flat of her hand and one light came on.

It was a brown, wooden lamp with a stain-covered shade, sitting atop a cheap wooden end table. Next to the table was a dilapidated, green couch with a multicolored, knitted afghan thrown across it to hide it's age, which it really didn't, as the three worn cushions that made up the seats sagged in the middle.

A small television sat across the room with bunny ears on top. Trudy hadn't seen a set of those in years, though the television looked like it had always had them.

The walls were white, though heavily marked, and the place smelled of age and decay. The bar would have been a better place to stay than this room. She hoped Tommy wasn't paying for the room, because it was quite a sight—that much was certain.

They moved to the couch, where Bruce dropped his friend. Tommy's heavy, woolen, brown sweater reeked of stale beer and cigarettes, and the cheap coffee table in front of them was littered with beer cans.

Tommy must've been on one hell of a bender before we showed up, thought Trudy. I thought Bruce once told me he was a teetotaler, having given up alcohol due to a memory problem a few years back.

When you'd forget everything important to you in one night, then it was probably a good idea to give up the booze. Obviously, he'd started drinking again.

"Do you have any coffee?" asked Bruce. Holding his friend's head in his massive hands, he gazed into the red-rimmed eyes. Through his tears, Tommy nodded toward his right. Trudy squinted in the low light of the single light bulb and saw there was what looked like another room. Must be the kitchen, she thought.

She hurried from the room toward the kitchen and quickly located another switch along the wall. The bulb was brighter in here; at least it allowed her to see the old white appliances. A stove with an unidentifiable substance stuck to one of the elements, a fridge that looked older than her, and a white porcelain sink with rust stains at the bottom.

There on the cracked gray linoleum countertop next to the fridge was a new coffeemaker. A tin of her favorite brand sat next to it. She moved to the coffeemaker, quickly found the filters, and started to brew a pot.

With that done, she made her way back into the living room.

"You found it, I assume," said Bruce, casting her a slight smile. He held his friend in his arms and the man now had both his arms firmly wrapped about Bruce as if he might suddenly disappear.

For all his coarse talk, maybe the guy was a fag. He was, after all, a musician. Bruce must've seen her look because he frowned and shook his head. No, she decided, Tommy wasn't gay, he was scared.

She threw him a disparaging look. They were here for his help, not the other way around. She flopped down on the tattered couch next to them and sighed heavily. She was tired already and they'd only just begun.

"This ain't fucking fair," she said.

"Who said it would be?" asked Bruce.

He cradled Tommy in his arms until the thin musician drifted off into a deep sleep. His snoring would wake the dead, thought Trudy.

Bruce easily lifted the smaller man and carried him to a closed door in the shadows opposite the kitchen. He pushed the doorknob and it swung open. He stuck his head in and nodded, then disappeared inside.

It was dark and Trudy felt a sudden rush of fear that he was out of the room. What if those guys—the ones trying to kill them—came back?

After several tense minutes, Bruce reappeared. His face was creased in thought. She recognized that look. He was formulating something. Probably something she wouldn't like.

"We're staying here until the heat's off. The truck is in the lot at the rear, so no one should see it. We'll wait until Tommy wakes and then decide what to do next."

Trudy knew that there was little she could say. What the hell else could they do? "I'll call Phil," she said. As she moved to stand up, Bruce held up one hand.

"No," he said. "I don't think that would be a good idea right now."

Trudy sighed. "Bruce, I think we need help, and Phil's the only one around right now who can help us."

He shook his head; his length of jet-black hair moved with the motion. "No. No fucking way." He was firm on this issue and she knew it. His mind was made up. She saw a glint in his eyes she'd never seen before. Not even when the previous sheriff of Fairview had held a gun to his head. Fear. This big, tough, pseudo-biker was afraid.

"Then I'm calling Flo, and don't even think about arguing with me. We need help."

He nodded. "I could really use a smoke," he said.

She smiled thinly. "Yeah, me, too," she said and raised one hand to grasp his left shoulder. "We're gonna get through this."

He lowered his eyes and nodded. With his thumbs now hooked on the pockets of his blue jeans, he looked like a big kid. She smiled to herself. *That's why I love this big guy.* Like a brother, she reminded herself. Like a brother.

At least I hope so, she thought.

First thing first, she needed a telephone.

CHAPTER TWENTY-TWO

CARL RICHTER OPENED THE DOOR OF THE BLUE CHEVY and stepped out into the rain-soaked parking lot of the Ambassador Hotel. His partner, Larry Glenn, needed to make a report to the boss. Their twin dark suits, white shirts, and dark ties made them look like that fictional team of alien hunters in that silly movie, or so someone once told Carl.

Carl hated anything stupid—people, movies, television—and wouldn't waste his time with garbage. Garbage needed to be erased from the world, and that was their job. They were the best CSIS hit team in the business.

Disappearing drug bosses, bikers who mysteriously went missing off ferries, and other assorted annoyances were all potential cases for Larry and Carl.

This job, though, was getting messy. Twin body counts and a lot of press coverage was something that made them nervous. The boss wasn't going to like that.

The local dicks were good, maybe too good. They might even pick up their trail. If they had one to follow. They were off the record. Even their pay was off the books, and they'd never even filed an income tax return, nor did they have any record in any federal government computer anywhere.

They did what had to be done to make sure justice was served. The pansy courts weren't doing the job, so they took care of society's ills. Whatever it took.

Side by side, scanning the way ahead with the occasional glance behind them, they made their way into the lobby of the hotel. The desk clerk glanced up as they entered but then quickly returned his eyes to the documents in front of him. He didn't paste his usual phony smile on his sallow features, as he would normally for guests. No, he'd decided these two didn't appreciate good manners, so he wasn't about to share the wealth.

Larry hung back, his arms folded in front of him, watching the people milling about in the lobby. Carl walked up to the desk, his polished leather shoes reflecting the light from the cheap chandelier hanging in the middle of the lobby.

Carl stood in front of the simulated oak reception desk, his hands at his sides.

"Any messages for us?" he asked in his deep voice.

The desk clerk cast a quick glance upward at him. "No, sorry."

Carl nodded then walked away until he was out of earshot of the clerk. He pulled out his cell phone and dialed the number he had memorized. The line rang twice at the other end before a bored male voice answered. "Control."

"This is Foxy Lady. Code twelve two six, scramble."

"Acknowledged. This is W. Thanks."

The proper code words had been given and received. All was well; they were to continue as planned. The expression in his pale blues eyes never flickered. They were dead eyes. No emotion. In their business, emotion got in the way of the job, and that would never do.

He put away his cell then headed for the elevator.

He and his partner entered the elevator to take them to their room on the sixth floor.

The Ambassador was an older hotel off the beaten path. It was comfortable, cheap, and small, with only six floors. They requested and got the top floor in the event a quick exit was required. The fire escape on these older buildings provided a good mode of travel when you need to move fast. It also made a good way to keep a threat in sight.

Carl and Larry's airborne training served them well when those skills were required.

Before opening the door to their room, Carl checked to make sure the hair he'd left to show if someone had disturbed the room was still in place. They'd made it clear to the hotel manager that their room was not to be disturbed. A crisp, new, hundred-dollar bill had secured his cooperation without further questions. Carl smiled at the thought.

Carl would've gone to two hundred, but their guy was a rabbit and readily accepted the bribe. Greedy little shit. Carl would've held out for at least three hundred, but then, he had balls.

The door swung slowly inward. It creaked softly as it moved on its oiled but old hinges. It was a sound normally inaudible to all but the trained ear.

Carl glanced at his partner. He had his right hand inside the left side of his dark suit, no doubt grasping the butt of his 9mm Glock.

It was a good weapon that had proven itself a useful tool in the past. Not this time, though. The mission was to be clean and leave no traceable clues. An ordinary steak knife in the hands of a trained expert, like Larry, is also a deadly weapon. There happened to be about a million knives in the world just like it, making it the perfect weapon. The untraceable, perfect weapon.

No, this would appear to be a murder committed by a person who knows cop procedures. Lowlife criminal gang members seeking to rid themselves of the competition, not highly trained professional killers.

They moved into the room, slowly and stealthily. Carl flicked the light switch near the door and the two double beds with the burnt-orange-and-brown pattern came into view, hurting his eyes just as they had the first time they'd entered this room.

The larger man moved like a cat to the bathroom door.

"You can put it away, Larry."

Apparently satisfied they were alone, Larry stuffed his gun in the shoulder holster then dropped his hand to his side and with practiced ease removed his dark suit jacket then threw the jacket across the room, where it landed on the arm of an overstuffed pea-green chair as if it were meant to be there. He flopped into the chair and picked up the TV Guide next to him on an octagonal-shaped end table made of pressed wood and covered with a dark laminate.

Carl moved to the bed next to a matching end table, where there was a beige telephone and a radio alarm clock with glowing red numbers. He eyed his partner as he dialed the same number as before. The phone line was no doubt scrambled so that even if it were bugged, the eavesdropper would have difficultly trying to translate the pops and whistles they would hear. Static was static.

"Go ahead, Foxy Lady," said a different voice, this time female. Carl hated these code names and secret code phrases, but he also knew they were necessary to a successful mission.

Sometimes he thought someone at headquarters was reading too many bad spy novels.

"Mission objective achieved on code two seven, triangle."

Larry didn't even look up from the guide. Like Carl, he knew they'd be waiting a long time before they received any new missions.

"Roger, Foxy Lady. Please hold."

Carl held his breath. Hold. That had never happened before. Something had changed. He raised one black leather shoe and tapped the side of Larry's leg. The larger of the two men cast him an annoyed glance until Carl mouthed that they were on hold for further instructions.

Larry's face paled and his eyes were suddenly intent upon his fellow operative. The TV Guide had been dropped into his lap.

"You are to proceed to two seven Surrey and observe, but do not engage target. Repeat, do not engage target. Code is orange. I say again, code is orange."

This meant extreme danger was anticipated with this target and extra caution was required.

Carl's pulse quickened. Finally, a target worthy of their skills. He raised his eyebrows at his partner and a grin spread across his face.

Larry mouthed "What?" giving his partner a look of annoyance at having to wait for the answer. Larry must've sensed the rising excitement that had suddenly filled the dank hotel room.

Carl shushed him by holding up one finger as the woman's emotion-free voice again came on the line. "The target is Sergeant Michael Harris, Detective, RCM Police."

CHAPTER TWENTY-THREE

MIKE HUNG UP THE TELEPHONE. What a strange call. He sank back into the comfortable cushions of the ergonomic chair the super had sprung for. It felt good after that old wood piece of shit he had suffered for years. That was the chair that must've been invented for purgatory.

He looked around the room at the other detectives; their heads were down, acting as if they were staring at their computer screens. Looked like a damn video arcade in here. Wonder if anyone needs change?

He smirked, then called to the new kid, Phillips, "Hey, Joey, you wanta get a cup of the thick and dark?"

The crew-cut, red-haired young rookie with the orange freckles that looked like a connect-the-dot game peered over the computer monitor in front of him and smiled. His forehead wrinkled when he did that.

He'd finally learned to leave his tie, which matched his maroon shirt, loose about his neck.

Yeah, thought Mike, ro*okies need an old hand to teach them the ropes.* At least that part of the job hadn't changed in the past twenty years.

Mike rose from behind his ancient oak desk and crossed the room to stand next to Joey Phillips' modern gray workstation.

"Sure. Sounds good," said Joey as he stood and reached for his navy suit jacket hanging off the back of his chair like it was a coat rack.

"You don't need that," said Mike. "We're only goin' as far as the cafeteria."

Joey looked puzzled for a second, then shrugged and followed Mike out into the corridor to the two elevators to the roof of the building, where the cafeteria was. The corridor was deserted except for the two men.

"I know," said Mike, smiling. "I usually like Starbucks, but I don't think we should leave the building right now."

Joey shrugged again and nodded.

They entered the elevator as it arrived, the ancient metal doors opening to admit them. Inside was simulated wood finish on the four walls.

Joey stepped in and Mike followed, his eyes narrowing as he watched the young officer walk to the rear of the car.

He waited until the door was closed before he pushed the button that meant the car would travel to the basement.

Joey looked surprised and Mike could see his hands tremble slightly before his body tensed. He was very much in shape beneath the baggy shirt and pants. It concealed what the kids called today a hard body. Mike knew surprise was the only weapon he really had other than experience.

Not that he wasn't in shape for a guy nearing his mid forties, but he also knew his reflexes weren't what they used to be.

The elevator stopped at the parking level and the doors opened.

"Mike, what the hell is going on?" asked Joey. He, of course, knew perfectly well, but he also knew that Mike was an old-fashioned guy who carried a cannon in his shoulder holster while he'd left his gun in his desk drawer.

"I want to show you something." Mike turned his back on the young officer and walked into the garage. The lighting was low and there were long shadows in every direction. Anyone could be in those shadows.

Joey stepped out and the elevator car doors closed behind him with a deafening slap.

The garage smelled of burnt gasoline and cigarette smoke. Some of the guys who hadn't managed to kick the habit yet liked to come down here and fill their lungs with the poison.

Mike walked quickly across the parking lot and stopped where the cement walls met to form a corner.

He held up one hand to stop Joey, turned, and grinned. "You can come out," he said.

Joey's eyes flitted back and forth. He saw no one until a person far shorter than Mike stepped from behind the corner and stood before them with a serious expression in her eyes.

"Huh…" Joey's eyes flitted between them, "Superintendent…I don't get it, what's going on?"

"Can we trust him?" asked Barbara. She glanced at Mike, her eyes hard and business-like.

Mike nodded. "Yeah, I think so." Mike leaned against the wall, a sardonic grin across his face as he gazed at the young detective.

"Okay, then." She paused to take in a deep breath. "Joey—Detective Phillips," she corrected herself to use his formal job title. Her dark eyes focused on his. "We have a situation, and Mike and I need your help."

Joey threw up his arms in relief. "Well why didn't you just ask…"

"It's not that simple," said Barbara, her voice a sharp whisper as she cut him off. Joey stopped and his jaw line hardened.

"We've been compromised and we think people are being framed for murders they didn't commit for a purpose we don't yet understand."

Joey frowned and gave Mike an enquiring look. Mike pointed at Barbara. "Wait'll you hear the rest. It's a doozy." He smiled and Barbara cast him a damning look to signal him to shut up. Mike just crossed his arms and kept the silly half grin on his face.

"If you help us with this, you can't talk to anyone about it, and I mean no one: not your fellow officers, your friends, your sweetheart, or your family members. You okay with that?"

Joey nodded.

Barbara cast a quick glance at Mike. "Mike and I are being followed because we're involved in the case he's working on and have direct knowledge of those involved. Do you know anything about it?"

"Only what I read in the papers, you know policy, we're…"

"Don't quote me policy, kid, I wrote the fucking thing."

"Sorry." His eyes drifted to the gray cement floor.

"We need someone who's not involved. Someone who can work quietly and without being detected."

"I don't get it. We're the good guys," Joey said. "We're the cops; we stop crime, not the other way around. At least, that's what I learned in cop school."

"Ah, to be so young and naïve," said Barbara with a heavy sigh. Her expression immediately turned serious. "Mike will brief you on the case to date and he'll update on a regular basis with any new information. For now, I expect you to use some of those cop school lessons to find additional clues and find out who's following us and why. For now you report to me through Mike, okay?"

"I have one question," said Joey.

"Yeah," said Barbara, with a trace of impatience in her voice.

"Who do you think it is?"

"I don't know, yet, but I've some suspicions. You just do your job and we'll all get out of this alive."

Joey's eyes widened and he swallowed hard, then looked to Mike for help.

"Don't ask me, kid. You're on the team now." He placed one large, heavily muscled arm around Joey's shoulders and guided the young cop toward the elevators to return to the first floor. Mike had a wry grin fixed to his chiseled features. Joey looked worried.

When they arrived back in the office, Mike had his best bored expression on his face. "Never enough break time around here." Some of the older detectives in the room of ten nodded and sighed as he passed and then went back to the latest report they were working on.

Mike dropped into his chair and put his black leather shoes, shined to a high gloss, on top of his desk with a loud thunk. "Ya know," he said, "I think we should go on strike." He locked his fingers behind his square head and looked wistfully at the white ceiling panels and began to hum softly to himself.

"Hey, Hammer," said Smity, a cop with a large beer belly that made sitting behind his desk a challenge every morning, who sat two desks away. "Knock that fuckin' shit off. I got work to do. Ya may have heard of it, real cop type stuff."

"Fuck you," said Mike happily. Smity rolled his eyes and went back to his hunt-and-peck on his computer keyboard.

Mike glanced at Joey, who raised his shoulders as if to ask him what he was doing. Mike winked slyly. He knew what he was doing. At least, Joey hoped so.

CHAPTER TWENTY-FOUR

<small>PHIL ANSWERED HIS CELL PHONE AFTER THE SECOND RING.</small>
"Singh."

"Phil?" It was Trudy.

"Oh, hi," he glanced around the coffee shop table at the other two detectives he was sitting with. He hoped he didn't look suspicious. "Hi, Rav, what's new?" He placed one hand over the phone's mouthpiece and mouthed it was his sister and excused himself from the table.

"What…?"

"Hold on, will ya?"

He quickly made it to the lobby of the building where there were people bustling by on their everyday lives. The world seemed to slow down for him. He was risking his job and probably everything else in his life even talking to Trudy right now. But, Flo…

"I'll call you back on a land line," Phil said, his voice barely above a whisper. There was silence on the other end of the line, then Trudy gave him the number.

He closed his cell and hurried across the stone floor of the lobby to a bank of four pay phones.

He reached into his trouser pockets and found he was out of change. The phone didn't take credit cards, but that was okay—he couldn't use one, anyway. Traceable. He searched in his navy suit jacket but he didn't have any coins in there, either.

He hurried back into the coffee shop and found the two other detectives embroiled in the latest hockey controversy. The place smelled of freshly brewed bean. He was a tea drinker, mostly, but the coffee still smelled good. Was he being a fool? Should he just forget about her and go back to his normal routine? He shook off the feeling. No, it wouldn't be right.

He stood over the two men. "One of you guys gotta quarter?"

They both looked at him quizzically. "Cell's dead," he said sheepishly.

Troy, the older of the two, reached into his pants and pulled two from his pocket. He tossed them on the table, where they clattered across the smoked, shatterproof glass top.

Damn thing showed every fingerprint of everyone who had come in the place for the last twenty-four hours. It was a standard joke among the detectives that they should always dust the place first if a crime was committed.

Phil hesitated, thinking about that joke, then picked up one of the coins and thanked Troy. Troy nodded and told him to knock himself out, then went back in the heated battle concerning the latest trades and who was the best player among the ones traded.

Phil hurried back in the lobby and was relieved the bank of phones was still unoccupied.

He inserted the coin and dialed the number. The phone rang once, then Trudy's breathless voice came on the line. "Hello?"

"Trudy, it's me. Phil."

He heard her muffled call to someone, then her voice came on the line. She sounded afraid.

"You okay?" he whispered.

"Why are you whispering?" she asked, sounding distracted.

"Wouldn't you be if you were talking to someone that every cop on the planet is looking for?"

"Oh…yeah…of course."

"What the hell is going on? You two are leaving a trail of bodies behind you a mile wide." He was getting annoyed now, so he checked himself and took in a deep breath of air.

"What do you mean?" asked Trudy.

"Do you recall reading in my file about that guy Logan, Spike Logan?" He didn't wait for a response. "He's been found floating in the Fraser River. Whoever put him there tied his hands and feet and tried to weight him down with a couple of cement bricks. Needless to say, it didn't work. And let me tell you, a body that's been in the river as long as he has isn't a pretty sight."

Phil could almost hear Trudy go white because of the silence on the other end of the line. Bruce came on the phone.

"What the fuck is that about Spike?" he asked, his voice angry. Phil didn't need this shit. He started to say something he'd probably regret, but stopped himself.

He'd be upset if his only alibi was gone, as well.

"You know what this means, don't you?" said Bruce.

Even though he couldn't see them, Phil nodded. "Yeah. Someone's cleaning house." His mouth hung open as he spoke and realization came over him, causing his hands to tremble. His family might be next.

He felt the rising panic inside him as he thought of his wife and kids, floating in the river facedown like Spike, or with a knife sticking from their backs like Bruce's cousin. He pushed the thoughts away. No, that wasn't going to happen—not while he had breath in his body.

***

The last of the day had receded as the sun dropped below the horizon and the first of the stars began to appear when Joey spotted the dark, four-door sedan with the two figures inside.

He was hunkered down behind the steering wheel of his Honda, a place he'd been for several hours, parked on the tree-lined street outside Mike's apartment. Mike was inside with the lights on and the television blaring, waiting for Joey to call him. The interior of his car smelled of stale coffee and donuts. A real cop's car, he smirked.

He flipped open his cell and hit the red "send" button. He'd had the number on the little liquid crystal screen ready to go in a moment's notice in case something went wrong. The line rang once and Mike's voice came on. Since he had caller ID, he knew who it was immediately.

"Yeah."

"Mike, there's two guys in an unmarked Chevy watching your place. I think they're waiting for you to leave so they can follow you."

"Okay, I'm gonna go out for dinner at Herbie's Place. You know it?"

"Yeah. On Twelfth Ave, isn't it?"

Herbie's was a little greasy spoon that Mike liked. Not exactly fine dining, but the food was decent. Being a single guy for so long meant Mike wasn't big on cooking for one.

Joey thought about his girlfriend, Alice. Damn, she's a good cook. Italian girls usually were pretty handy in the kitchen; their mommas made them that way.

"Yeah. You follow." Joey was going to take an alternate route and park two blocks from the restaurant, then walk the rest of the way. There was a coffee bar across the street where he'd sit and keep an eye on them. It was a risky plan if they planned to take Mike out right on the way, but it couldn't be helped. "I expect these guys are very good, so be careful."

Joey flipped his phone closed. The lights inside Mike's apartment went out immediately.

He waited, feeling rising excitement in his gut until he saw Mike exit through the front door of the four-story walk-up. It was an older building, built in the '60s. The front door was an oak-and-glass type, with a metal bar across it that ran corner to corner. The outside of the building was gray stucco with embedded sparkles of shiny sand.

The rows of large picture windows offered the residents a good view of the street.

Mike walked to his red Corvette and unlocked the driver's door with the keys that were already in his right hand. The car was a '70s model, fire-engine red with a tan interior. The gull wing shape wasn't Joey's favorite model of the car, but it was powerful, with faster than average pickup from a standing start.

Joey heard the quiet of the street interrupted by the rumble as the Corvette's V8 engine came to life. For emphasis, Mike tapped the gas pedal twice and the engine noises echoed off the low-rise apartment buildings that lined Oxford Street.

As expected, Mike didn't glance in Joey's direction as he put the 'Vette in gear. He let the clutch out and pulled away from the curb, and the powerful car seemed to leap forward like a caged animal now released.

Joey watched as the dark sedan started its engine and the headlights came on. The car pulled away as Mike approached the end of the street, where there was an intersection.

Joey could see the tag number on the sedan and he wrote it down in the notebook that sat on the passenger seat of the Honda.

He waited until the two cars were gone and silence was again over the street before he started the little car's engine. It purred in comparison to the two larger cars that had just pulled away.

He smiled and shifted the car into gear and slowly let the clutch out. He drove to the corner and made a right. The other two cars would've turned left here, taking the more direct route.

Yeah, he thought, these guys are good, but we're better.

As they'd pre-arranged, he soon arrived at the place where they agreed he'd park. It was outside a row of small retail shops on Broadway. Mike would already be at Herbie's, two blocks over on Twelfth. He locked the driver's door of his sky-blue Honda—the other doors were already secured—and walked the two blocks.

Not too quickly, as Mike instructed him, so as to appear out on an evening stroll. The air was pleasant tonight, filled with the smell of flowers from the flower boxes that lined the street. The city made a point of decorating during the tourist season. That was over now, but the locals would reap the benefits for a while yet.

The coffee shop had six white plastic tables out front, surrounded by matching chairs. Joey went inside and ordered a small coffee. The pretty young blonde behind the counter smiled warmly as he paid.

He grinned and nodded his thanks, then went back outside and sat at one of the tables.

At one of the other tables were two dark-haired men in blue jeans and plaid work shirts. They wore matching waist-length navy windbreakers, unzipped and hanging open. They each wore what appeared to be brand-new brown leatherwork boots.

He would've thought they were twins except one was considerably larger than the other. They didn't acknowledge him as he sat down. They were talking to each other in low tones.

They look like lumberjacks, he thought, except the shirts looked freshly pressed. He noted that their hair was cut military-style short, like army crew cuts. He pondered that for a second, shrugged, and lifted the paper coffee cup to his mouth and took a sip of the hot, black liquid. It tasted freshly roasted, something he appreciated.

Cops love fresh brew.

He glanced at Herbie's across the street and saw Mike sitting in a booth by the window, apparently reading a newspaper. Good, he'd look relaxed to the two tails.

Scanning the area, he didn't see the sedan they'd come in. Maybe Mike lost them. No, that couldn't be, as Mike said these guys were pros and they knew how to tail a guy.

He sat for a while, wondering what he should do next. He decided to call Mike. He flipped out his cell and dialed Mike's number. He glanced up to see Mike put down his paper and pull his cell phone out.

"Hello?"

"Mike, I don't see the two guys anymore. I think maybe you lost 'em."

Rookies. "Not possible. They'll show. Don't you worry."

"Okay." Joey flipped his phone closed and put it back in the holster on his belt. He didn't have a jacket on; it was too warm for that. Consequently, he didn't have his gun on him; it was secured in the glove compartment of the Honda.

The light had completely faded now and the seating area was dark except for the interior lights of the coffee shop. He glanced at the table where the two-pseudo lumberjacks were and saw they were gone. He smirked.

Still no sign of the two tails. What had happened to them? Maybe they weren't as good as Mike seemed to think they were.

"Don't move," said a husky voice behind him. He tensed as he felt what could only be a pistol barrel being held against his neck. "One sound will be your last," said the voice.

"Okay," said Joey, his voice tight. He wasn't afraid, just startled at being spotted. It had to be the two marks they'd been following.

"Get up."

The inducement was increased pressure of the pistol barrel on his neck. He stood and was shoved forward lightly by a large hand in the middle of his back. He heard another set of booted footsteps.

There were two of them.

It could only be them.

Joey thought he might try to take them on, but the gun in his neck would make any fight a short one. He relaxed his body as he realized he had no choice in the matter. Surely they wouldn't kill a cop. No one was that stupid.

He was herded to the rear of the coffee shop; an unlit alley smelled of urine and rotting garbage where he stopped and stood, his hands hanging loose against his sides.

"Well, what now?" he asked after several seconds of waiting. No sound except the disembodied bark of a dog a long way off. He slowly turned his head and saw he was alone.

He heard sirens. The cops in this patrol zone were converging on them. Not that it would've mattered. Like many murders all they would've been in time for was to take the crime scene photos and put up the yellow police tape at either end of the alley. He frowned. A sense of relief washed over him. This had been a warning.

These guys were good, scary good, too good. They weren't cops, that much was certain. They were better than cops. And he hadn't even seen them. Now he was mad, and Joey didn't like being mad. And he didn't relish having to tell Mike he was right about these two.

"Fucking assholes," he breathed.

CHAPTER TWENTY-FIVE

PIERRE LAVOIS SAT IN THE OFFICE OF THE HEAD OF CSIS for the Pacific Region. Pat Reynolds, his roommate and best friend at Carlton University, was the same age as Pierre but looked considerably older. His baldpate with a fringe of black and gray hair and facial wrinkles the size of the Fraser Canyon were evidence that the intervening years hadn't been kind.

Right now his gray eyes sparkled as he gazed at his old chum. They hadn't seen each other in the past five years, and the new prime minister's visit was a welcome change to his usual humdrum days. Not being in central Canada, replete with its power brokers, meant that his days could be long and uneventful.

The only external threats to national security here were drugs and Asian gangs. His small force kept the lines open to their counterparts in Asia and on the American west coast.

"Pierre, it's so nice to see you again," said Pat, his hairless face split in a grin.

Pierre smiled warmly. "Yes, my old friend, I share your sentiments. I am, however, here on a matter of some urgency and…" He hesitated and leaned forward, the smile disappearing like an early morning haze from his pale skin. "Is our conversation being recorded?"

Pat nodded. "We record everything around here." He eased back in his high-backed leather chair to contemplate his friend. The chair was new; Pierre could smell the leather from across the dark oak desk. The white wall behind Pat contained a number of plaques with RCMP crests and a half dozen framed certificates citing him for various recognition awards.

The soundproof room was windowless. Not surprising, its location was in the basement of the Bentall Tower number three, of four. CSIS needed to be out of sight and out of mind, so their location was kept low profile and away from other police operations. The press didn't know about this place, and Pierre's driver had stopped outside the freight elevator to let him ride to the basement level. Wellman had led him to the proper unmarked door. He sat ten feet away from where the two men were, in the outer waiting room reading an outdated issue of People magazine.

"I want this conversation to remain between us alone," said Pierre.

Pat frowned and steepled his fingers, his elbows resting on the cushioned arms of his executive chair. His striped red power tie and white shirt made him look like most executives, except his job was to stop terrorism or other international crimes from infiltrating Canadian society. It was something he was very good at.

"Okay," he said, after several seconds of studying his friend's serious expression. This was against the rules and the boss could technically fire him for this, but he trusted his friend and knew he wouldn't be asking if it wasn't important.

He reached for a button underneath his desktop. It would shut off the cameras and microphones hidden in the walls of the room. All except his personal record, one the CO didn't know about, which didn't form part of the official record. "Always cover your ass" was the motto in government circles. One of the certificates behind him on the wall was a fake with a pin camera in one of the large dark letters built into it. That one would keep going and go into his personal files, just in case.

"Okay, we can talk."

Pierre's shoulders visibly relaxed. The tension in his shoulders eased and he smiled again. "Thank you, Pat. I knew I could count on you." He paused to collect his thoughts. What he needed from Pat was highly unethical, but they were the only two people on the planet that had to know.

Pat studied Pierre quizzically. Here was the prime minister of Canada, who needed the services of a minor station chief of a backwater like Vancouver. Yes, they were old friends, and maybe, just maybe, he'd get a juicy favor in return, depending what his old pal wanted of him. He'd eagerly anticipated Pierre's arrival after his assistant had called him this morning. This was very unexpected.

"It's this business with my son."

Pat nodded. He knew of the case from reading the papers. It was a local matter and not something his section would normally get involved in. The inspector in charge of the SCU had called him a couple of days ago, complaining about his office interfering in her officer's investigation of the murder, or as it had become, the string of murders. Of course, he denied any of his officers were making any enquiries, which as far as he knew, was true. Certainly not on his orders. It seemed that fact might be about to change.

It seemed to him that, other than the PM's son's wife, most had been scum-of-the-earth types that very few people would miss. Now suddenly the PM needed him to straighten out this mess.

"How can I help?" asked Pat.

"I need your team to make some enquires with your U.S. contacts and find out more about this biker. I think the name was Bruce Carstairs. He's been thus far able to elude capture since they let him out on bail. You know these liberal courts these days."

Pat shrugged and smiled. Yeah, he knew it only too well. Democracy had its price, and a soft judiciary was one of them.

"Yeah, I think I can do that. What exactly were you hoping to find out? I know the type; most of them are heavily involved in organized crime. You know: prostitution, drugs, gambling, liquor, and the usual stuff. I doubt you'd find anything remarkable about this guy."

Pierre shifted uncomfortably in his seat. Pat knew it was well padded, so it wasn't physical discomfort that was bothering Pierre.

"There's something different about him. He's got a friend helping him. Someone on the inside. Someone who knows more than your average run-of-the-mill biker should. I want to know who that person is, because I suspect there is more than one lone wolf biker behind his sudden disappearance from radar."

Pat contemplated his friend. He knew him well, and even behind the politician's shield—the one he'd erected in order to hide his true feelings and thoughts—Pat was able to see the eager idealist university student he used to be.

He had been able read that guy then, and right now he knew Pierre was only telling him part of the story. There was much more behind all this that Pierre wasn't telling him. He decided to play along for the moment and see where it led. Besides, with no "official" record of this meeting, he had plausible deniability on his side.

"Yes, Pierre, I'll help you," Pat said finally, his dark eyes studying the PM's face. Pierre looked visibly relieved at his friend's agreement.

He eased back in the chair and sighed. "You don't know what that means to me," he said. "I'll pay you back, old friend, don't you worry."

"I was hoping you'd say that," said Pat with a smile. Pierre grinned. Being prime minister had its privileges. No doubt some of his ministers hated the fact he selected a low-level station chief like Pat, who was also his old college pal, suddenly vaulted to the seat of power, but as far as he was concerned they could all go to hell. He was the PM not them.

Pat said he would contact him by tomorrow morning at the latest with the information concerning the biker. Then the two men agreed to share lunch together in the dining room of the Vancouver Hotel and catch up on each other's lives.

***

Wellman studied the pictures of the Hollywood elite's toothy smiles as they partied at some inane awards event that was designed to give the simpletons a chance to strut the latest Bill Blass tuxedo or Versace gown. Pasty-faced creeps, he thought. Got nothin' better to do.

He glanced at his watch and sighed. It had been almost an hour since they'd arrived in this dark hole in the ground. Why couldn't the secret organizations have their offices on the twentieth floor? A view would be nice for a change.

No, they had to live in the dark corners away from the light. Intelligence, he smirked. Oxymoron when it involved the cops. They were such dumb-asses who knew nothing about real justice.

Justice was best left to real men like the ones who were busy cleaning up the mess that Willie had created. The PM expected Wellman to fix the PM's son's mistakes without ever telling him how he did it. One day Wellman knew he would be rewarded for his loyalty.

He was expecting a call soon to tell him that the situation was under control. Those meddling SCU types would soon be off the case and then the investigation would die on the vine and be placed in the unsolved file forever. After that, there were just two more loose ends that needed to be taken care of.

The boys would make sure that was done, then they could move on to the next mission and he'd be secured in his post for the foreseeable future. He eyes narrowed and a twisted grin spilt his dark complexion. Power was an aphrodisiac and something once gained was hard to give up. The PM would keep him close.

He hoped the old man was almost finished; he was getting hungry.

The door opened and Pierre Lavois came out followed by the CSIS guy, whom he didn't recognize, laughing and joking about their school days. Inside, Wellman grimaced, but he kept his face impassive and looked on with mild interest like a good assistant.

"Wellman, I'd like you meet one of my oldest friends, Pat Reynolds." Pierre stepped aside and the balding man with the wide grin on his face stuck out his hand in greeting. Wellman smiled thinly and shook the man's hand. It was firm and dry.

"Wellman, here, is my executive assistant. Kind of a walking appointment book, if you will."

Wellman nodded, keeping the thin smile on his face as if he didn't care what the prime minister called him.

In the very near future, things were going to change around here, and then the PM wouldn't be joking about him in front of his friends anymore.

"Wellman, use that cell phone of yours to get us a reservation at Griffith's for lunch." Wellman glanced at his watch. It was eleven thirty; that would make it difficult on a Friday to get a reservation. Griffith's was one of the finest restaurants in the city and was in high demand for the local business crowd on Fridays.

Pierre shook his head and glanced at Pat. "I am the prime minister of Canada, after all…"

Wellman caught his meaning and immediately dialed the number of the desk at the hotel. The concierge would make it happen. If not, heads would roll; that much was certain.

Pierre laughed and Pat joined in as the two men headed for the door. Wellman followed, still on his cell phone, berating the hotel desk clerk to put the concierge on the line immediately. They would get their table, even if it pissed off everyone at the hotel, or he wasn't much of an assistant. And of course, he'd get another table close by. Being the man behind the power gave him certain privileges. He smiled inwardly.

CHAPTER TWENTY-SIX

MIKE STARED AT JOEY FROM ACROSS HIS DESK, his expression glum. Joey sat slumped in the chair, his head back and eyes closed. He wasn't asleep, but like Mike himself, the kid looked damn tired. His hands were stuffed in the pockets of his faded blue jeans. Mike was staring at the coffee stain down the front of Joey's navy-blue Harvard sweatshirt, with a hood behind his head that he was using as a pillow.

Mike's red-rimmed eyes testified to the fact that he, too, needed some sleep, but what had happened earlier in this long evening had unsettled both detectives' nerves. How the hell had the sons of bitches gotten wind of the tail? Were they so good they could pick up a tail that wasn't following them? It didn't make sense. They'd been careful in planning this, how had they failed? The super wasn't going to be happy.

Joey thought the two sets of footsteps could've been faked, but Mike didn't think so. No, the car definitely contained two men, and they were definitely following Mike.

These guys were way beyond his league and one thing was certain: they could take both of them out before they could do anything to stop them. This bothered Mike. He was a cop, damn it, and a good one, and he didn't like being toyed with.

The incident in the alley made him realize they were being sent a message to back off on the case, or else. Whatever the "or else" was, it certainly wasn't milk and cookies. Mike glanced at the wall clock, with its white face and black numbers and dashes. The hands moved slowly across the face, counting down the seconds as it neared three a.m. They would make their report to the inspector at seven, when she arrived.

"Joey," he said slowly.

Joey's head dropped to rest on his chest, his dark eyes, with the matching dark circles beneath them, looked into his.

"You gotta get off this case, and I mean right now." He'd been saying this, like a broken record, for the past two hours; but the young detective wasn't being pushed out the door no matter what he said. The younger man wanted to see it through to the end. He was mad and wanted to get even with the bastards who had threatened him.

Mike was sure the kid's pride would get him killed one of these days, and he didn't want that weighing on his conscientious if this was the case that ended the young guy's career permanently.

"Mike, I don't give a shit. I'm not letting those sons of bitches scare me off." To punctuate his point, Joey suddenly drove his fist into the top of Mike's desk with a loud thump that echoed off the still walls. The plastic file trays stacked three high jumped off the desk, spilling paper in a torrent across the desk.

They were alone, after all, so Mike let it pass without comment.

He leaned forward to rest on his arms. "Look, kid, we've covered this already. These guys are obviously far better trained than we are and they will kill both of us if we aren't careful."

Mike thought he could smell the anger from Joey. His eyes were wide and the look on his face was like one of those scary kids' Halloween masks, or those psycho wrestlers on TV, except his was all too real.

"I said I don't give a shit," said Joey angrily. He was losing it, the kid was getting under his skin, or maybe he was right. "I'm not gonna let you take these guys on alone."

Mike sighed and leaned back. As he did, he picked up an orange, wooden pencil and ran it between his fingers like a cigarette. It was at times like this that he regretted quitting the filthy habit. His eyes dropped to the floor, then he lifted them to gaze into the kid's. "Who said anything about me working alone?" He'd dreaded this all night. They were about to open a door that should remain locked, or at least ajar. Their careers, and maybe their lives, were on the line.

Joey's expression relaxed. "What are you talking about?"

"I have an idea who might be able to help, and it's risky. Kinda like working with the enemy."

"What…?"

Mike leaned forward and dropped the pencil with a clatter on his desk. It rolled across to fall off the other side onto the tiled floor as if to punctuate the tension in the room.

"If I tell you what I have in mind, there's no going back. Understand?"

Joey nodded, his interest piqued.

"Okay, here's my plan…"

They spend the next three hours going over the details.

They argued some of the points back and forth, like two matadors fighting the bull in the ring, until Barbara arrived.

The three sat in her office discussing the final plan. They argued with her and Mike assured her it would work. She nodded as they left her office.

"And close the door behind your sorry asses!" she shouted at them as they left her office.

Joey's expression when they left her office had morphed into a wide smile. He looked like some kid on Christmas morning, finding that much-wanted item under the tree.

Mike's expression was grim and he could see Barbara shaking her head in wonderment through the glass door to her office. They turned and walked back into the squad room full of amazed Mounties. They weren't used to the boss getting mad at any of the officers. She was a team player and understood the tough choices cops made everyday to get the job done.

What the rest of the room didn't know was that the plan, once activated, could mean the end of hers and Mike's and Joey's careers.

If things went really bad, a nice funeral courtesy of the taxpayer, thought Mike. The chances of this succeeding seemed slim and none.

Barbara picked up her telephone receiver and made the call that would get the ball rolling. Her hands trembled ever so slightly, then solidified as she pushed each button, not from fear but from anger and resentment. She didn't want to be a cop anymore if this was the way things were going to be. She knew the phone was tapped. It was a fact she counted on. Whoever was listening was about to get an earful.

Five miles away, Phil Singh picked up the telephone's receiver from its cradle on top of the radio alarm clock on the nightstand next to his bed.

He hesitated and glanced through narrow, sleep-filled slits at the alarm clock on the nightstand. The glowing red numbers showed that it was just past seven thirty in the morning. Who the hell was calling him this early and on his day off?

"Hello," he said in a hoarse whisper. He cleared his throat.

"Is this detective Philip Singh of the Vancouver PD?"

He didn't recognize the voice, though Mike once told him his new commanding officer was a woman. Could this be her? If so, why would she be calling him? He sat up and moved to the edge of the bed, dropping his bare feet to the ornate, imitation Persian throw rug on the floor.

Ranjit, sleeping peacefully beside him, stirred slightly but remained in dreamland. He rolled his eyes. Thank God for small mercies. He didn't need to explain why strange women were calling him at home. It had been bad enough when Flo Henderson called about Trudy until he'd explained how he knew the Sheriff of Fairview. He'd never given his wife reason to suspect him of infidelity and he wasn't going to start now.

"Yeah, this is he," he said in a whisper, cupping the receiver in one hand.

'This is Inspector Barbara Kelso of the Serious Crimes Unit, RCMP. We need to talk. Can you come down to my office today?"

Phil knew Mike worked for the SCU, so this had to be his boss. What would she want with him?

"What's this about?"

"I'll explain when you get here. Please, Detective, it's important."

He sighed. When someone of her stature used his title, it was almost an unwritten rule you had to be courteous in kind. And the Mounties needed his help to boot? Well, that was just too much of a temptation.

"Yeah, okay, I can be there in an hour." He knew the way to the RCMP Surrey detachment.

"Look forward to it," said Kelso and the line went dead.

Phil stared at the receiver for several seconds, then shook his head and hung it up on the top of the radio alarm clock.

Ranjit, lying face down on the pillow, her head to one side, murmured, then one sleepy eye opened. "Going somewhere?" she murmured, her voice partly muffled by the pillow. He smelled her perfume-scented skin and momentarily hesitated. He could simply ignore the inspector's phone call. Or could he?

He rose from their queen-sized bed to stand beside it in his blue striped boxers and white tee shirt, his favorite sleeping attire. "Yeah, sorry. I have an appointment in an hour. Shouldn't take long."

"Okay," she said with a small sigh. Such was the life of a cop's wife—a role she'd long ago come to accept. The one eye closed. She'd be up in another half hour to get the boys off to school.

Damn, she's a fine woman, he thought as he strode to the en suite bathroom, where he'd have a quick shower and shave.

***

Phil arrived at the Surrey RCMP detachment with five minutes to spare. He'd even had time to drive the boys to school. He parked his car in the lot and headed toward the entrance. Before he got to the twin smoked glass doors, Mike Harris intercepted him and held his right arm in an iron grip.

"You don't wanna go in there," said Mike, his face a grim mask.

"I don't?"

Mike shook his head.

"Then where do I want to go?"

"With me."

Mike let go of Phil's arm and hurried down the three cement stairs as if a ghost were chasing him. He glanced back, his gaze fixed on some unseen enemy. His black leather cowboy boots barely touched the steps, he moved so quickly. He was headed back toward the path leading to the parking lot. Phil, his head still swimming with the suddenness of Mike's harried appearance, followed. He very nearly had to run to keep up with the big man.

Once in the parking lot, they got into Mike's red Corvette and were soon out onto the main road to the sound of screeching tires as Mike stepped hard on the accelerator.

"Whoa, buckaroo," said Phil, his fingers wrapped in an iron grip on the door handle. They were slumped low in the bucket seats, but with a glance at the speedometer, Phil could see they were quickly passing sixty miles per hour. The car was built before kilometers were the standard of measurement for a car's speed. All he knew was that, regardless of how you measured it, they were going too damn fast.

The car fishtailed slightly as they rounded a curve leading into the tunnel of tall fir trees that lined both sides of the road. Mike's angry eyes flitted to either side of the road, and as the car straightened out, he again stomped hard on the accelerator, leaving a rooster tail of fallen leaves in their wake.

"Mike, is this really necessary?" asked Phil, who by now figured his life had passed before his eyes at least twice already. The intersection with the traffic light was just ahead. Mike didn't say anything; instead, he kept his eyes fixed on the road ahead.

As they approached the intersection, the light changed to yellow. Phil was certain Mike would try to blow through, but he must've decided the risk was too great because he suddenly hit the brake pedal hard and the car's nosed dipped.

Phil was thrown hard against the seat belt he'd been smart enough to put on.

The brakes screamed and Phil could smell the burnt rubber of the tires as the car gradually slowed. Phil looked up to see they were fast sliding toward the lights that were now red. Mike must've seen it too, and come to the same conclusion. They weren't going to stop in time. Phil watched a full-sized station wagon, complete with a big blond dog and three kids, come into the intersection in front of them. Now what the hell were they supposed to do?

Phil glanced at Mike, who gripped the wheel so tightly his knuckles were blood red. The glint in his eye told Phil that Mike didn't like to lose. Phil hoped Mike never lost anything he was determined to beat as he felt the car accelerate.

***

Carl stepped out of the four-door Chevy sedan onto the pavement. His work boots felt like they didn't fit right. Kind of tight around the ankle. He glanced at his partner Larry as he exited the passenger side of the plain-Jane automobile. Carl decided that the next time they rented a car when on a mission, he would get it. Larry was too conservative. A damn, plain blue Chevy was like saying, "hey, we're a couple of cops" or something. Even though they weren't cops, at least not real ones, anyone looking at the plainness of the car with its black-wall tires would certainly think so.

And these outfits. Lumberjacks, for God's sake. Larry was a real dumb-ass. Carl shook his head in disgust. First time he comes to B.C., and Larry seems to think everyone here is a lumberjack or a fisherman. At least they didn't smell like fish. *Thank God for small graces,* thought Carl.

He walked around the front of the car to the sidewalk and stood gazing down the street. Nope, no tail. Okay. He nodded to Larry as the big man turned to look at him. He'd been checking the opposite side of the street for the same thing. He nodded and the two men walked into the lobby and scanned it as well. Once they were satisfied, they hurried into the elevator and waited until the doors closed to say anything to each other.

"You like these duds," said Carl.

Larry shrugged his broad shoulders. "Yeah. Kinda comfortable, don't ya think?"

Carl rolled his eyes and they rode in silence to their floor, where they exited and headed down the hallway to the room they shared. The housekeeper passed them with her cart containing stacks of plain white towels, toilet paper, soap, cleaning supplies, and a cloth basket to hold the dirty linens she collected each day. She smiled thinly as the two men passed her. They acknowledged her with a nod, but their expressions remained passive.

She glanced at them and frowned. They hadn't asked to have their room cleaned once in the four days they'd been at the hotel. They'd left instructions with the front desk that their room was not to be cleaned unless they asked for it. They insisted no one enter the room unless they were there. Thus far, they'd not called for anything but food. She decided that the next time they were out, instructions or not, she was going to clean their room. Otherwise, when they left, there would be a real mess for her that could take up her whole day and mean other guests would suffer. Her responsibility was to make all the guests happy with their rooms, not just these two macho creeps.

She hurried away to the next room on her list.

Carl scanned the door and found the hair intact, as usual, in the doorframe. He slipped the key into the lock. Larry went in first, followed by Carl.

Carl locked and dead-bolted the door behind them. The so-called locks wouldn't hold up to a frontal assault, something they knew very well, but if someone kicked in the door, this might give the milliseconds they'd need to get their weapons out.

Carl moved to the bed and picked up the telephone while Larry slipped off his navy-blue windbreaker and flopped into the overstuffed chair across the room. He rested his meaty hands on the arms of the chair and stared vacantly at his partner.

Carl dialed the number as before. After two rings, a female voice came on the line. Must be the guy's day off, thought Carl. Wish we got one of those sometime.

"Foxy Lady, code one, two, seven, razor, orange," said Carl into the receiver. The code was changed every day, and every day Carl would memorize the new day's access code.

"You're on scramble. Go ahead, Foxy Lady."

"We observed the target and did not engage; however, there was a complication." Carl hesitated and glanced up at Larry, who shrugged his broad shoulders. That made his leather shoulder holster, with the butt of his 9mm showing, move against his massive chest. He patted the gun and flashed Carl an evil smile.

"We were followed and had to send a warning to the tail. We think it was local law."

The line was silent for several seconds and Carl almost thought the line dead when the woman spoke again. Her tone suggested she wasn't thrilled with this new development.

"Got that, Foxy Lady. Hold position for further instructions."

The line went dead with a resounding click. This meant they were to wait at the hotel until they were contacted by control. The people in charge, whoever they were—sometimes Carl wondered if they were the they everyone always talked about in the abstract—would decided what Carl and Larry would do next. One thing was for sure: their lives were suddenly more complicated.

Carl replaced the receiver in its cradle. "They said we were to wait for instructions. We'll have to order room service again."

Larry rolled his dark eyes and began to loosen the laces of the brown leatherwork boots he wore. "What's on the fuckin' tube?" he asked, annoyance evident in his deep voice.

They'd been eating in for the past several days and Larry had told his partner earlier he hoped they could try one of the local restaurants. He already had one picked out. Chinese place with the mundane name of Hong Kong Palace.

"Sorry, pal, but us being tailed by that punk cop complicated things," said Carl, who'd also stopped to take off his boots. "What do you want?"

They'd seen the menu so many times they knew it by heart. Nonetheless, Larry always ordered the same thing. "Cheeseburger," he said in a monotone voice.

Carl rolled his eyes. Why couldn't Larry try something else? Carl'd tried the pasta and a steak and ... yeah, he'd tried the cheeseburger. In this fleabag, it was the best thing on the menu.

"Yeah. I think I'm gonna have the same thing," Carl smirked. He hit the button for room service. A friendly female voice came on.

He ordered the food and two cokes to wash it down and then sauntered to the television and flipped it on.

The batteries in the remote control were gone due to Larry's insistence that commercials had to be exorcised from programs by flipping the channel each time one came on.

He pulled the shiny metal "on" button and the box came to life. The late news was on and they stared at it dull-eyed, waiting until one of those late night talk shows would come on. They both like those, though Larry complained every time a commercial came on. One thing about those shows was they had a lot of commercials, and they seemed to run at the same point in each show.

As the news was ending and the sports guy was on summarizing the latest baseball scores, there was a knock at the door.

Carl moved to the door and engaged the metal bar across the post to make sure no one could surprise him. Larry had his holster off now and the butt of his automatic sticking in the seat cushion next to him as a precaution. In their business, caution was second nature.

Carl peeked through the crack in the door and saw a man in a waiter's uniform with a white table-cloth-covered cart with two silver-colored metal tops and two bubbling glasses of coke. Everything looked normal, so he stepped back and disengaged the metal bar.

The door swung open and the waiter smiled broadly, his perfect white teeth glowing in the lights of the hallway.

"Room service," he said cheerily.

"Yeah," said Carl as he stepped back to let the waiter into the room.

The waiter wore the usual white shirt and bow tie, but his blue jeans seemed out of place.

"Missed a laundry day, did we, pal?"

The waiter smiled warmly at Carl's attempt at sarcasm. "Sorry, sir, how did you know?"

Carl smiled wryly and Larry removed his meaty fingers from the butt of his hidden pistol and turned his attention to the TV as the music signaled the start of the late night show. Carl stopped suddenly and started at the waiter. "Say, didn't I just see you on TV? The news...."

Silently, before he could say anything more, the waiter lifted one of the two metal covers off the white china plates to reveal a large, black pistol with a silencer attached to the barrel lying on the plate.

Carl's eyes went wide as he realized they'd been had. He started to say something to warn his partner, but was cut short by the report of the gun as it went off in the small hotel room with a muffled thump. Larry stared at the bloody, dark red gash that appeared in the middle of his chest. His eyes rolled back in his head and he slumped forward in the chair.

Carl stared at the barrel of the gun as it was turned in his direction. He heard it fire again, just before a dark hole appeared in the center of his forehead like a third eye. His last thoughts were ripped away from him as the bullet traveled through his brain and out the back of his head to create a decorative spray of blood and brain matter on the door behind him.

He fell backward from the force of the impact to land on his back on the short, blue shag carpet. Blood gushed from the wound in the back of his head, quickly creating a dark stain on the floor. His heart would soon realize his brain was no longer sending signals and that, too, would stop.

After engaging the pistol's safety and donning a pair of white surgical gloves, the waiter stooped over one of the men and released his pistol from its holster, then replaced it with the one he'd just used to kill them after wiping it clean of his prints and removing the silencer.

He pulled the white shirt he wore out of the waist of his blue jeans and slipped the gun into the waistband in the small of his back. He then pulled a white cloth handkerchief from his right pocket and wiped down the lid of the metal cover and gingerly stepped around the stain on the rug, wiped down the door handle, and with the handkerchief, closed the door behind him.

He'd removed the plastic-coated card on the inside door handle and slipped it over the doorknob. It read, PLEASE CLEAN ROOM. He smirked.

He then walked casually to the elevator and pushed the "down" button with a handkerchief-covered finger. He checked in both directions and was satisfied that he was alone in the hallway. Within a few seconds, the elevator door opened and he stepped inside. The door closed and the hallway became quiet once more.

CHAPTER TWENTY-SEVEN

MIKE PICKED UP THE TELEPHONE RECEIVEr from the cradle next to his queen-sized bed. As he did so, he cast the dark blue quilt aside. He hadn't slept much, his mind going over the day's events. Joey was asleep on the couch in the living room. He'd insisted he stay so they could get an early start on phase two. Phil Singh was in the spare bedroom, where he'd spent the night tossing and turning. He'd already called Randy and told her he wouldn't be home for a couple of days and not to worry.

When Mike had filled him in about the events of the previous evening and explained the plan he and the inspector had devised, Phil had readily agreed to help. His boss wouldn't be too happy about his working with Mounties, but tough shit.

They had narrowly missed that station wagon, but Mike was convinced that they had to lose any possible tails. For the first time in his career, his ability to differentiate an enemy from a friend was being put to the test. The real issue in question, though, was how high up the cover-up went.

"Yeah," he said groggily into the phone.

"Mike?"

""Yeah."

"It's Sam Closter. I'm at the Ambassador Hotel, room 602. I think you better get down here. Inspector Kelso is here already, and she says she wants you to act as an advisor on this investigation."

Mike shook his head. "Listen, Sam, I'm kind of busy on something else right now and—"

"Nope, she insists. What the boss wants, the boss gets, you know that." Sam didn't sound too pleased himself, but orders were orders.

Mike sighed. "Okay. Tell her I'll be there within the hour. Shit, I don't even know what this is about."

"Double homicide. Two John Does," Sam said.

Mike's face paled. "Tell her I'll be there in forty minutes or less." He hung up the phone. He suddenly felt wide awake, as if he'd received a caffeine injection.

He dressed quickly in white socks, jeans, and a gray tee shirt. He hurried into the living room and found Joey asleep, curled in a fetal position facing the back of the green, overstuffed couch. He rocked him and Joey's head of greasy red curls popped up. The curls had bunched to one side of his head, and his unshaven face made him look like a bum down on his luck.

"What time is it?" asked Joey with a yawn.

"Seven thirty."

Joey's head dropped to the couch and he pulled the thin beige blanket tighter around him. "Fuck. Another hour, okay?"

"Nope. Sorry, bud. The inspector wants us in on a double homicide in less than an hour."

"Aw, shit, do we have to? We go other stuff to do and she knows it." Joey sounded like a whiney little kid—something Mike had hated since he was a kid himself.

"Come on, let's go." Mike pulled the blanket off Joey, revealing he was wearing the same clothes from the day before. He smelled as sweaty and greasy as he looked.

Joey sat up and rubbed the sleep from his eyes. This kid's just a baby, thought Mike. I should've talked him out of being involved. Too late now.

"I'm gonna wake Phil, and I expect you to be ready when I come back." Mike wagged an index finger at the younger man, who grinned as he stood and stretched his weary muscles.

Mike opened the door to the second bedroom and immediately heard the soft snoring coming from the single bed against the far wall. The room had thick, forest-green curtains, so it was dark. He walked over to the bed and found Phil fast asleep. Good, he thought. He was finally able to get some sleep. He was lying on his back with the covers halfway up his chest.

Mike placed one meaty hand on his right shoulder and shook him. Phil looked so peaceful he hated to wake him, but he had little choice.

Phil's eyes popped open so suddenly Mike felt himself tense a little.

"Everything okay?" asked Phil. His dark eyes were alert and searching.

"You always wake up like that? You scared the shit outta me." Mike grinned.

Phil shrugged and sat up, the covers falling away into a heap in his lap. He, too, wore the clothes from yesterday, not having bothered to get undressed.

His worn black Nikes sat side by side on the floor at the foot of the bed, ready to be leaped into on a moment's notice. His service revolver sat in his brown leather shoulder holster on the nightstand next to the bed.

"When you have kids, you have to be able to move fast," said Phil with a wry grin on his dark face.

Phil glanced at the white-faced alarm clock and squinted to read the time in the dim light of the room. "Hey, it's early," he said, his eyes narrowed and his body visibly tensed. "Something's happened, hasn't it?"

Mike nodded.

"Does it involve Trudy?"

"Nope. I'll fill you in on the way."

"Where we goin'?" His eyes were curious.

Mike sighed." Murder, as usual, my friend."

***

The three detectives arrived at the hotel with Mike and Phil in the front seats of Mike's Corvette, and Joey crammed, like a sardine in a can, into the tiny back seat meant for tennis rackets, not people. Not normally a problem, as Mike didn't play tennis.

Joey barely had enough room to squeeze his compact body behind the two front bucket seats. Fortunately for him, the young detective didn't yet suffer from secretarial spread, though he complained bitterly all the way to the hotel. He wanted, or more properly threatened or pleaded with Mike, depending on his level of discomfort, for them to stop at the office and pick up his Honda or Phil's larger Chevy.

Mike threw Phil a mischievous wink as he explained that unfortunately time was of the essence and they needed to get to the hotel as quickly as possible.

With the speeds they traveled, Phil realized the RCMP homicide detective wasn't joking, even though he tried to give the outward appearance he was.

They arrived at the Ambassador Hotel, stopping the car in front of the weathered burgundy canopy. A stone walkway led to the glass doors that opened into the hotel lobby. There wasn't a doorman to assist them, so Mike knew this wasn't one of those hoity-toity hotels. It was the kind of place he might even stay if he needed a place to lie low.

Good thinking', you pieces of shit, he thought as he turned off the engine.

Flowers lined the horseshoe-shaped driveway. The mixture of scents from the roses and other fragrant flowers filled the air. At least the place smells better than it looks, he thought with a grim smile.

He nodded at Phil as they threw the wide doors of the car open. Joey crawled out from behind the front seats to stand near the passenger door and stretched his arms and back. "Ow, son of a bitch," he said. "It hurts." His legs and arms cracked loudly.

Mike slapped him on the back with one meaty hand, causing him to stagger slightly, then catch himself by resting one hand on the car's shiny hood. "Come on, old timer."

Mike climbed the two steps at the end of the stone path that led from the half-moon driveway to the lobby. "And keep you mitts off the paint job," he said with a chuckle.

Phil gave the young cop a shrug and a grimace, and together they hurried after Mike into the lobby of the old vine-covered building.

Once inside, Phil smelled the musty odor of the place and saw that the burgundy carpet that lined the lobby floor, obviously installed at the same time as the weathered, faded canopy outside the main entrance, was worn threadbare in several places. The hotel had seen better times.

They headed to the front desk. A weasely looking man with a pencil thin mustache, wearing a plaid sport coat with a silver colored nametag, stood watching them cross the lobby. His brown hair was slicked back like it'd been freshly oiled. On his pale, thin face was the fixed smile of someone who obviously hated customer service and should be actively seeking work in another field. His eyes were bland and seemed to barely contain intelligent life.

Mike and Phil recognized the dull expression, having seen the same look many times in the course of their work.

The false smile faded as Mike threw his badge in its worn, black leather wallet on the pine desk. It landed with a thump. The man gazed at it and pointed immediately to the bank of three elevators to the right of the desk. "Room 602, 6th floor."

The last was intended as an insult, as if they couldn't surmise the floor number from the room number. Phil gave the desk clerk a withering look and concluded the guy had little use for cops. No wonder, he thought, in a fleabag like this.

They ignored the man's sarcasm and silently hurried to the nearest available elevator car. Fortunately, one was already there with the doors open. Once inside, Joey pushed the floor number, finally feeling the blood circulating in his veins again.

They got off the elevator at the correct floor and followed the sound of voices down the empty hallway until they found an open doorway, guarded by a uniformed constable.

He nodded to Mike as he approached, stepped aside, and let the trio of officers enter the room.

Inside were two detectives, a photographer, and an oriental-looking man wearing a navy-blue jacket with the word "CORONER" in large, yellow, block letters across the back. They were all wearing white, rubber, surgical gloves.

Standing near one of the victims, writing something in a black notebook, stood one of the detectives. His badge wallet was sticking out of the breast pocket of his rumpled, green, pinstriped suit jacket.

The coroner tech spotted the three new arrivals and tossed them each a pair of white rubber gloves. The three detectives knew procedure well, so they quickly donned the gloves with practice, as they had many times in the past.

The room's air was permeated with the metallic smell of drying blood.

Sam Closter's beer belly rode the belt around his waist as if it was about to spill over onto the floor in a heap of jiggling gelatin. In one chair, with his head resting on his chest and a red gash the size of a fist, was victim number one. Phil glanced over to see another victim lying on his back, his eyes still fixed on the ceiling overhead.

He concluded that this had happened fast. They hadn't expected it.

Phil immediately saw vic one had the handle of a gun sticking up from the seat cushion beside him and vic two wore a shoulder holster with a similar weapon still strapped in tight.

"What we got, Sam?" asked Mike.

The beer belly looked up at him, a bored expression on his jowly, gray face. "Two vics, both dead by gunshot wounds." The coroner tech glanced at Sam and gave him a disgusted expression. Sam sighed and rolled his eyes.

"All right, sorry, Wally," said Sam. "Allegedly shot in the chest," he paused to point at vic one, then pointed to the middle of his own forehead with one gloved finger. "And one in the head, though," he added with a sideways glance at Wally, "the coroner will confirm the cause of death."

"What else?" asked Phil, trying to not sound impatient.

Sam frowned. "Who the fuck is this?"

"Sorry, Sam. This is Phil Singh. He's with VPD. He's helping me on a case. Joint task force kind of thing."

"Don't tell me this is related to another case. I hate when this shit happens," said Sam. Shaking his head in disgust, he wrote something in his notebook.

"Sorry, Sam, I can't discuss the other case until we have a direct link confirmed."

Sam glanced up and snorted. His brown eyes cast Mike a look as if to say, "Yeah right."

Mike shook his head, his expression serious.

"You using my name in vain again, Harris? Inspector means it, Sam. Inspector's orders," Barbara Kelso said, as she came through the apartment door, her almost-floor-length tan trench coat covering a green pantsuit and white dress shirt.

A scarf was around her neck, patterned in leopard spots. Her short, blonde hair was neatly combed into place. Mike always marveled at how she managed to look so business-like, no matter what time of day it was or where she was. Even at a fucking crime scene, she managed to look like she was about to give the commencement address at some university.

This broad has more class in her baby finger than the Prime Minister of Canada. He almost dismissed the thought, when something suddenly occurred to him.

"Hey, Joey, will you join me in the hallway for a minute."

Barbara caught the look in his eye and nodded to him to go ahead. She put her hands in the pockets of her trench coat and moved to stand over the body of vic two.

"Yeah, Mike, you talk to Joey while I talk to Sam, here, about his weight management program." She arched one eyebrow as she gazed at Sam's beer belly.

The detective looked at her wide-eyed as his complexion became a shade of crimson. Phil stood off to one side and watched the inspector about to tear a strip off one of her detectives

Once they were alone in the hallway, Mike let Joey in on what he was thinking. "Listen, kid, did you ever complete the background check on the first vic? The daughter-in-law of the PM?"

Joey shrugged. "Yeah, I think so. But I don't know what that's got to do with anything. She's dead, for God's sake, and we know who did it." Joey gazed into Mike's eyes and recognized what he saw. "You're not sure, are you?"

Mike shook his head. "No, I'm beginning to think this trail of corpses is trying to tell us something. I think whoever is behind all these murders is trying to frame this Bruce Carstairs guy, for a reason I don't yet get; but I think its related to this girl's background."

Joey shrugged. "So what do ya want me to do?"

"Go back to the office," he reached in his jeans jacket pocket and pulled out his car keys. "Take the 'Vette, and Phil, and bring her file to my place in about an hour. I'll meet you there with the inspector and we'll decide the next steps." He looked thoughtful. "I think we've missed something. Something important."

"But, Mike, those files are supposed to stay in the office. I'm not supposed to…"

Mike threw the younger man a withering look.

Joey grinned and nodded, then went back into the hotel room to retrieve the Vancouver detective. They soon rushed past Mike, headed for the elevator. Phil glanced at Mike as they blew past him. His face was grim. He knew his job was on the line for sure now, and wondered how he'd ever explain all this to his Sergeant. Taking a protected file could also mean jail time for them all.

Mike smiled and shrugged as they passed him on their way to the elevators. He then walked back into the hotel room, where Barbara was continuing to give the coroner's tech and Sam a hard time. He smirked to himself. Boy, was she good.

"Excuse me, Inspector." Barbara stopped in midsentence and glared at Mike. She obviously didn't like some of the responses she was getting.

"Yeah, Mike, what is it?" Her eyes crinkled at the corners and he realized she was enjoying this little dangle-from-the-hook routine.

"We have an urgent matter to attend to elsewhere," Mike said while maintaining a straight face.

She nodded, then turned her attention back to Sam. "You got my card, right?" she asked the rotund detective sternly. There were beads of sweat on his greasy forehead and his puffy cheeks were the color of a fire engine. He nodded and patted his suit jacket with his right hand.

"Okay," she wagged one finger alternately at the two murdered men. "You call me when you have some idea who these dead guys are—or were—right away, on my cell. Got it?"

The two detectives nodded sharing a nervous glance. Neither knew whose responsibility it was to call her.

Without another word of instruction, she turned and grabbed Mike by the arm and led him from the room.

Once out of sight of the two men in the room, she winked at Mike from the corner of one eye. He chuckled lightly.

They entered the elevator, the doors closed, and Barbara's shoulders relaxed. "That was the most fun I've had in a long time. I don't get out enough; that's all there is to it."

Mike chuckled in reply.

"So where's Joey and that VPD cop? Singh, is it?" she asked.

Mike nodded. "Yeah, Phil Singh. Good cop. Been on homicide in Vancouver for five years. Solved a lot of cases."

Barbara smiled thinly, her eyes focused on the row of white numbers as they lit up on an aluminum strip over the elevator door. The confined car smelled of stale urine. "Then why isn't he a Mountie?"

Mike chuckled, then continued with his debrief as the elevator continued its slow descent. "Joey and Phil have gone to the office to get the first vic's file. I told them to meet us at my place…"

"You did what?" asked Barbara with a shocked expression on her suddenly pale face.

Just then the doors decided to open on the lobby floor and all conversation ceased. Mike knew Barbara was a consummate professional and she wouldn't air their differences in so public a place.

On the way outside, he thought about what he was going to say. Her wrinkled brow and head down, coupled with a glare, and with her hands stuffed in the pockets of her trench coat meant she was downright pissed off.

Once they were outside, she'd let him have it with both barrels. Wouldn't be the first time one of his superiors took a chunk of flesh off him, and certainly wouldn't be the last. His next job might be pumping gas or maybe making license plates at the penitentiary, but no doubt he'd piss off his boss there, as well.

The smell of the roses that lined the hotel driveway leading to the entrance reception area assaulted him as they let the twin, clear glass doors close behind them. Mike concluded it was the one redeeming feature of this dump.

She whirled to face him, her eyes angry. Her voice was surprisingly calm. "I don't need to know this, do I." She arched an eyebrow.

He looked at her in amazement. He'd never seen her back down before. It suddenly dawned on him.

Mike played his hunch. "If the file on this broad were to mysteriously disappear, then re-appear at say…my apartment, and let's say you happen to be visiting a sick friend at my apartment and the file was there… But of course, you didn't know that and we discussed the information in the file that was missing from the official files, no one would have to know, would they?" He grinned.

She grimaced. "Close enough," she grumbled. Looking around, she said, "Where's your 'Vette?"

"I lent it to Joey. Mind if we take your car?"

Barbara smirked. "You really know how to push your luck, don't you?"

"Yeah. I am a little devil, aren't I?"

Barbara waved one hand toward her black Lexus, parked near the front entrance. "Get in," she said, walking around the car to the driver's door. Mike heard a beep as she disengaged the locks of the big car with the remote attached to her key ring. Simultaneously, they opened the driver's and passenger's side doors and stepped inside.

Once seated, Mike reached over his right shoulder and pulled the seatbelt into place and secured it.

"Don't trust my driving?" asked Barbara with a wink.

"It's the law. Or don't you know that?" asked Mike with a grin.

She smiled and turned the key in the ignition and the big V8 engine came to life with a barely detectable tremble.

"Are you sure this thing's running?" asked Mike.

Barbara smirked, then put the car in gear and they started down the horseshoe-shaped driveway to the main road and headed for his apartment. She knew the address because she liked to know where her officers lived in case one was needed on an urgent case. Sometimes the closest cop to the scene of the crime was the best cop for the job.

They drove in silence for a few minutes. It was as if they both needed to catch their breath. The police band radio that Barbara had recently installed proved a low backdrop of constant buzzes and routine calls as the cars scattered across the city went about their nightly routine duties. One thing about this case was that it was far from routine.

"So what do you think?" asked Barbara, her dark eyes focused on the road ahead.

"Barbara, I think we got a whole shit-load of trouble to dig our way out of before this mess is resolved. We may be on the bread line before this is over, but damn it, I'm not about to let anyone off the hook. I don't give a shit who they think they are."

Barbara sighed. "I hear you, Mike, but who the hell do you think is behind this? What possible reason could these two schmucks have to kill the prime minister's daughter-in-law?"

"That's why I asked Joey to get her file from the office. I think the answer's in there."

Barbara nodded and they drove the rest of the way in silence.

CHAPTER TWENTY-EIGHT

FROM THE PASSENGER SEAT OF THE BRITISH RACING GREEN CORVETTE, Phil Singh felt a tremble on his right hip. Joey steered the car around the traffic as they raced from the RCMP station. Phil had the file they'd clandestinely removed from the station inside Joey's jacket in his lap. It was a small folder with the word "CONFIDENTIAL" stenciled across it in large, black capital letters.

He felt slightly sick as the powerful car swayed through traffic. He wasn't sure if it was the kid's driving or what they'd just done that made him feel this way. For his part, Joey looked like a kid on Christmas morning. Inwardly, Phil cringed. Young kids always love their toys. Mike must be a big kid to have a car like this. As that movie cop liked to say, he was too old for this shit.

The vibration on his hip was there again. He realized it was his cell phone. He pulled the silver-and-black phone from his belt and hit the red button.

"Singh," he said, pressing the phone to his right ear.

The reception wasn't the best because he could hear a slight buzz in the background. "Phil, it's Trudy," was what he heard clearly, jolting him.

"Trudy, thank God," he breathed.

Joey glanced at him, a serious expression on his face, his brow wrinkled.

"Where are you?" He had to shout because it was noisy inside the car due to the growling engine.

"You—have—yell," said Trudy. The signal was breaking up but he understood what she meant.

"Yeah, sorry. I'm on the road and its kinda noisy here." Joey shot him a withering look and shrugged. "So where are you?"

"I'm—Bruce and—Tommy—musician—"

"You're not that clear, sorry, but did you say you're with a musician?"

There was a garbled response.

"Sorry, Trudy, the line is getting worse. I hope you can hear me okay at your end. I'm gonna give you an address. Write it down and we'll meet you there. And don't worry, it's safe." He gave her the address of Mike's apartment.

He heard another garbled response, but it sounded like "Okay," before the line went dead.

"Well?" asked Joey.

Phil placed his cell back on his belt before answering. "I hope so." His jaw set in determination.

He then grabbed for the door handle to steady himself as they floated around another corner. His stomach flipped and he had to swallow hard to keep from vomiting. Maybe they wouldn't make it to the apartment after all.

The cell phone rang again. Phil exchanged a brief look of surprise with Joey then answered the call.

"Detective Singh, it's Barbara Kelso. I need your help."

***

"Phil?" asked Bruce from where he sat on the worn couch. The room still smelled of the bacon and eggs she'd made for them to eat.

Tommy had taken two bites then run to the bathroom to lose whatever was in his stomach to the porcelain pony. Not that there was much in his stomach. Afterward he collapsed onto the couch on his back.

Bruce had sat down and made a pillow for his old friend. He cradled the musician's sleeping head in his blue-jeaned lap.

Trudy nodded. "Yeah. He wants us to meet."

Bruce rolled his eyes. "Yeah, right. Listen, you may think he's okay, but he's still a cop and I'm still a murder suspect."

"All right. How 'bout I go alone?"

"They'll still arrest you. You're an accessory after the fact, or something like that."

"You watch too much TV," said Trudy with a grin.

He smirked and his face flushed. "Yeah. You be careful."

"You bet your ass." Trudy crossed the room to the little rickety wooden dining table where her jacket hung off one of the two mismatched plastic chairs. Her purse hung with it.

"Do you think the truck is okay to drive?"

"The guy shot out the window, but the engine is okay. But the shattered window might be a signal to a passing cop to be snoopy. You know what they're like." Bruce grinned.

Trudy frowned and slipped her coat on, then hung her purse off one shoulder. "How do I look?"

"Like shit." It was true; her clothes looked like they'd been slept in, which they had, and her hair was matted and dirty. She'd been afraid of the bathroom and hadn't done more than use the toilet. Even then, the grunginess of the room made her cringe every time the urge struck her.

"Aren't we the little charmer?" she asked sarcastically while tying her hair back into a ponytail. She'd removed a red cloth-coated hair band from her purse for that purpose.

He smiled warmly. "No, really, Trud," he said, his voice becoming soft with his inner gentleness shining through the tough-guy exterior. "You look fine. I mean, under the circumstances." He waved one hand in the stale air. "This place might as well be a ratty prison." He nodded his head grimly. "You're right, we gotta do something. We can't hide here forever."

He grimaced. "It's just that I feel kinda useless. I mean, you're the one taking the risks."

She shrugged. "Listen, Bruce. You and I been through a lot together and we've faced some pretty shitty situations. I'm not gonna stop until we get outta this mess. You got me?"

He saluted. "Yes, ma'am," he said sternly with a twinkle in his blue eyes.

Trudy's pale face brightened and her eyes drooped at the corners. "You didn't kill anyone. I know that and Flo knows that. This guy Phil seems to me to trust us because Flo does, God only knows why, but we need to hold on to that belief and trust this guy now. I mean, we gotta trust someone sometime, ya know?"

Bruce nodded.

Trudy headed for the door to the hallway. "I'll call you later. I promise." She kept her back to him as she closed the door behind her. Once alone in the hallway, she closed her eyes and leaned back against the wall, her head tilted back. She took a deep breath to steady herself and then opened her eyes and raised her hands to eye level. They were shaking badly and she had the urge to take a pee. Damn, I'm scared, she thought. Even more so that that time on the beach in Fairview. "I've gotta get fucking control of myself," she whispered softly to herself. "Come on, old girl, you can do this."

She forced herself away from the yellowing wallpaper covering the hallway and started, on wobbly legs, toward the stairs leading to the pub below.

She passed the bartender, who smiled warmly as she went by. She smiled thinly and, she was sure, none too convincingly. He nodded and went back to cleaning something out of sight behind the large teak bar.

Once outside, she took in a deep breath of the salt air to steady herself, then walked around the two-story building to the rear parking lot where they'd left Rocky's blue pickup. As she rounded the corner, she found the shattered rear window was still visible. A sound like someone talking on a portable radio met her ears. She stopped, holding her breath.

She then moved against the side of the building, placing her hands flat on the wooden siding. She inched toward the corner of the building and saw a police car parked where she couldn't see it from the front of the building.

A lone uniformed cop was inside the white police cruiser, his eyes focused on his notebook. She moved back along the building out of sight. Damn it, Bruce was right; the cops did see the shattered window as a smoke signal of trouble.

She rushed back to the entrance to the pub and headed up the stairs two at a time.

The eyes of the startled bartender watched her. She hurried down the hallway; it seemed to take her forever. She burst through the door to find a surprised Bruce standing over Tommy, lying in a fetal position on the floor crying.

Bruce's face was flushed and he looked ready to pounce on her.

"What's wrong?" she asked, her voice breathless. She realized she hadn't had much exercise lately and even that short run had almost winded her.

"I heard someone running. I thought there might be a threat?" He looked bewildered; his fists were in balls and were blood red. Tommy was moaning and his arms were clenched tightly around himself.

"We gotta get outta here. The cops found the truck. One of 'em's in the parking lot behind the building right now."

His eyes went wide. "Oh, shit." Bruce glanced down at Tommy. He wasn't exactly dressed for going out, with his stringy, grease-covered curls of brown hair and black, stained tee shirt. He wore no shoes or socks on his dirt-covered feet. At least he had a pair of drab, olive-green cotton trousers on.

As for himself, he had his Daytons on as usual, blue jeans, and his leather vest over a gray tee shirt. His uniform was at least intact.

"Oh, shit," he said again, his eyes wide. He glanced at Tommy's .45, sitting on the end table, and almost dismissed taking it with him. They were in enough trouble already. "Fuck it," he muttered under his breath. He slipped the gun underneath his tee shirt in the small of his back. There was the sound of a siren in the distance. The cop had radioed for backup. Time was short and they had to get the hell and gone away from the place.

216

"Well, I guess we're putting your pal Phil to the test together after all."

Trudy nodded as Bruce picked Tommy up in his heavily muscled arms like a newborn baby and carried him to the front door. Bruce had noticed an old fire escape off the opposite side of the building from the parking lot, where they wouldn't be seen leaving.

They hurried down the steel stairs, the odor of rotting garbage drifting up from the large, open, garbage bin near the bottom of the stairs. Trudy felt her stomach heave at the strong smell, but steeled herself and followed Bruce to the bottom.

Tommy was still moaning. "What the fuck is the matter with him?" Trudy asked in a hoarse whisper.

"If you drank and didn't eat, what do you think would happen to you?"

Trudy nodded knowingly. Bruce shrugged.

They hurried away to the street and flagged down a yellow cab coming toward them. Fortunately, it was available.

The driver rolled down his window. He was a dark-skinned man, who looked to be about thirty. He was smoking a cigarette. His eyes were droopy, as if he hadn't had a lot of sleep lately. He wore a blue, pin-striped dress shirt and no jacket.

"Yeah?" he asked. His accent indicated he was East Indian.

"We need to get to Surrey," said Bruce, still cradling Tommy in his arms.

"Hospital?" asked the man, nodding toward Tommy. "There's one closer than Surrey."

"No," Bruce shook his head. "No, we're goin' to a friend's place."

The guy shrugged and they got into the back. Bruce laid Tommy on the seat as Trudy moved around to the street side of the taxi and got in.

Then Bruce got in while Trudy held Tommy's thin frame out of the way.

The cab driver reached for his radio mike. "Two seven, away," he said, then keyed the mike button twice as he returned it to the slotted holder that held it while not in use. The interior of the taxi was clean, with plush, powder-blue seats, though there was a lingering odor of tobacco smoke.

Trudy told him the address.

The driver nodded and pulled away from the curb. Trudy glanced at the driver's identification card and hack license attached to the rear of the seat. The guy's name was Parmjit Dhillon.

"You been driving long?" asked Trudy.

Parm flicked his dark eyes briefly at the rearview mirror. "About five years," he said.

"Meet some interesting people in this business?" she asked, intentionally attempting to keep her tone of voice light.

Parm shrugged as they headed up a hill toward the King George Highway to head north. They passed houses, parks, and schools. How normal the world seems sometimes, thought Trudy.

"You married?"

Parm nodded. "Yup, with two children."

"Boys, girls?"

"One of each."

Bruce caught her eye, then nodded toward the driver, then outside. They weren't going very fast, and numerous cars were passing them. Something seemed wrong.

"Parmjit, is it?" asked Trudy.

"Parm." The man nodded, keeping his eyes focused on the road ahead.

"Why are we going so slow? You're not trying to pad the fare, are you?"

"Of course not," he protested his voice had a tremor in it.

Trudy could see his hands twisting tightly on the steering wheel.

Bruce nodded at Trudy, then eased forward until his lips were right behind Parm's right ear. "If you don't step on it, when this car stops, I'm gonna kick the shit outta you. Understand me?"

Parm nodded and the noise coming from the Chevy's V8 engine increased and they began to pull away from the cars around them. Trudy saw Parm's eyes flit to the rearview mirror, beads of sweat formed on his knitted brow.

Good, she thought, *he's scared*.

"He signaled the dispatcher that there is trouble in the cab," said Bruce.

Parm began to visibly tremble now and he fidgeted in his seat.

"Keep you eyes straight ahead, ol' buddy," said Bruce.

Parm nodded.

"What are you talking about? I heard him say he was away, that's all."

"He keyed the mike button twice, which is the universal cab driver call for help. His dispatch will have called the cops by now."

Bruce rested one meaty hand on Parm's right shoulder. "Listen carefully, Parm. I don't want to hurt you, but as you probably guessed by now, we're in some shit here and if you want to see those kids of yours again, we need your help."

Parm nodded.

"Good. Do you know a back route to the address she gave you?"

Parm nodded again.

"Then that's what you'll do, and you'll keep your mouth shut. Got it?"

This elicited another nod from the frightened driver. The car turned onto another street away from the main road and sped up. No doubt he wanted to get rid of this fare as fast as they wanted to get where they were going. His trembling left foot pressed the GPS activation button sending the dispatcher an emergency signal and a signal so the taxi could be tracked.

***

"Did you hear that?" asked Barbara, suddenly startling Mike to alertness from his dream-like state. The lack of sleep over this case was beginning to catch up with him. The light ride of the expensive Lexus wasn't any help. Smooth, comfortable ride, just like his bed.

"What…?" he blurted.

"The emergency dispatcher says there's a cab indicating the driver has activated his distress beacon in Surrey. If I know thing about these people it's very likely it's our dynamic duo. Those two they attract trouble like moths to a flame."

'You barely know these people, inspector. Except form the file…." His voice trailed off as Mike realized she had read the file and that she suspected something was wrong with the investigation.

Barbara ignored Mike's comment and picked up the mike from the bracket on the side of the radio. "Dispatch, this is Superintendent Kelso. What was the 10-20 for the cab call?"

A bland male voice read out the address again.

"Roger." Barbara let go of the squawk button, then placed the mike back on the side of the radio. She glanced at Mike. "We're in serious shit. Get Joey on the line."

She stepped hard on the gas and steered with one hand as she pushed the button to roll down the driver's window.

When it was down, she opened the lid on the armrest between them and pulled out a portable light.

Mike plugged it into the specially designed receptacle on the dash and she placed it on the roof of the car. She flecked a switch on the dash and the light began to flash. Cars ahead of them pulled over and she managed to speed up further.

"We need to get there ahead of them."

Mike nodded. This whole thing could be bust if the wrong people got hold of Trudy and Bruce, and they knew it. No witnesses, no resolution, and the careers of some good cops in the toilet for good measure.

***

Across the city in his office, Superintendent Pat Reynolds glanced up from the intelligence report on Middle East terrorism when he heard Inspector Kelso's voice. He wrote down the address on a yellow Post-it note and immediately picked up the telephone. He punched the phone number he'd memorized on the white buttons. A man's voice answered.

"I know where they are," he said, then read the address off the note he'd made. The line went dead with a click as the person at the other end hung up.

Pat replaced the telephone, then reached into the bottom drawer of his desk. He kept a gray steel ashtray for just such occasions from his days as a smoker, a hobby he'd given up more than fifteen years ago. The bottom of the ashtray was blackened.

He placed the Post-it note in the ashtray, then opened the top drawer of his desk to retrieve a pack of matches. The logo on the matches was for his favorite beer.

He struck a single match, lit one edge of the note, and watched the orange- and blue-tinged flame quickly consume the note. The room now reeked of sulfur.

"Well, that's it, Pierre. I've done my bit," he murmured to himself.

He rose from the desk to carry the ashtray into the private washroom attached to his office. Sometimes being high enough in a government job did have its perks. He washed the remnants of the blackened note down the sink. He then walked back to his desk, sat down in his chair, and went back to reading the intelligence report.

He wouldn't give the matter another thought.

CHAPTER TWENTY-NINE

THE TAXI STOPPED TWO BLOCKS from the apartment building. Bruce gave the driver an extras forty bucks on top of the fare and told him to forget he ever saw them, or he'd find him and his family and make them all pay. The guy drove off to the odor of burnt rubber.

"You think he'll go to the cops?" asked Trudy.

"Yup," said Bruce with a nod. Tommy hung off his right arm, his bare feet on the sidewalk. He'd become a little more aware of his surroundings but was still in pretty bad shape. Bruce would have to prop him up until they made it to the apartment building.

The one good thing was that Trudy hadn't been able to understand Phil enough over the bad connection so neither they or anyone listening would know the apartment number. She always assumed someone would be listening. That, at least, might buy them some time.

They hurried down the sidewalk, passing rows of low-rise three-story apartment buildings. The kind with no elevators commonly known as walk-ups.

Trudy scanned the addresses and saw that at least they were in the right block number, just two streets over from where they needed to be.

They cut between the buildings so they could avoid intersections with inquisitive passersby until they stood across from what she hoped was the right apartment building. It looked much the same as the other gray stucco structures in the neighborhood.

They could see an unoccupied red Corvette parked in front. There were no lights visible in any of the six apartment windows they could see. They watched for a few seconds and Trudy then made a tentative step out onto the sidewalk and looked in both directions. No cop cars, nor was there anyone sitting by themselves in parked cars nearby.

Good, the cops hadn't arrived yet. There might be time. She waved one arm to signal to Bruce to come out so they could make a dash for the apartment.

Just as they arrived on the front step, a flashing light appeared down the street. They froze. This was it, they were trapped.

A black Lexus with a light stuck to the roof over the driver's side of the large car pulled up and stopped. The passenger window, comprised of dark, one-way glass, rolled slowly down.

Trudy almost fainted when she saw Phil's smiling face appear from the shadows beside the car. "Trudy, thank God," he said. "Get in. All of you."

"Is this your car?" Trudy asked.

"Loaner." Phil aimed the remote control attached to the key ring and pressed a button. There was the soft click as the car's doors unlocked.

Bruce, still holding up his friend, rushed to the door behind the driver and pulled it open with his free hand.

Trudy climbed in behind Phil and helped Bruce push Tommy to sit between them, then closed the doors. They sped away just as a siren began to warble in the distance.

"That was close," said Trudy with a small sigh.

Phil turned his head slightly to study her with the corner of one eye keeping the other on the road. "You look like shit," he said, visibly concerned.

"Why do I have to meet all the charmers today," she said in mock disgust.

"Sorry, but that's not what I meant…" Phil began to protest.

She raised one hand to stop him from speaking.

"As the kids say, Phil, talk to the hand and see if it gives a shit." Trudy chuckled and Bruce threw her a withering smile. Tommy's head lolled forward and Bruce pushed him back into the leather seat.

"Trudy, my name's Barbara Kelso." Trudy froze as a woman's voice erupted from the car's interior speakers. "We need to talk."

Trudy cleared her throat. "And who are you, Ms. Kelso?" asked Trudy, immediately suspicious, her eyes narrowing. She cast Phil a look of fear. The tension and adrenaline hadn't left her body yet.

"I'm Mike's boss, and hopefully a friend." Barbara paused to let her words sink in. "We're going to meet at a place I know and see if we can get to the bottom of this mess."

Trudy nodded, suddenly feeling a sense of relief come over her. "So you believe us?"

"I am beginning to."

A cell phone went off in the car. "Hold on, Inspector." Phil pushed a button on the steering wheel. It was a hands-free phone. "Singh," he said.

A man's voice came over a hidden speaker. "Detective, it's Wong with the coroner's office."

"Go ahead."

"We've been unable to ID those two vics from the Ambassador. However, the guy from the river, Logan, he was killed with one of the guns on the vics at the hotel."

"You sure about this, Wong?"

"Positive ballistics match." He sounded a little insulted by the inference that he might be mistaken.

He cast a little sideways smirk at Bruce who grunted.

"Okay. What about the gun that killed the two vics? What kind was it?"

"Interesting one there, actually." Wong had warmed to his subject. "A model 1911 .45. The kind that was used up to the '70s by the U.S. military. I checked with the firearms registry in Ottawa, and discovered there are only five such weapons registered in B.C."

Phil appeared impressed. The killer had gone that extra mile. "Great stuff, Wong. I'll make sure to tell your boss about this, okay?"

"Thanks. Please let me know if you need anything else."

Phil hit the button with his forefinger to disconnect the line.

"That doesn't mean it's not a stolen or smuggled gun, you know," said Barbara who had been listening to the conversation while on hold.

"Yeah, I know," Phil said, with a twinkle in his eye. "But I'm willing to bet it is a registered gun that killed those two guys."

Trudy gave him an amazed look. How did he know that?

***

They arrived at Barbara's beach house at four o'clock in the afternoon.

The house had been built back in the 1930s and had since been renovated several times by the successive owners that last being Barbara's ex-husband.

The green-and-white siding made of aluminum to beat the winter rainstorms and keep the active insect population from invading, looked clean and bright. Fall was coming but the flowerbeds still bloomed with the last of the summer foliage. The sun was low in the western sky at this time of day and made the property seem to glow. The sandy beach was across the paved, two-lane road, which was lined with wooden telephone poles, their wire humming from the electricity pulsing through them.

As they exited the luxury car, Trudy heard the call of seagulls flying above the vast expanse of gray beach that stretched over the horizon on both directions. Other cottages lined this side of the road and all had an unobstructed view of the flat ocean beyond. The sheltered bay would be relatively calm, at least until the wilder winds struck from the north.

The air and sounds made Trudy feel immediately homesick. Barbara sensed her mood. "I love the ocean, don't you?" she asked, a smile playing across her tanned features.

"Oh, yes," said Trudy, "I certainly do."

They stood side-by-side, watching the seagulls playing their games in the air over the beach. Bruce, still holding Tommy upright, came up behind them.

"Can we forget the mutual admiration society and go inside?" he asked. "We might be seen, and I, for one, feel a little naked out here. "

"Yeah, sorry," said Barbara, leading the way to the white front door.

It had a crescent-shaped, fogged-glass window set into the top, more for decoration than practicality. Just as she raised her hand to the door latch, the door suddenly swung open to reveal the smiling face of Mike Harris. Joey was visible standing behind him, his hands stuffed in the pockets of his jeans.

"Inspector, how nice to see you," he said brightly, tongue obviously planted firmly in cheek.

She pushed him aside with a scowl on her face. "Cut the comedy, Harris. Help Mr. Carstairs with his load, will you?"

Mike's smiled faded and he helped Bruce and Phil guide Tommy to the living room. The furniture was in a tropical motif, with wicker chairs and a matching couch, all with large, burgundy cushions. Throw pillows were arranged along the back of the couch of the same material and color.

Together they placed an almost-comatose Tommy on the couch on his back. Bruce used one of the pillows to cushion his head. Tommy's eyes were closed and immediately he curled into a fetal position and began to snore lightly.

"He's a real wreak," said Mike, stating the obvious and earning a withered stare from Bruce.

"All right, now that we're all here, we need to figure out what the hell is going on," said Barbara, immediately taking charge.

"Hold on," said Bruce. "Who fuckin' died and made you the boss?"

Barbara crossed her arms over her chest and shifted her weight onto one leg. She gazed into the big man's eyes.

"You think because I don't have a dick I can't be in charge, is that it? Up until now, you've been on your own and you've pretty much fucked it up, don't you think?"

Bruce's expression softened and his shoulders relaxed. Trudy came over to him and wrapped one arm around his broad shoulders. "Listen," she said to him. "I trust these people," she waved one hand at the assembled cops in the room, "to get us out of this, okay?"

Bruce nodded at her. "One thing I wanta know before we go any further."

"And what's that?" asked Barbara.

"Why are you doing this?"

Mike stepped forward and held one hand up to his boss, who nodded. "I think I can answer this for all of us here." Behind him Joey, Barbara, and Phil all nodded. "We're cops, and someone is trying to make us all look bad and make fools out of us. If there's one thing cops hate, it's being made fools of. The son of a bitch behind these murders is gonna pay, and we know for sure it isn't any of you." He pointed at Tommy. "Except that guy, maybe. Who is he?"

They turned and looked at Tommy, who had abruptly sat up on the couch and was alert. His eyes were wide as he stared at the group staring back at him. He looked frightened and confused.

"Huh…where am I?" he asked.

***

After they'd calmed him down from his initial confusion, Bruce explained how he'd found Tommy Roper in a room above the Pelican Bar and Grill. Tommy gazed dumbfounded at his friend. He had no recollection of anything past two nights ago. All he seemed to be able to recall was that that night was to be his last gig at the pub, and then he would head back to the states. There was a job lined up at a small nightspot in Seattle off Pioneer Square.

"What's the last thing you recall?" asked Bruce. The group was seated around the long, natural wood, stained table in the dining room. It was a ten-foot long pine table, which could be extended with two leaves in the middle to fourteen feet. Trudy made them some coffee and they sat listening intently to what Tommy had to say. Somehow his story seemed to fit with the incongruities of recent events.

Finally, he finished his story by saying that the next thing he remembered was waking up here at the beach house to the sound of seagulls calling to each other.

Bruce leaned forward in his chair to rest his arms on the table, his dark eyes locked on Tommy's red-rimmed, blood-streaked eyes. Between his arms sat a large, brown, glazed coffee mug with the words stenciled in yellow on the side, "HAPPY EASTER."

It was the largest mug in the mixed bag of mugs Barbara kept in the kitchen cupboards. She said they collected the mugs at flea markets that are why no two were the same. The smell of warm, fresh-brewed coffee wafted through the room.

For her part, Barbara stood with her arms crossed, leaning against the doorframe that led to the kitchen, watching the group's reactions to the conversation.

"Tommy, do you remember me and Trudy meeting you in the hallway at the Pelican?"

Tommy shook his head, his eyes pleading with Bruce to help him remember.

"You met us with a gun in your hand and you mumbled something about men in black, like in the movies."

Mike glanced at Phil with a surprised look in his eyes, but they both silently agreed to let the conversation continue without interruption.

The interrogation was going just fine without them. Too bad this guy was off his nut.

Tommy silently shook his head and his shoulders made a slight shrugging motion. He raised the coffee cup before him with two trembling hands and took a tentative sip of the warm, sugary—he liked three spoonfuls in his coffee and a double shot of cream—beige-colored drink.

"Who gave you the gun?"

"What gun?" asked Mike? He couldn't hold himself back now.

Bruce reached behind his back and removed the .45 automatic, model 1911, from the small of his back and dropped it on the table. It clattered once, and then came to rest in front of him.

Mike, Joey, and Phil stared at the gun wide-eyed. Until this moment they'd not realized, nor even considered, Bruce was carrying a gun. It dawned on each of them that they had somehow abrogated their responsibilities by not searching Bruce and Trudy when they'd first encountered them.

Barbara chose this moment to walk up to the table and snatch the gun from in front of the large biker before anyone could move. "Bruce, Trudy, do you have any more weapons on you that these officers haven't already confiscated?" She glared at Mike, who averted his eyes from her steely gaze.

His face flushed. He cursed himself for being so stupid.

"No," said Trudy. "That's the only one."

"I had that," said Tommy in wonderment, clearly confused. "How the fuck…"

"Who gave it to you?" asked Bruce, his dark eyes still focused on his friend, as he seemingly took no notice of the tension in the cops surrounding him.

Tommy frowned and his eyes narrowed. He slapped the side of his head as if to jar some buried memory loose in his drugged brain. "He does that sometimes," said Bruce dryly for the benefit of the group. "Come on, buddy, you can do it. Think."

"I was in the club singing my songs, and on my break I met someone...."

Tommy's eyes closed and his face reddened. He squished his face as if he'd bit into a fresh, sour lemon. Finally he relaxed his shoulders and his eyes opened. He shook his head of greasy, brown curls. "Nope, I can't fuckin' remember." He laid his thin arms across each other on the table and dropped his head, resting his forehead on his arms.

Bruce grabbed him by the hair and pulled him up to his eye level. His fierce glare registered on Tommy's face as fear.

Mike thought about jumping in to help, but one glance at Trudy, sitting there impassively watching Bruce, made him decided to wait and see.

"You fucking piece of shit," said Bruce, growling the words like they were being shredded by his deep voice. "My cousin is dead, and I've been framed for the murder of a girl I didn't even know. People are dead; Tommy, and you sit there and tell me you don't remember? Come on, man, you must do better that that. I want a name, or at least a description of the guy who gave you the gun."

Tommy's eyes watered and he began to tremble uncontrollably. Bruce let go of his hair and he remained upright, facing the immense biker. "They'll kill me," he whispered.

"Who?" asked Mike?

"The Angels."

"The Hell's Angels?" asked Mike.

"Yeah," said Tommy, sitting back in the wooden chair and crossing his thin arms over his chest. His chin sat against his chest, his eyes focused on the wood finish of the table.

"Was it a guy out of Calgary who you met that night in the pub?" asked Trudy. Everyone in the room, including Bruce, turned to stare at Trudy. Tommy sat, his eyes wide, staring at her. His jaw hung open.

"How did she know?" asked Tommy.

"A biker from Red Deer tried to kill me on the way up here. At a motel I stopped at on the way. Fortunately, the Washington State Police arrived in time to stop him." Trudy kept her eyes focused on Tommy. "His name is Simon Renault. Do you know him, Tommy?"

He nodded and his eyes welled with tears. Bruce's eyes went wide and he cast Tommy a dark glare. The anger on his face would make most men's knees tremble. For his part, Tommy lifted his hands as if in surrender. "B, you gotta listen. Simon came to me and said that two guys were after anyone who knew you and he said they would kill me. He gave me the gun. He said the guys were with a secret branch of the cops and no one would ever see me again once they got ahold of me. Please, you gotta understand."

"Then why did you threaten us with the gun?" asked Bruce.

"That part isn't Simon's fault. He sold me the smack, yeah..." he hesitated, his eyes wild, "but I took it later. I thought they were after me, I guess..." His voice trailed off into silence.

Bruce scanned the cops around the table. He signaled with a nod of his head they should leave room.

Once they were alone Bruce said, "Let's let Tommy sleep it off. He's a wreck." Barbara nodded and Mike went to fetch the musician. He was back in ten minutes.

"But we need to find out where this Renault is and who he's working for. I don't think it's the Angels. This isn't their style."

"I concur," said Barbara from where she stood. Mike, Joey, and Phil looked doubtful. "Okay, gentlemen, we need to do three things. First, Mike, I want you to call the detachment and have someone run Renault through CPIC. Second, Trudy, call you pal Flo in Oregon and ask her to see what the WSP did with Renault for the attempted murder complaint; we need to make sure we're dealing with the same guy. And finally we'll review Cherie Lavois' file to see what we can find out, which is where this little venture was headed in the first place."

She scanned the group for any dissent and was satisfied with the eager looks of people who wanted to get to the bottom of this mystery. Tommy had his head down again, resting on his arms on the table. She smiled thinly. "All right, let's get to work, people."

Two hours later, the group reconvened to review the evidence at the same pine dining table.

"So, who is Cherie Lavois?" asked Barbara.

Joey flipped open his black notebook and read from his notes where he'd summarized the material in the file folder. He'd learned to only make note of relevant facts based on the investigation to date.

"Married a little over a year ago to the middle son of Prime Minister Lavois. The son's name is William, an engineering student at UBC. According to witnesses interviewed by the investigating detective, he's known as a party guy, as apparently is, or was, his new wife, also a student at UBC. Her major was in theatre." He paused to flip the page. "The marriage was a quickie at city hall. Ummm..."

"How was she killed?" asked Mike, listening intently.

Joey scanned his notes and flipped another couple of pages over. He nodded. "Yeah, here it is. Strangulation. With something thin, probably wire of some kind. Nothing was found at the crime scene that matched the marks on her neck."

"Sounds like a pro to me," muttered Phil.

"Bruce could've thrown it in the bushes that line the road from the house," said Mike. "Don't forget it's in a remote corner of south Surrey. Lotta bushes round there. Were the bushes on either side of the road searched?"

Joey nodded. "Yeah, first thing I checked when the forensic guys said they found nothing in the house. In the investigating officer's report, there was reference to a team of five officers who scoured the road, and the bushes along it, for two days before they gave up. Still, it's possible, however unlikely, that Bruce could've thrown it far enough into the bushes that they couldn't find it."

Mike shook his head and grinned at a visibly annoyed Bruce. They were talking about him as if he weren't in the room. "Naw, I think the killer of the girl was a pro, no doubt in my mind. Not enough to convince a jury, but I'm reasonably satisfied."

Joey continued. "Okay, on the day of the murder, dispatch reported they received a call at 6:03 in the a.m. saying there had been a murder and gave the address of the biker's party house. The caller was male but refused to ID himself. Being as it was a biker hangout, the NCO on duty decided to set up a roadblock to stop anyone leaving the house while the ERT moved in to secure the premise."

Barbara nodded. By the book.

"The girl's body was found in the bed. She was nude and her blood was chock full of uppers and alcohol. A lot of alcohol. If she'd been driving, she'd have been arrested at least twice. No wonder she was out cold when the killer strangled her."

"What was that?' said Bruce.

"Yeah, the coroner's report said she was out when she was strangled. Why, is that important?"

"Might be," said Bruce. "I got to the party kinda late, after midnight. This girl wasn't there yet. Spike gave me the mickey not long after I got there, then I don't remember very much. Maybe they killed the girl elsewhere and brought her to the house and dumped her beside me to make it look like I did it. What they didn't bank on was I'd wake up and split before the cops found me with a dead girl next to me."

"Anything's possible," said Mike. "Joey, is there any evidence that the body was moved?"

Joey shook his head.

"Okay, that's enough speculation. What about Renault?" asked Barbara with one eyebrow raised.

Trudy had found a pad of legal paper in a drawer of the roll top desk in the den and used it to make notes from her conversation with Flo Henderson. "Flo told me the Washington cops let him go after he made bail the next morning. He left town and they have an outstanding warrant for failure to appear. He's a Hell's Angels associate, not a full patch member. Yet. Probably done this to get his full colors." Bruce once explained to her the hierarchy in the biker clubs. "Anyway, he hasn't been seen anywhere down south, so they think he split back to Red Deer. Is that around here somewhere?"

Mike glanced at Joey, who smiled. "Nope," he said, "it's one province over, in Alberta."

"Oh." She had no idea where Alberta was, but she surmised it wasn't close from their expressions of amusement.

Mike spoke next. "I had Closter run Renault through CPIC, and his record is mostly small stuff in Alberta, though there was one interesting one in Vancouver: a month prior to the murder, he was picked up for assault at a local bar out by UBC, one the students like to frequent. A place called Barnaby's on Fourth Avenue."

Barbara looked thoughtful. "Interesting. Maybe we should run the serial number of the .45 and see what we get on that."

Mike grinned. "Way ahead of you, boss. It turns out the gun is registered to another UBC student named Philips. His daddy's one of the newspaper mogul Philips's."

Joey whistled softly and Mike threw him a glance to tell him to shut up. He clamped his mouth tight and made a zipper motion across his lips, eliciting a smile from Mike and Barbara.

"The campus detachment reports that Philips' gun was stolen about the time Renault was arrested at the bar fight."

"What about the charges against him?" asked Joey, now heavily engrossed in the story.

"Dropped. And the NCO in charge at UBC I spoke with said he didn't have any details to explain why charges were stayed against the guy, only that they were. Smells to me like political interference." Mike leaned back in his chair and crossed his massive arms. He had an arrogant smirk on his ruddy face.

Barbara studied the group, her expression grim. "Well, it looks like we have to find this Renault guy before someone else does. I'm sure, after the murder of Bruce's cousin and the pile of bodies this has become, he doesn't want to be found facedown in the river. The question is, where do we start?"

What she didn't share with them was her discovery that the political interference was so high up in the organization. She was also sure that there was a mole in her own unit. She didn't know who it was yet. Until she had some certainty, she was going to keep her thoughts and opinions to herself.

"I know a place we might look," said Bruce after several seconds of silence.

Mike patted him on the shoulder. "Ya know, I knew somehow this big guy would come through." His expression changed to a frown. "So where do we go?"

Barbara moved to an empty chair at the table and sat down. "Okay, Joey, I want you to go back to the detachment and keep your eyes and ears open."

Joey gave her a wounded expression, to which she raised one hand. "I need you there, Joey. None of the other guys on the floor will suspect you of being involved in this mess. Let's understand something: we're sticking our necks out a mile here, and at any moment they could be chopped off."

Joey nodded.

"Okay, next. Phil, I need you to go to that restaurant in Vancouver and find out what you can from anyone there about the fight involving Renault and then go to UBC and talk to the student who had his gun stolen. In the meantime, Mike and I will go with Bruce and see if we can track down Renault. Questions?"

"Yeah, what about me?" asked Trudy. Her arms were crossed and her expression hard. Bruce knew the look in her eye; he'd seen it before. The head cop better play this right or she was going to have a fight on her hands.

"You stay here. It's going to be dangerous," said Barbara.

Bruce looked at his friend sympathetically. "I agree, Trud, the guy did try to kill you once before. And it sounds like he's one nasty piece of work."

Trudy shook her head. "No fucking way. I'm going with you to find that guy Renault. I didn't come this far to sit back and wait for you guys to save my butt."

Barbara sighed. "All right. How about you go with Phil?"

Trudy thought about it for a couple of seconds. "Well, if that's all I can do, then okay. But I want to be in on the arrest when you catch whoever's behind this. I wanta kick him or her in the ass. Hard."

This drew a round of relieved chuckles and knowing glances. Everyone in the room felt pretty much as Trudy did. Barbara knew that wasn't likely, but she agreed, nonetheless, to let Trudy tag along with Phil Singh. She had no power to stop her from accompanying him, nor did he have to agree; though Phil, who also felt the assignment was routine, readily agreed with a shrug.

Trudy watched Barbara take Phil aside to have a brief whispered conversation. He came back his eyes hard, his lips a grim line. "Besides," Phil explained to the inspector, "I could use the company."

"What was that about, Phil?" asked Trudy.

"Housekeeping," he said without further explanation.

A knot of worry formed in Trudy's guts. There was something going on here far bigger than she knew and it made her nervous. But she also knew she had to see this thing to the end no matter what happened.

Trudy and Phil left first.

CHAPTER THIRTY

P HIL AND T RUDY ARRIVED OUTSIDE B ARNABY'S just as it was
getting dark. Joey had dropped them off at the detachment parking
lot so Phil was able to retrieve his car. Phil parked his silver Firebird
in a spot that was open on the street right in front of the entrance to
what he called the neighborhood pub. It looked more to Trudy like a
yuppie restaurant than any bar she'd ever seen.

As they stopped, two young men, probably in their early twenties
by the clothes and the long side burns, came out the door laughing.
They turned right and walked away down the street.

"Place looks like the one Joey described. A hangout for the
university set."

They got out of the car and walked up to the door. There were
windows with wooden frames, each with a group of small panes
separated by a cross work of wooden slats, that lined the street side of
the pub. There were planters hanging below the windows filled with
fragrant flowers in a variety of colors and types. The flowers were
beginning to wilt, with fall just a few weeks away.

Flower season was almost over.

There were twin wooden doors with clear glass windows set into the top half and the name Barnaby in stylized green lettering painted on the glass.

They went through the doors and were greeted by the sound of laughter and music playing in the background. If you could call it music; Trudy called it rap crap.

Most of the tables were empty. Phil smiled at Trudy, then walked up to the bar; she followed close behind, studying the students sitting in captain's chairs at the scattered wood tables. Young students sat at each table, engrossed in their conversations, oblivious to the two older folks who had just intruded in their territory.

When they reached the bar, they were greeted by a smiling female bartender wearing a sleeveless powder-blue top with spaghetti straps, her white bra straps visible. Her long, poker-straight, auburn hair hung over her tanned shoulders. Around her waist, covering a pair of blue jeans, was a white apron.

She had a wide smile fixed across her tanned complexion and her brown eyes sparkled with amusement as they approached her. From the lines around her eyes, Trudy knew she was considerably older than her clientele.

She leaned on her hands on the bar as Phil reached for the wallet in his back pocket. He flopped the brown leather wallet open on the bar so his badge was clearly visible.

"Hi, there," he said cheerfully.

The bartender's smile faded and she frowned, stood upright, and crossed her arms over the swell of her ample bosom.

"Hi, yourself," she said. "What can I do for you, Officer?"

Trudy glanced around them and noticed one young man in the corner, watching them from the corner of his eye as if he was trying to not look at them, and watch them at the same time. While keeping one ear focused on the conversation, she stepped back from the bar and turned to watch the pub's patrons. Occasionally she glanced in the direction of their observer.

"I was wondering about a little dustup you had in here a couple of months ago. A guy was arrested. A biker named Simon Renault, you know him?"

She shook her head. "Nope."

"How about the fight, you recall that?"

She looked thoughtful for a few seconds, then shook her head. "Nope."

Phil smiled. "Well, I'll tell you what; how's about I check some IDs of some of your customers? To make sure they're all of legal age. I'd hate to see you lose your license. If the provincial liquor inspectors get word from a trusted member of Vancouver's finest otherwise, they might have to come down here everyday." He arched his eyebrows. "To see for themselves."

The woman frowned and her cheeks flushed crimson. "Yeah, I remember the fight," she said, more a growl than actual words.

"Good. Now we're getting somewhere. There was a kid in here that night named Philips, you know him?"

The bartender glanced to her right before she answered. She nodded tentatively, with a worried expression across her face.

Suddenly the guy Trudy had been watching bolted from his chair and ran toward the doors. Trudy surprised herself by intercepting him and sticking her right foot in his path. He tripped, landed on his face, and slid face-first across the floor, leaving a trail of blood as he went until he slammed into a post near the front doors.

He moaned pitifully.

Phil turned around and gazed at the injured young man. "I don't think that was a wise idea, Trudy, but what the hell." He pointed at the kid lying on the floor, who had now sat up and was holding his bloody nose pinched between two fingers of his right hand. His watery eyes reflected his pain.

"Nathan Philips, I presume," said Phil with a grin.

The young man nodded.

Phil turned to face the stunned bartender. "Thanks." He reached into his pants, pulled out a gold-colored coin, and tossed it on the bar. It rattled on its rim, then settled flat. "Here's a loonie for your trouble."

He walked over to the man on the floor and lifted him up by his left arm until he was standing, then pushed the door open with his free hand. "You comin', Trudy?"

She nodded and cast a small smile at the bartender.

The bartender's yell was cut off as the door closed behind them. "Fucking cops…."

Trudy could see her angry look through the glass in the door. With each holding one arm of the guy between them, they carried (more dragged than carried) the bleeding young man to the side of the Firebird, where Phil shoved him against the side of the car. "Hold your head up and keep the pressure on the bridge of the nose. The bleeding will stop in a few minutes."

Phil pulled a pale green handkerchief from the inside pocket of the tweed sport coat that he kept in the trunk of the Firebird for when he needed to be undercover. The jacket was the kind with patches of suede on the elbows. Trudy teased him, saying that it made him look like some mad professor with a tweed jacket and blue jeans. Phil joked by telling her the look was the idea.

He gave a faux hurtful look. He handed the handkerchief to the kid kneeling on the ground. "Use this," he said.

Philips took the offered handkerchief with an angry glare. He wrapped the piece of cloth around his damaged appendage and managed to push himself up the side of the car with one hand until he stood leaning against the door.

"Why did you run, rabbit?" asked Phil.

"I want my lawyer," said Philips. His voice had a nasal quality to it, no doubt from the damage to the length of bone between the nostrils having been bent like a pretzel.

"I don't think your daddy would like seeing you arrested as an accessory to murder, do you?" asked Trudy, jumping in to add to the kids misery. Phil looked momentarily surprised, but decided to say nothing and let her talk. They weren't here to arrest Philips, they wanted information; but the kid didn't need to know that, now did he?

Philips sighed. "No." His lean shoulders slumped. "Listen, I had nothing to do with it."

"With what?" asked Trudy innocently.

"You know—the murder." His black- and blue-rimmed eyes—visibly swollen now and beginning to turn various shades—betrayed his puzzlement.

"You mean Cherie and Spike Logan?"

"Who's Cherie?" asked the kid. Obviously, these university brats spend more time partying than watching the nightly newscast or reading the newspaper. His father would be so ashamed, thought Trudy.

"Never mind her. Did you meet Spike Logan here about two months ago?" asked Phil, deciding to step in. Philips' response to Trudy's question meant he had met Spike.

There was now a link that begged to be explored.

"Yeah. My roommate, Willie Lavois, and me. Who the fuck is Cherie?" Philips was getting agitated.

"His wife, numb-nuts," said Trudy.

"Who, him?" Philips pointed an index finger at Phil. He really didn't seem to know whom they were talking about. Time to change tactics with this pukelet.

"What happened to the gun?" asked Phil.

That caused Philips to drop his eyes to the sidewalk and slump against the side of the Firebird.

"You won't tell my dad, right?"

"No, we won't," said Trudy. Phil's eyes narrowed and he gave her a warning look to keep quiet.

"I sold it to Spike—for beer money." His voice was barely above a whisper, but they heard him loud and clear.

"You did what?"

"Listen, pig, I'm not proud of it, but I was a littler short, and besides, Willie told me to bring it with me to the bar that night. He said we'd shoot logs down on the beach after we left the pub."

"What happened to make you sell it?" asked Phil, his voice calm and businesslike.

"We drank a lot of beer and we were a little short of bucks, so… Willie spotted Spike—I found out his name the next day, Willie told me. He was sitting on a stool at the bar. He said he wanted a gun so I sold it to him. That's all. I didn't shoot anyone. You gotta believe me."

Phil placed one hand on the kid's shoulder. "Yeah, kid, I believe you." He nodded at Trudy and walked around the car to the driver's side. Philips stepped away from the car as Trudy pushed him aside, then climbed into the passenger seat, slamming the door behind her.

The last they saw of Nathan Philips was in the rearview mirror, in Phil's case, and in the passenger's side mirror, in Trudy's case. He was waving a fist at them, holding his swollen nose between his red-tinged fingers of the other hand. Trudy couldn't read lips, but if she could, she was certain he was using some words that were not in a university text to describe them.

"Where we goin'?" asked Trudy, casting a glance at Phil. The Firebird weaved its way through the heavy traffic of Fourth Avenue. Until the '90s, the area had been occupied by aging hippies, and tie-dye boutiques and natural food stores had been replaced by trendy coffee shops and high-end designer specialty stores. The once cheap boarding houses had been replaced by tony condos with ever skyrocketing prices.

"We have to find the Lavois kid. I think Philips was covering for his buddy back there." He turned to look at Trudy and grinned. "The little punk doesn't have the balls to even shoot the gun at trees." He turned his gaze back to the road ahead as he avoided a dark blue Mercedes two-door. "I think Philips was set up."

"What do you mean?"

"Lavois wanted him to meet Spike Logan and sell him the gun."

Trudy's eyes went wide. "Oh."

***

After they'd followed the road to Dunbar Street, Phil made a left and drove until he turned right onto Sixteenth Avenue, then followed it through a forest of trees until they came to a nest of low-rise buildings. There were lecture halls, faculty offices, and dormitories, and all the amenities a modern university had to offer.

Unbeknownst to Trudy, Phil had kept William Lavois' dorm number in his notebook since he'd decided to assist Mike with the case. He felt having Lavois' address was somehow important. Now they would test his gut feeling.

They pulled into a side street and stopped in a parking lot across from the three-story dorm building where Lavois lived when not in Ottawa with his parents.

They parked the car, then walked across the now dark street. The streetlights were few in this area, something the student council often complained about to the board of governors due to safety concerns for female students.

Once across the street, they walked up to the building Phil indicated and stood outside at the intercom. Phil pressed the button of security.

A male voice answered. "Yeah."

He sounded a little bored, thought Trudy.

"Detective Phil Singh, Vancouver PD."

"Wait there," said the voice after a couple of seconds.

They stood gazing around the empty street until a large man—he was at least six-four or -five if he was an inch—wearing an RCMP uniform appeared in the lobby from the elevator.

He walked up to the door, his hand on the brown leather holster on his belt. He didn't have his hat on, but he was wearing his black, bulletproof vest over his brown uniform shirt. His shirt was open at the collar and his uniform pants had a yellow stripe running down the outside of each leg. His black leather boots were polished to a high shine that reflected the lights in the lobby. He opened the door with one meaty hand.

"Identification," he said, his expression somber.

Phil reached in the back pocket of his jeans and pulled out his wallet. He handed it to the Mountie, who took it, then let the door close. They watched him through the glass wall that separated them as he checked the badge and then flipped open the wallet to check Phil's departmental ID card.

Apparently satisfied, he then opened the door and stood aside to let them enter the lobby. It smelled of dust and wet running shoes.

"Who's this?" asked the Mountie, indicating Trudy.

"Consultant."

The big cop nodded. Police departments often used consultants in investigative work. Every working cop knew this, so it wouldn't be a surprise.

"What can I do for you?" asked the big man, who towered over both of them. His chest was broad and his brown hair was cut so short it made him look more like a marine than a police officer.

"I understand William Lavois lives at this address. Is that correct?" asked Phil.

"I cannot confirm that." Obviously his orders were to protect the prime minister's son and he wasn't to discuss with anyone outside the security detail where or when Willie Lavois was or wasn't.

Willie Lavois was a spoiled brat who made these cop's lives hell. He frequently gave his security detail the slip, and they, being proud members, were fed up with the little son of a bitch. This was something they didn't discuss with, or admit to, outsiders. Certainly not to a local cop, who couldn't make the grade as one of the Queen's cowboys. It was a given among RCMP members that all locals wanted to be Mounties. They were the elite among Canada's police forces.

Phil smiled as he placed his wallet back in his pocket after the large man handed it to him. "I happen to know he lives here, at this address, and I need to speak with him immediately."

"What's this about?"

"Murder," said Phil, as the smile disappeared from his face.

The Mounties' brow wrinkled and he looked thoughtful for a few seconds as he considered Phil's words. He knew his NCO would raise hell with him if he obstructed a murder investigation. It was the one thing that would get this local inside, and he knew it.

"Yeah, okay. Follow me." The RCMP officer led them to the elevator, where he pushed the button to go up. The bulb inside glowed to life, then immediately winked out. The elevator hadn't left the main lobby while the cop was speaking to them. The doors slid slowly open and the three entered the car.

The doors closed just as slowly and the elevator lurched beneath Trudy's feet, then began to gradually move. She could hear the mechanism click as it moved upward. There wasn't any elevator music. Trudy felt a little relief at that, though the silence was deafening to her.

"How long you been working here?" she asked, keeping her eyes focused on the red numbers over the doors.

"Two years," said the cop with a shrug. The boredom of the duty didn't seem to matter to him. Bodyguards were babysitters, and guarding a politician's kid was sometime hell if the kid in question was a "problem child" like Willie.

"William ever give you any trouble?" asked Trudy

The cop nodded, but said nothing. She concluded he wasn't supposed to discuss such things with anyone outside the detail.

"Why didn't you seem surprised when we said we were asking about a murder?"

The big man ignored her question.

Phil threw her a look to tell her to keep her mouth shut. She grimaced.

Finally the elevator car lurched to a stop, and after a pause, the doors began their slow, almost painful, slide open. Once in the hallway, it was a short walk to the dorm room for the two university students. Even William Lavois, it seemed, had to share his room. No doubt the boy they'd met at the pub had been security screened until they knew what color underwear he wore on Tuesday when he was eleven.

The door was closed, so the constable knocked twice. Silence greeted them. The cop reached into his pants pocket and pulled out a shiny steel key ring with a clip on the end. It had the same symbol as his uniform patch near the shoulder of his uniform.

The door opened inward, and with the large Mountie in the lead, they entered the room. Inside there was a bed, unmade, the sheets tangled with a green quilt, the pillows mashed and strewn haphazardly about the bed. The walls were lined with brown wooden bookshelves filled with textbooks. From the titles, Trudy discerned they were engineering texts.

There was a reading lamp next to the bed, still on. There were no shoes or jackets on either of the recliners that sat opposite the bed. There was another bedroom off the first and a communal bathroom, which Phil and the Mountie quickly searched and discovered were empty.

While they did that, Trudy walked over to the nightstand next to the bed and saw there was an ashtray with some gray ash in it. She reached down and touched the ash and felt it was warm.

The cop and Phil came back into the bedroom, having found no one.

"Our rabbit's gone. Just left," said Trudy.

"Fuck," said the Mountie. His face was flush with anger.

"That little son of a bitch does this all the time." He laced his hands on his hips, one resting on the butt of his holstered pistol.

"Does this a lot?" asked Phil.

"A lot," said the clearly frustrated cop as his block-like head scanned the room.

"How long is he gone, usually?"

"Sometimes days."

"Where's the best place to look for him?"

"The Pit. And I'm going with you."

"Yeah," said Phil, with a smirk and a knowing glance at Trudy.

Trudy crossed her arms over her chest and fixed a stare at the big Mountie. She frowned. "I still want to know why you weren't surprised when we said we were investigating Cherie's murder."

Phil rolled his eyes. "Trudy…."

The big cop held up one hand to stop the surprised Vancouver detective. "It's okay. I don't mind," he said with a sardonic grin.

"Well?"

"Anything that kid is involved in doesn't surprise me. He's done just about everything that a spoiled brat can, including manipulating his parents. Besides the arrest of the biker seemed a little too convenient to me. "

"How about if I told you he was involved in at least one murder that we know of?" asked Trudy. From the corner of her eye she caught Phil's eyes pop slightly and knew the signs of his body tensing.

The Mounties' expression changed to surprise and his blond eyebrows went up. "Now that would be a new one. Cherie?"

"Did she live here?"

"For a month, then she left to live across the campus at another dorm. They didn't get along too well. Outside the bedroom, if you know what I mean."

Trudy nodded. "That's one thing I know something about."

"Let's go," said Phil. "Who's going to drive? I mean, there's no point in taking two cars, is there?"

"Let's take mine," said the Mountie. "After all, I know the way—believe me, you can easily get lost round this place. Especially at night."

It was agreed. They'd go together in the constable's police car.

***

They arrived at the campus bar known as The Pit. It was a place where students who weren't studying or in class hung out. On weekends there were live bands and dancing. There was a food service that served what most college or university students lived on for their four years: burgers, pizza, and beer, which were food groups as far as the university crowd was concerned. Though how anyone could call a veggie patty a burger was beyond imagining.

They entered the noisy establishment that was filled with students, intent on their conversations. The place was surprisingly free of cigarette smoke. Herbie Kochel, the constable, had introduced himself on the drive over. He explained The Pit was non-smoking as decreed by student council.

Trudy had no way to know where they were or how they were going to get back to the dorms.

The smell of greasy burgers permeated the air.

The students didn't look up from their mugs of beer as they passed. They walked slowly through the crowded room. The latest rap song blared from hidden speakers, making the room conversationally challenged.

Phil and Trudy knew what William Lavois looked like, but they stuck close by Herbie as he scanned the young faces. Finally he pursed his lips and nodded at a knot of young men surrounding one of the raised tables at the far end of the room. He strode across the room toward them.

Lavois spotted the constable looking at him and slumped in his chair with what Trudy would call a wiseass grin across his face. His pale gray eyes glared at the angry cop. He wore a navy-blue sweatshirt, worn, tanned Dockers, and had a dark red baseball cap backward on his head. In his left earlobe was a metal stud.

He sat with three other similarly dressed young men, who threw furtive glances at each other. The presence of the cop made them uneasy. Willie appeared arrogant and relaxed.

Phil and Trudy followed Herbie up to the table, where the mountain of a man towered over them, his brow creased in an angry glare.

"Where have you been?"

"Right here," said William, with the wave of one thin hand. He smirked and the three other men chuckled nervously.

"You're not supposed to go anywhere without me," said Herbie, even though he knew from experience it was useless. "You're father is saying he'll have me pulled if you keep this up."

"You don't get it, do you, pig? I don't need a babysitter. I can take care of myself." Willie had leaned forward in his chair and spat the words, his face twisted in disgust.

"You boys get lost," said Herbie to the other three young men. "And take your drinks with you before I check your ID."

The three young men bolted from their chairs with their mugs of beer clasped in their trembling hands. They looked pleased to be as far away as they could get from the cop.

Each had a relieved expression on his face.

"What the fuck…?" asked William.

Herbie sat down in one of the still-warm chairs with one index finger pointed at Willie Lavois' face. "Shut your hole. These people have questions for you and you're going to answer 'em. Got it?"

Willie slumped in his chair and scowled at the big cop like some high school kid who'd just been turned down by the prom queen.

Phil and Trudy each took a seat. "Hello, Mr. Lavois. My name's Phil Singh." Phil pulled out his wallet and showed his badge and identification card. "I'm a homicide detective with Vancouver PD, and this is Trudy Wilson." He motioned toward Trudy. "She's helping me with the case."

"About time you guys were doin' something about it," mumbled William. "You guys can call me Willie. Everybody does."

Trudy thought she could feel the cold shield of ice enveloping the young man begin to melt, though he still seemed guarded, especially in his eyes. They continued to be hard and unemotional.

Philo shook his head. "No, we're not here to investigate your wife's murder. We're here about a couple of men who were shot to death in a hotel last night."

Willie crossed his wiry arms over his white tee shirt and shrugged. "What's this got to do with me?"

"Your roommate said he and you sold a gun to man who we suspect was involved in your wife's murder."

There was flash of surprise at the corners of William's eyes, then they went hard again. He shifted in his chair like someone with numb bum. "Yeah, we sold his gun to some biker guy, what of it?"

Trudy felt a sudden flash of anger emanate from Herbie. He obviously hadn't known there was a gun in the dorm room Willie shared with Philips.

"The gun killed Spike Logan—the biker you two sold the gun to—and the two men in the hotel," said Trudy. Phil would be mad she spilled everything they knew and added some embellishment to shake Willie's confidence. She knew from they way Willie was behaving he might give up more than he normally would if she pushed him a little.

Phil glanced at her, surprised at the sudden interruption.

"I had nothin' to do with those," said Willie. A single bead of sweat appeared on his forehead and his hands appeared to tremble slightly before he dropped them underneath the table.

His dull eyes clouded with doubt. Sensing Willie's increased agitation, Phil decided to help Trudy a little and see what else was behind door number two. "Ballistics confirmed that Spike and the two as yet unidentified men were killed with the same gun," he said his voice calm.

Willie's eyes flitted toward Herbie, whose features were fixed in a scowl, and then back at Phil. "You don't have the gun?" he asked.

Phil shook his head. "Not yet." He smiled thinly casting Trudy a knowing look. "We will soon." Trudy realized he was lying hoping Willis would reveal something useful.

"What do you want from me?"

"We'll need you to testify in court that you witnessed Philips sell the gun to Spike Logan," said Phil.

Willie looked visibly relieved. He shrugged and an easy grin came over his pale features. "Yeah. No problem."

Phil stood. Trudy cast him a startled glance, then stood. Herbie remained seated. "You comin'?" Phil said to the Mountie.

"Naw, I gotta stay with this little puke and keep an eye on him."

Willie scowled. "You watch your mouth. You know who I am, for fuck's sake."

Herbie cast him a withering glance. "Yeah, right. I don't give flying fuck anymore. I'm gonna ask to be transferred off this duty. It's a real pain in the ass. I'll ask the boss to send a meaner cop than me, one who knows how to keep you on a tight leash."

Herbie glanced first at Trudy, then Phil. "You guys need a ride back?"

"Nope, we'll find our way on our own. Thanks anyway."

"Suit yourself," said Herbie with a shrug.

Trudy followed Phil out the main doors of the pub until they were in the night air outside. It smelled slightly of the ocean, sending a brief wave of nostalgia over her.

They walked down the three cement starts to the path that led down the side of the building. There were hooded, amber streetlights atop steel poles that provided light along the path. "Phil, how're we gonna get a ride back if we don't call a cab? It seems to me it was a long way from the dorms."

"Yeah." He nodded. "Hold on until we get to the other side of the building." They continued along until they came to two doors that were opposite the entrance to the pub. These were the doors used by the staff to come and go, and where deliveries were made.

Phil stepped out of the light of the streetlights and stood at the corner, out of sight of the two doors. Trudy stood beside the detective, clearly perplexed.

"What's going on?"

He shushed her and spoke in a whisper. "I know who did this. I know what the hell is going on."

Before she could respond, one of the doors burst open and Willie Lavois came running out and down the stairs, headed away from the building. He cast his gaze around him, but was unable to see Phil and Trudy standing in the shadows.

Phil held one hand up to signal Trudy to remain silent.

They watched the younger man until he got into a British racing green, two-door sports car. Trudy didn't know what kind it was, but it was probably one of those Japanese cars made in California. The car's engine roared to life, followed by the sound of screeching tires as it sped away. Phil's gaze followed the little car until it disappeared down the access road.

The door from the pub slammed against the side of the building as Herbie, with a flushed face and wild eyes, burst from inside.

Phil stepped out from the shadows. "We have to follow him."

Herbie knew immediately what Phil was talking about because Trudy had trouble keeping up with the two men as they ran back down the cement path to the parking lot.

Trudy gasped for breath by the time they were in the Mounties' cruiser and racing away from The Pit. The lights on the roof of the car cast their red and blue glow over the streets that made up the campus roads.

"Where's he going?" Trudy managed a gasp and a cough as her breathing steadied and her heart rate finally slowed.

"To get the gun."

"What gun?"

"The one he stole after he killed Spike and those two men at the hotel."

CHAPTER THIRTY-ONE

Herbie called in for backup and to report the pursuit of William Lavois. Phil explained to her why he was so certain that Willie Lavois was behind the murders.

He explained that once the forensics was completed on the two dead men they would find that one of the guns found on them had been recently fired. They would also find that the hands of the man found with the fired weapon wouldn't have residual powder burns on his hands.

"That means he didn't fire the gun. That means…" said Trudy her eyes wide.

Phil nodded and grinned as he glanced at the speedometer on the dash in front of Herbie and saw it pass one hundred twenty. They were now on the straight stretch headed toward the city. Cars in front of them pulled over as Herbie hit the siren. The big man had both hands on the wheel, one at the bottom, the other on the side.

"Yup. It means Willie shot them, then stole one of their guns and left the murder weapon right under our noses, expecting we wouldn't test them. Of course, we would, as standard forensic procedures."

Herbie nodded in agreement, his eyes focused on the road ahead. "But who killed Cherie?"

"That, I'm afraid, is a little tougher to prove, but I suspect Willie hired these two men, then killed them as the only link to his wife's death." He grinned. "That's only speculation, though."

Trudy nodded. This case was turning into a real fucking mess. The kid was jealous of his wife so he hired two pros to take her out then tries to cover up the whole thing. It amazed her to what lengths people would go sometimes. Why not just divorce her?

As they rounded a curve, they spotted the little red car parked next to the road on the paved shoulder. "That's it," said Phil, though Herbie had already begun to slow the cruiser. He turned off the siren but left the light bar on as they pulled up behind the little car.

There was no sign of Willie.

They got out and Herbie spotted a break in the bushes off the road. "Once you leave this road," he explained, "there is a forest that falls away from the road down steep inclines. There are numerous trails through the forest of evergreens and oaks. The underbrush isn't too thick in some places."

"We need to find him," said Trudy.

"I can call in the dogs," said Herbie.

"No time," said Phil, shaking his head. "We have to go into the bushes and follow him or he'll destroy our only evidence against him. All we have right now is circumstantial and we need physical evidence.

"I'm going in there," said Phil in a determined voice.

"Me too," said Trudy.

Phil sighed. "Herbie, did you call for the cavalry?"

The big Mountie nodded.

"Then Trudy will wait here for them while you and I go get the kid." Trudy scowled. "No rebuttal allowed," he said, patting her on the shoulder.

The two men disappeared into the underbrush, leaving her alone, standing beside the cruiser. She slumped against the side of the car with her arms crossed. She heard the two men's curses as they broke branches while making their way in the dark. They each had a flashlight that Herbie kept in the trunk of the car.

Soon Trudy was alone with her thoughts and the sound of cars speeding by, going in the other direction. A few cars passed and slowed to gaze at her standing alone by the police car, then sped away. The drivers and their passengers had puzzled expressions on their faces. After a couple went by, she chose to ignore them.

The sounds of Phil and Herbie gradually disappeared.

"Don't move, bitch," said a voice behind her that she immediately recognized.

"Listen, Willie, they have nothing on you, yet," she said slowly.

"You're lying," he said. "I should kill you right now."

She felt fear shoot through her and her knees felt suddenly a little weak, like she'd been drugged. "I'll drive you anywhere you want. You name it."

"Funny," he said, "that's exactly what I was thinking. Now get behind the wheel." She felt the prod of the gun's muzzle against the small of her back. She got into the police cruiser and realized the keys were missing. Willie was walking around behind the car to the passenger side.

She thought of her options. *If I tell him there are no keys, he'll kill me. If I try to get away, and he's faster than I am, so he'll certainly catch me. He's a lot younger than me and probably in better shape. Either way I'm dead.*

Trudy had left the car door open, so she bolted onto the road and headed across the four lanes of traffic toward the other side, hoping to reach the safety of the woods before he could shoot her. Bullets were faster than humans, but she hoped his surprise would be in her favor.

"Hey!" she heard him shout behind her. She didn't look back but kept her feet pumping. Her breathing was harsh and ragged in her own ears.

Her heart nearly stopped when she heard a shot from behind her. The sound was surprisingly loud. It seemed louder than last time. She stopped and took a deep breath and didn't feel any pain.

She put her hands up above her head and closed her eyes tightly, waiting for the next shot to rip through her, sending her into oblivion.

Nothing happened, so after several seconds she opened one eye and turned her upper torso so she could see the police car.

She spotted a silhouetted figure kneeling down at the rear of the car. Another figure lay face down on the ground.

She turned and slowly walked toward the car. It was then she saw it was Phil Singh kneeling over a figure in a navy-blue sweatshirt wearing a red baseball cap.

Herbie came up beside her with his service pistol in his right hand, casually aimed at the figure on the ground.

In the dim light, Trudy saw Phil slip his still smoking service revolver into the holster in the small of his back under his jacket.

He then stood and gazed at the late William Lavois, son of the prime minister of Canada.

She moved forward as if she were in a dream, not noticing the cars coming toward her. The cars braked, their tires squealing loudly. The drivers honked their horns at this crazy woman impeding their progress.

Fortunately, the motorists had slowed due to the flashing police lights. For some reason, people loved to gawk at accidents and wrecked cars. Maybe they hoped to see someone they knew, or maybe they were relieved that the accident didn't involve themselves or anyone they knew, or maybe it was a morbid fascination with death.

Perhaps this explained the proliferation of reality shows and professional wrestling on television. No matter, they were going slowly enough to be able to brake in time to avoid hitting Trudy Wilson.

Trudy crossed and stood next to Phil beside the young man who lay on the ground at their feet. In the middle of his navy-blue sweatshirt was a wound pooled with red. His arms and legs were splayed in an awkward fashion, like a mannequin hit by a truck. He wasn't moving, and Trudy knew without asking that he was dead. She was enveloped by an eerie sense of déjà vu as she gazed at the young man's cooling corpse. How did she get herself in these situations?

She hadn't even been after the guy, yet somehow she seemed to be the one who was in the crosshairs, until someone saved her. Last time it was Rocky, this time Phil Singh. She felt a surge of anger at Willie Lavois. He'd abruptly ended the lives of real people. People who were loved. His wife may not have been the best wife on the planet, but did she deserve to die?

Trudy knew from bitter experience it took two people to make a successful marriage work. Had he even taken the time to look in the mirror at his own behavior? Probably not.

"So what now?" she asked.

Phil shook his head. "I don't know. I just don't know."

***

Sixteenth Avenue was blocked off going west into the city by a plethora of emergency vehicles, all bearing flashing light bars of red and blue lights. The coroner's van was present, along with police cars from Vancouver and the RCMP detachment at UBC. Also present were the Chief of Police and the Chief Superintendent responsible for E Division, which encompassed all of British Columbia and the Yukon.

Standing next to Herbie's cruiser were Trudy, Phil, Mike, Barbara, and Bruce. So far, the press had been kept at a distance with a promise of a joint news conference by the chief and the head of the RCMP. Trudy knew the shooting death of a sitting prime minister's son would create a firestorm of speculation.

"What happened?' Bruce whispered in Trudy's left ear. He was standing next to her, watching the cops and forensic team working the shooting scene. They were running yellow tape and wearing white surgical gloves as they stepped gingerly around the shrouded corpse of Willie Lavois.

"I don't know, exactly; I think maybe I had a mild aneurysm or something. It's all like a dream to me," said Trudy. She stood with her hands in the pockets of her jacket. The air was cool now that they'd been standing in one place for a while and she wasn't running for her life.

Mike moved closer to them. "The chief and the superintendent want to talk to you guys. They've already spoken us," he motioned toward Barbara, Phil, and Joey, "and they aren't too happy you civilians are involved."

Bruce and Trudy nodded. She couldn't imagine the chief and the superintendent were happy with them at all in the circumstances.

They walked toward a distinguished looking man wearing a navy-blue police uniform, with brass buttons running down the blazer and yellow-gold piping on his peaked uniform cap, and a balding man in beige golf slacks, a bulky mahogany sweater, and white Nikes.

They couldn't have looked more opposite if they'd planned how they were dressed.

The balding man smiled warmly as they approached, while the man in the uniform scowled, and seeing his colleague's face, gave them a brief but professional smile, the corners of his mouth upturned slightly. The balding man had a cup of steaming coffee in his right hand in a paper cup from one of the chains Trudy had seen near Phil's house.

The uniformed man was a good two inches taller than the other.

"Hi," said the balding man. "I'm Superintended John O'Reilly, RCMP. This is Chief Owen August, Vancouver City Police." He held out his right hand and shook each in turn, as did August. Each man's handshake was dry and firm.

O'Reilly sipped his coffee and turned to gaze at the shrouded body. "Damn shame," he said. August nodded grimly.

"Not really," said Trudy, deciding to take the plunge and satisfy this man's obvious fishing expedition. She knew they'd done nothing wrong, so why not?

"What do you mean by that?" asked August cautiously, his dark eyes narrowing.

"That little son of a bitch killed three people that we know of, and probably some we don't know about."

O'Reilly nodded.

"You're talking about his wife," said Augst, nodding toward the corpse.

"That and another biker named Renault," said Trudy firmly. Time to go for broke.

This time O'Reilly's eyebrows went up. "How are you so certain?"

"Chief Augst, your man Phil Singh and I figured out what Lavois was up to and who he killed based on the evidence. I'm fairly certain you haven't found the body, living or dead, of the man who tried to kill me down south. I smell cover-up, and frankly, as an American citizen, I don't much appreciate being accused of something I didn't do, and I don't like being a visitor in your country and some asshole," she pointed at the gray cover over Willie's body, "trying to kill me."

O'Reilly stifled a laugh and his blue eyes sparkled with delight as Augst squirmed and straightened his uniform jacket.

"I've got business elsewhere," said Augst, then walked away toward the forensic team and began to bark orders to the cops standing around, both his and the RCMP. Herbie crossed his arms and glared at the chief, but said nothing.

O'Reilly turned toward the two. "Let's take a walk." He indicated the path along the side of the road leading away from the scene. His big, friendly grin made Trudy relax her guard.

"Okay," she said

The three walked away slowly as O'Reilly let them in on what they'd discovered when Barbara had gathered all the evidence together. No, Bruce wasn't involved in Cherie Lavois' murder, he was free to go. He himself had woken the crown counsel at home earlier and explained the situation.

The crown would file the motion to stay proceedings in the morning.

One thing he said he wouldn't—Trudy suspected it was more couldn't—discuss was the political matters related to the case.

They were closing the murder investigation because Vancouver Detective Phillip Singh killed the person responsible in the performance of his duty and that was that.

Trudy asked and was granted her request that the officers involved not be disciplined for their part in resolving the case. She suspected they were in serious trouble for deviating from established procedure.

Though he couldn't guarantee anything about Phil, Superintendent O'Reilly agreed to Trudy's request, with the understanding that he would intervene on Phil's behalf with the Vancouver chief.

They shook hands with smiles all 'round, then the superintendent bid them good-bye and headed back to his black Lexus and sped off.

"How the hell did you manage that?" asked Bruce with a look of admiration. "I thought for sure those cops' asses were in the ringer."

"Just call it skill, bud," said Trudy. "Come on, let's go tell the others."

***

Superintendent O'Reilly's cell phone, set in the steering wheel of the luxury car, rang. After two rings, he answered on the hands-free system. "O'Reilly," he said.

"This is Reynolds. Is it done?"

"Yeah."

"Okay, I'll take it from here." The line went dead and O'Reilly hit the button to turn off the cell. He drove the rest of the way home in silence, wondering what he needed to do to work on his golf swing to fix his recently developed slice.

***

Wellman hung up the telephone after speaking with the PM and smiled to himself. The PM's son wouldn't create any more trouble for them. Now he could get on with his plans at a big promotion when the PM left office. He had proved his loyalty and he was certain the PM would take acre of him.

He better, thought Wellman as he took the next briefing file from his in basket. Or he'd have to explain his involvement in his son's unfortunate death to the press and parliament.

Right now there was work to do. All would fall in place. In time.

CHAPTER THIRTY-TWO

FIVE DAYS AFTER WILLIE LAVOIS' DEATH, Trudy, with poor, tired Tommy in the passenger seat, his head resting against the door, and Bruce, riding behind her truck on his beloved motorcycle, were on their way south along the King George Highway, headed for the border and home.

Phil and Randy Singh and their two children had been heaven-sent the way they treated them after all that had happened. Phil, in particular, was pleased that Flo's faith in her friend had panned out and that he was still a cop, a profession he loved, even though Randy wasn't too happy with the hours or the dangerous aspects of the job. She'd nearly fainted when she'd found out Phil shot Willie to save Trudy's life.

It still bothered her that Phil had been involved in something more than she knew but he refused to explain in more detail so what could she do but speculate. He seemed such an honest man she doubted he had done anything illegal.

A couple of days into their respite from all the excitement, Trudy had received an urgent call from Flo. May Carpenter had cleaned out Trudy's bank account and skipped town with the butcher, Mr. Swinson.

Why couldn't she ever get a break? When she asked where Rocky was when all this happened, the answer was the same as usual: he was at the bar or sleeping it off at home.

Trudy gathered up her lost sheep and headed for Oregon. Tomorrow was another day. She sighed. Loyalty has a price. Glancing in her rearview mirror, she spotted Bruce astride his motorcycle, his long hair trailing behind him in the breeze from beneath his helmet. One she would happily pay.

Trudy Wilson will return.

ABOUT THE AUTHOR

International selling author, Russ Crossley writes science fiction and fantasy, and mystery/suspense as well as their various subgenres.

His latest science fiction satire set in the far future, Revenge of the Lushites, is a sequel to Attack of the Lushites released in 2011. The latest title in the series was released in the fall of 2013. Both titles are available in e-book and trade paperback.

He has sold several short stories that have appeared in anthologies from various publishers including; WMG Publishing, Pocket Books, and St. Martins Press.

He is a member of SF Canada and is past president of the Greater Vancouver Chapter of Romance Writers of America. He is also an alumni of the Oregon Coast Professional Fiction Writers Master Class taught by award winning author/editors, Kristine Katherine Rusch and Dean Wesley Smith.

Feel free to contact him on Facebook, Twitter, or his website http:www.russcrossley.com. He loves to hear from readers

OTHER TITLES FROM 53RD STREET PUBLISHING YOU MAY ENJOY

http://www.53rdstreetpublising.com

Other books by the Author

Razor and Edge Mysteries
The Kidnapping of Billy Buttons
String of Pearls
Death by Clown
Beggin' For Murder
Ragged Ice
The Grand Central Mystery
A Strange Case of Undead Murder

Jazz Stiletto Mysteries
A Day Without Sunshine
Skullduggery
Instrument of justice (first published in Over My Dead Body online mystery magazine)

The Amanda Dark paranormal mysteries
Hook Island
Grind Manor
Moonrise Diner

The Trudy Wilson Mysteries Novels
Bad Loyalty
Shear Murder
Buzzcut coming in 2015

Novels
Attack of the Lushites
Revenge of the Lushites

My Zombie Prince
Antique Virgin
The Fire In Their Hearts
with R.S. Meger (from Champagne Books)
Zomopolis
The Last Serial Killer

Short Stories
Countdown
Shoeless Moe
Round Up At The Burger Bar:
The Story of Trixie Pug, Parts 1, 2, 3, 4, 5, 6, 7, 8, 9
Five Minutes
Blossom Queen, Barbarian
The Secret
The Family Line
End of the Flies
Death by Magic
The Penguin Sleeps With The Fishes
Only The Worthy
Hero For A Day
End of Empire
Strange Bedfellows
Big Business
A Perfect Crime
The Wise Guy and The Pirates
In Search of the Perfect Cup
T.I.N. Men
The Legend of G and the Dragonettes
The Incredible Mr. Fix-It
Lock Stock and Barrel
Divided Loyalties
Cave of Wonders
A Family Empire
Until We Meet Again
Dragon Rising
Solitary Man

The Keel Mountain Conspiracy
Angel on My Shoulder
Heroes of Old
The Great Bicycle Race
Tikka's Big Day
"My Partner the Zombie" —
Hungry For Your Love Anthology
(St. Martin's Press)
Big Hairy Deal
One Red Shoe
A Bad Day in Lunden Texas
Bloody Betty, Queen of the Pirates
Mirror Image
Dangerous Waters
Cape Disappointment
Boomerang
The Watcher of Wayburn Street
The Apprentice
Drip!
A Beautiful Friendship and The Parrot of Doom
Robine's Diary
The Christmas Club
Loose Ends
Splatter Pattern
It Takes Two
Lexicon
Replacement Parts
Sidekicks
Lost Stories
Time and Space

Anthologies
Tales of Urban Fantasy
Five Tales of Bizarre Detectives
Tales of Mystery and Suspense
Tales of Weird Fantasy
Spies, Detectives, & Heroes

Tales of Twisted Crime
Tales of The Unexpected
Tales From Space
10 by Russ Crossley
Round Up At The Burger Bar: The Story of Trixie Pug,
Parts 1- 5 The Beginning
Worlds of Science Fiction and Fantasy
More Tales of Mystery and Suspense
Ladies of the Jolly Roger
Justice Served
Love Stories
Ladies of the Jolly Roger with R.S. Meger
The Adventures of Razor and Edge:
Five Tales From The Quirky Detective Team

Non-Fiction
The Writers Tools - The Synopsis

Also available now from 53rd Street Publishing

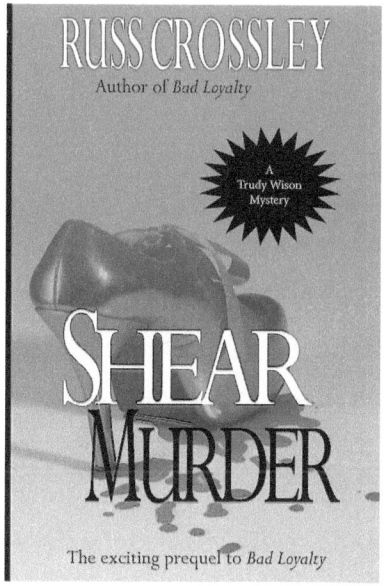

RUSS CROSSLEY
Author of *Bad Loyalty*

A
Trudy Wison
Mystery

SHEAR
MURDER

The exciting prequel to *Bad Loyalty*

In this exciting prequel to Bad Loyalty we first meet hairdresser, Trudy Wilson.

Trapped in a marriage to a drunk for a husband she faces a failing business and a dead woman, Sharon Carstairs, she's suspected of murdering

To clear herself and find the real murderer Trudy joins forces with Sharon's biker brother, Bruce. Join them on a terrifying ride to a highway of fear, murder and conspiracy to discover the terrible truth. A truth they both fear.

Feel free to contact me on twitter or facebook. I'd love to hear from you.

This title is available in an electronic edition at various web retail sites. The trade paperback is also available from your favorite book retailer.

The following is an excerpt from Shear Murder now on sale.

ONE

MARCH, AND THE SALTY, ICY WIND BLEW HARD across her face as she walked toward the locked glass door of the Hair Club beauty shop in the Bricktown Plaza. At least the metaphorical wolves from the bank had finally disappeared from the door. Sharon Carstaris had made that possible, not her own business acumen.

Trudy Wilson sighed as she brushed the stray strands of mouse-brown hair away from her face, then pulled her key ring from her jacket pocket. The burden of debt she'd been carrying was finally beginning to disappear from between her narrow shoulders.

The lights inside the shop were set on dim as she had instructed Sharon to leave them each night at closing time. The local cops patrolled the parking lot at night, and they liked to be able to see inside without getting out of their plain white cruisers—the ones with the row of red and blue lights atop a bar on the roof.

Trudy thought of Sharon Carstairs, with her pleasant smile and her flowing blonde curls. The golden cascade down her back made her look younger than her chronological age.

Sharon's girl-next-door attitude belied her true nature. Behind that innocence, Sharon held her secrets close, locked away from prying eyes.

Trudy had hired the 40-ish blonde some six months ago, and soon realized she didn't know much about Sharon.

What Trudy did know was that her and her husband Rocky's cash reserves were nearing the end. Bankruptcy had been hounding their every waking moment for months and would have continued if it weren't for Sharon and her client list.

At first, Sharon seemed to be the answer to all her problems.

Sharon said she had worked for a few different shops in Newport over the past twenty years. She volunteered no specifics about her previous employers and Trudy didn't press her. Ignorance, at times, was a useful thing. The only thing Sharon did tell Trudy was that she had moved up the Oregon coast to get away from what she called "family problems."

Trudy, being new to the business world, felt she shouldn't pry, so she let it go without checking work or personal references and hired the pretty blonde.

The shop consisted of six chairs, with Trudy and Sharon working two of them. The other four were unused for the moment.

Trudy had moved to Fairview from Seattle five months ago, specifically to open her own hair shop. Prior to moving, Rocky had owned a small auto parts supply company, and had been reasonably successful. He had sold the business so they could enjoy the country lifestyle here on the Oregon coast. Unfortunately, he hadn't had a job since arriving and had become depressed and retreated into a bottle.

To compound her money troubles, small-town people take quite a time to accept new people moving into the area, and as a result, Trudy had had few customers.

The addition of the sunny, blonde-haired stylist, with her tight black leotards and loose fitting tee shirts, which did little to disguise her ample breasts, had made all the difference. Sharon was a welcome sight to the men in town. Consequently, business began to increase at a steady pace shortly after she arrived.

Sharon was quickly building a clientele. Men would stop and talk, especially when she washed the windows or energetically swept the brick sidewalk. There was Mr. Keelson, the bakery shop owner with the fringe of gray around his mostly bald head, and Mr. Williams, the postman who stopped by on his route on Tuesdays. They were among the many admirers of the buxom blonde. Mr. Johnson liked his chestnut brown hair cut short. He'd been a client since the first time he came in and Sharon made him laugh.

At the supermarket, while elbow deep in the apple bin, Trudy overheard two women extolling the virtues of the new hairdresser from Newport at the Hair Club. She knew then she'd made the right decision.

Slipping the bronze key into the lock on the door, Trudy turned it and heard the familiar click as the bolt disengaged. Pulling on the aluminum handle, she entered the shop. The air inside wasn't really warm, but it was warmer than the air outside, and it washed over her. It felt good against her cold, pale skin as she stepped inside.

It was quiet after the door closed. The noise of the wind and the early morning traffic on the distant highway faded. The air was thick with the chemical smell of perm solution mingled with last night's floor cleaner, filling the air of the little hair shop.

Trudy walked to the back, where the office was located. An ancient wooden coat tree sat just inside the doorway. She hung her thin navy windbreaker before hitting the bank of light switches with the flat of her hand. Rubbing her hands to chase away the cold for the umpteenth time, she wished she had the money to buy a warmer coat.

The fluorescent lights crackled as they came to life and the shop again breathed to life.

The furnace was on a timer, and the fan began to purr as the furnace started to push warmer air into the six hundred and twenty-three square foot space. Rubbing her pudgy fingers together, she tried to increase her own internal temperature.

Glancing in the mirror over her station, she caught a glimpse of the middle-aged woman with brown curls falling down the sides of her full face and the rosy cheeks of her delicately applied blush. After counting her brushes and combs and checking to make sure her two electric clippers were plugged in, one for the longer cuts, the other for the finishing sideburn trims, she returned to the tiny office at the back of the shop.

Sharon had left fresh coffee in the coffeemaker's basket, just as she did every night. Trudy smiled to herself. Good girl—no, good woman, she corrected herself.

Filling the urn with water, she poured it into the coffee machine. She flipped the switch on the side of the white plastic potholder to the on position. The glow of the red light meant it was on and working. There would be fresh coffee in ten minutes. Good thing. She really needed a cup today.

She and Rocky were scheduled to meet with Mr. Simmons at the bank today. They had to renegotiate their loan repayment schedule. The hair shop had consumed most of their resources. If only Rocky would come out of his winter slumber and get a job. Once he got a job, it would really help to ease her worries about money.

Her husband complained constantly about the attitude of the townspeople toward newcomers. "They won't hire outsiders," Rocky explained.

At least for now, they had some cash flow from the shop. This allowed them time to work out a plan with the bank before they sank below the red line into bankruptcy. Trudy sighed.

The bell over the front door tinkled. It had to be Sharon.

Exiting the office, Trudy found Sharon standing over her workstation, playing with a new brush, a replacement for the one she'd brought with her from Newport. Sharon claimed someone had stolen it off her station, but Trudy sensed Sharon had broken it or lost it somehow.

"Mornin'," said Trudy in her light, musical voice.

"Uh... hi," Sharon said, her blue-green eyes focused on the combs and brushes laid out in a neat row on the surface of her mauve-colored station. The drawer was open, which she slapped shut as soon as Trudy appeared. Her shoulder-length blonde hair, usually perfectly coiffed and combed into place, was ruffled and had a windswept look.

Sharon glanced up, and the dark circles under the woman's eyes made Trudy cringe.

"I'd like the day off. I'm not feeling well."

Trudy wondered why she hadn't just called in if she needed a day off. "Of course. Do you want me to call your appointments for today?"

"Yeah."

"Are you okay?"

Sharon shook her head. Something was obviously wrong, but if Sharon wouldn't share, there was little she could do about it.

Turning away, Sharon hurried out the front door and disappeared into the bustling mob of tourists starting their early morning shopping. Trudy watched Sharon. Her eyes were focused on the ground, causing her to almost knock over an old lady with a cane who shouted at her as she passed. Sharon didn't meet anyone's gaze.

Walking again to the back, her rubber-soled Nike's squeaked across the tiled floor. She entered the small, whitewashed office and sat in the worn secretarial chair.

Reaching out, she pulled her thin, black, nylon smock from the coat tree next to the desk.

The coffeemaker was almost finished. The hot, black liquid would feel good going down. At least their financial situation might finally begin to turn the corner.

Walking into the shop, she stopped to study Sharon's station. She considered opening the drawer, then decided not to. She made a point of not invading her employee's privacy. Trust is earned, not given, her father used to tell her when she was a girl. The new brush looked familiar, though.

Picking it up, she studied the logo. A very expensive brand, one that Sharon could never afford. Her eyes narrowed when she realized where she'd seen this before.

Rocky had bought one just like it on their last visit to the wholesale beauty supply store. She shook her head. Couldn't be. Not with all the complaining she did about her drunk of a husband. If he and Sharon—

The bell on the front door tingled brightly, breaking her train of thought. Mrs. Evanston walked through the door, grasping her heavy aluminum walker in her gnarled hands. Covering her gray hair was a thin, pale blue scarf to hold her wispy hair in place, just as she wore it every week.

Trudy glanced at her watch. 9:05. Right on the nose, as usual.

"Hello, Mrs. Evanston." Trudy forced a wide smile to her lips, though she didn't feel particularly happy at the moment.

"Hello, yourself."

Mrs. Evanston had been Trudy's first customer shortly after she'd opened for business and had been a regular ever since. She was a wily old lady of at least eighty, who only came in on seniors' discount day: Tuesday.

Mrs. Irma Evanston had married a wealthy eastern industrialist and that he died shortly after he retired and moved to Fairview.

Even if it weren't true, Mrs. Evanston was a very unpleasant and difficult person to deal with. And the cheapest woman Trudy had ever met.

"Where's Sharon?" Mrs. Evanston asked, stopping by the coat tree near the front desk long enough to remove her long, green, floor-length overcoat. Shaking the excess moisture from the coat, she pulled off a steel hangar, then used it to hang the wet coat on the rack. It would be dry before she left. Mrs. Evanston always booked an hour and a half for her roller set.

"On a day off, Trudy said, without elaborating.

Trudy glanced at the appointment book on the front desk as she passed it while helping Mrs. Evanston to the sinks where she would shampoo her hair. They would move back to Trudy's station for her to set the curlers, then Mrs. Evaston would move to one of the dryer chairs.

Odd. There were no appointments booked for Sharon today. It was the first day in the past few weeks she didn't have a least one perm and several haircuts on the schedule. It was almost as if Sharon had planned for a day off.

Trudy made a mental note to speak to Sharon about it tomorrow.

***

The day ended with Trudy doing five roller sets and five haircuts, mostly walk-ins, none by appointment. People needing haircuts, passing through tourist towns, weren't big tippers, and certainly didn't tip well enough to keep the doors open.

At five o'clock, after locking the front door as she turned to leave the store, she was nearly knocked over by a wall of man muscle.

The man, well over six feet tall, blocked her way. He smelled of motor oil, and she stared at a wide chest covered by a black tee shirt and a leather vest. Lifting her gaze, she looked up into oil-black eyes and a toothpaste smile framed by a short, scraggly beard. A thick mustache covered his upper lip and his long black hair, draped over his massive shoulders, gleamed in the fading daylight.

The evening breeze must have sprung up because Trudy shivered as the cool air washed over her.

"Uh, sorry," said Trudy.

"Are you Trudy Wilson?" asked the man mountain. His deep, resonant voice vibrated off the walls of the covered walkway.

His voice matched his size.

"Yeah." She nodded, certain she looked like a deer in the headlights of an eighteen-wheeler.

"I'm Bruce. Bruce Carstairs."

Trudy's eyes went wide. "Oh. Carstairs. You know, Sharon?"

"Yeah, she's my sister. I'm lookin' for her."

Trudy took a step back so she could see his dark eyes better. The easy smile and his thick thumbs hanging off the pockets of his faded blue jeans made him appear relaxed.

"She left early. Sick," said Trudy.

"Do you know where she lives?"

Trudy had to think about that one. Was this guy really her brother? And if he was, why didn't he know where she lived?

"Uh…"

He interrupted her before she could reply. "I know what you must be thinkin', who is this guy really?" Unhooking his right thumb off his front jeans pocket, he reached into his back pocket.

A wallet with a stainless steel chain attached appeared in his hand. Flipping it open, he pulled out a Washington State driver's license, which he handed to her.

Studying it, she saw sure enough the license photo was his picture and the name was the one he'd given her. Handing the license back to him, she watched as he expertly slipped it inside the billfold, then stuffed the wallet back in the rear pocket of his jeans. Crossing his arms, he gave her an earnest expression.

"I can take you there if you like," she offered. At first she wondered if she should, but he seemed nice and he seemed okay.

"Okay." He nodded, his face splitting into a warm smile.

If this was what bikers were really like, then all those lurid stories on the TV were dead wrong. Swallowing, she realized her mouth was dry. Dead wrong?

www.ingramcontent.com/pod-product-compliance
Lightning Source LLC
Chambersburg PA
CBHW020240180626
46810CB00006B/2285